Books by Abraham Polonsky

The World Above
A Season of Fear
Zenia's Way

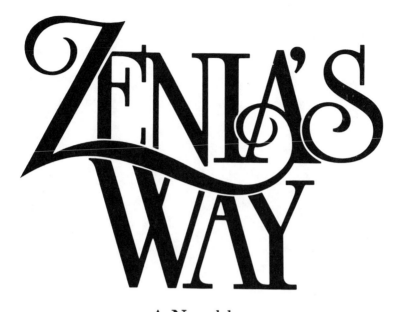

ZENIA'S WAY

A Novel by

Abraham Polonsky

Lippincott & Crowell, Publishers • New York

FIRST EDITION

Designed by Ginger Legato

U.S. Library of Congress Cataloging in Publication Data

Polonsky, Abraham.

Zenia's way.

I. Title.

PZ3.P77Ze [PS3531.O377]   813'.5'4   79-24884

ISBN 0-690-01896-7

80 81 82 83 84 10 9 8 7 6 5 4 3 2 1

Part I

Mambrino's Helmet

1

In those days on hot summer nights the mothers used to call their children home across the empty lots. Names mingled with meteors, with lions, with the perfume of flowering burdock.

In the lots we had our own names for the plants that thrived there, guinea rhubarb, sore-eyed daisies, stinkweed, sour grass, pepper pods and so on. Burdock we just called the weeds. Year by year it spread everywhere, being the climax weed of our lots. Where the lots were deep and rich, it grew more than eight feet tall, with wide foot-long leaves, coarse up close but beautiful as the weed spread for the sun, loaded with twigs of burs whose purple sticky flowers besieged our whole neighborhood with their fragrance.

"Arctium lappa, Linnaeus," my pharmacist father called it. "The dried lappa is used as medicine, a diuretic. Some folks, and doctors too, say it's good for the blood. In the old country, people stripped the stalks to make a food of the inside. But it's a strong laxative."

We used the dried stalks for spears and arrows in our make-believe fights based on the movies we saw every Saturday afternoon at the movie house on 180th Street. William Farnum and his brothers were my favorites.

We lived and played in a landscape of lots, old neighborhoods with older villages tucked within them, the great zoo, the Botanical Gardens, the Bronx River and the Bronx Lake, miles and miles of empty lots where once there had been farms, where still a farmhouse stood isolated among the flowering weeds with

3

its trim garden, grape arbors or wisteria vines. My Aunt Zenia and I used to explore north, taking trolleys to the wild fields of Westchester to pick berries and hunt snakes when she had a free day from Fordham Hospital, where she was ending her internship.

On the night federal agents raided my friend Laura's house, we were playing in the lots, and I was the last one free when the mothers began to call their children home.

Three prisoners, crouched shoulder to shoulder on the curb, were suddenly on their feet, restless to escape from the base chalked out under the streetlight. The four guards had long since given up searching for me and now stayed close to the base against any last-minute run I might make. Eager to win, they began to chant in unison over the prisoners' screams of protest:

> "Come in, come in,
> Wherever you are.
>
> "Come in, come in,
> Wherever you are."

Laura called my name, "Ram, Rammy." I was at that moment nearby but hiding high above them.

When the street was laid out, long before we moved up to that neighborhood across from the zoo, the city had blasted through a whaleback of Manhattan schist. So beyond the slate slabs of sidewalk a wall of rock rose some fifteen feet up. Through the burdock there I could see the prisoners, the roving guards, the streetlamp whose light was just a little higher than my eyes. No one looked up, for everyone knew there was no way down. I could, of course, sneak along the descending hill to street level but I would then be a good fifty feet from the prisoners' base.

With weeds below to break the fall, the fifteen-foot jump was hard but not impossible. One leap and the prisoners would be free, running in all directions just as the mothers called again and the game ended. I daydreamed the triumph of this jump from above. But now, the moment here, the street barely visible below as I crouched safely in the man-high weeds, I knew I could never do it.

Once again, the guards began to chant, "Come out, come out, wherever you are," and I could hear Laura angrily arguing with them.

I began to crawl down the hill, but even as I gave in to the fear of jumping, there I was at the very edge of the cliff looking clearly down upon the base, the prisoners, the guards, while I hurtled through the air. Laura saw me as suddenly did all the others. No one moved, appalled by the sight of this flying figure who would be broken, maimed, crushed in this movie of life.

I had forgotten my plan to jump close to the wall and hit the weeds. I struck the ground running and nothing gave, nothing: into the base and still running in a wild outcry everywhere, my name, shouts from the surprised guards and prisoners. I fled across the street and down the bocci path.

Gaining on me were Laura's light steps.

On Garden Street a tangle of bodies tagging, escaping, and by now everybody laughing with excitement at the surprise of the crazy jump from above the base. The game was in fact over, for the voices of the mothers were calling again, name by name. And the boys calling out to each other were going home.

With Laura close behind I now swerved into the dark mystery of the lot and then silently moved around Casanova's garden. We disappeared like swimmers into the sea, going down into the ocean of weeds. I crawled with barely a sound to lie panting a few feet from the fence of Casanova's garden, and as I stopped, Laura was behind me, lying close, one of her legs over mine, shoulder to shoulder, lying there in the greatest silence we could achieve, not to be followed, not to be seen, gone.

We could hear the steps of the departing players. We could hear the voices and then nothing.

The game was over for tonight and I let myself breathe. There was a sharp pain in my right ankle. But it wasn't broken. I knew I could never do this again. No one would do it again. And now I felt the fear of dying, of being hurt, of being maimed, and I looked at Laura, whose face was close to mine, breathing her breath and knowing the warmth of her body but not really seeing her in the darkness and the late surge of terror at what I had done.

Casanova grew enough vegetables to sell in the Italian section that lay farther north from where we lived. His fence was made of high staked wire with here and there an old door colored green, yellow, brown, with a proper gate lifted from some commercial enclosure, made of steel with a thick chain and heavy padlock. Within he had built out of abandoned boards a small but windowless hut with a locked door, inside which he kept his tools, his fertilizer, his pots, and where he had placed an old cushioned lounge chair, almost like a small couch, where he sat, very tall, very fat and to me very old, and smoked and drank his wine every day. Here he worked his vegetable garden. But now all was dark and still and we lay there for this last private moment which was our secret and were ready to go when we both smelled cigarette smoke.

I could hardly see her face. I saw the whiteness of it and the polish of her secret eyes. Again the smell of cigarette smoke close at hand. We froze as rabbits freeze or even great tigers and lions when a mystery that means danger becomes chemistry in the flesh and the spirit runs in fright.

Tense. Lifeless. Listening.

The smell increased.

There were two people in the hut. We could hear the bodies.

I could see that the steel fence gate was chained and padlocked as usual. I could see even in the darkness that the door to the hut was closed. I couldn't see if it too were padlocked.

Now the voices. Two men smoking Sweet Caporal in Casanova's hut in Casanova's garden. It was possible that tramps, hoboes, drifters might have climbed over the wire fence and broken in to sleep in Casanova's hut, as sometimes such strange creatures wandering from the outside world drifted through the

6

private world of our lots and stayed the night in a boarded-up wooden factory which naturally we children also had penetrated. Those men left not only the marks of their sleep but like wild animals urinated and defecated in some corner, leaving crunched newspapers, scraps of food, open cans, Sterno tins and bottles still rank with Prohibition alcohol. The filth of their passing was the world outside that sometimes drifted in. Here these two men had broken into Casanova's garden.

We lay in the intimate silence of our bodies touching, our spirits one, our legs locked, our hands holding, while we listened to the voices of strangers in Casanova's hut.

"Much longer?"

"Soon now."

The men spoke to each other in crushed voices, secure in the knowledge of the closed hut, the great locks and the loud humming of insects of the night.

They weren't New York voices. One of them, the tenor, sounded like someone from Laura's mother's part of the Midwest. The other had the voice of an Irishman, but with the tone of New England, of Boston streets and Boston slums.

"Any moment now," said Midwest.

"They're late," said Boston.

Around us fireflies courted in the darkness. There was light shining from the shaded windows of Laura's second-floor apartment. In the darkness, that shielded light was bright enough for us, lying in the weeds, to see the vegetable shapes that inhabited Casanova's garden. There was also an overflow from the streetlights, the cosmic radiance of this moonless night. All added together in the deep of the empty lots to create a universe for those living in the darkness to see as if there were light.

I could breathe the anxiety of Laura's breath and feel the pulse of her blood.

Inside the hut, the heavy bodies of alien men moved. The dirt crunched beneath them.

"The kids gone?"

"Gone."

7

"You play ring-a-levio?" asked Boston.

"Chase the White Horse we called it," said Midwest.

"Time," said Boston.

Grinding steps in the hut now, grinding the smell of tobacco and cigarettes into the dirt. The bodies moving. The door of Casanova's hut opened quietly although to us lying in cover it was noisy. Two great shapes appeared. Both wore straw hats, their faces white in the filtered light suffusing the darkness of the lots. Big men smelling of bay rum and tobacco. The chains banged like bells. They opened and relocked the padlock on the gates. On Garden Street two automobiles suddenly drew up. This was startling at this hour, for only one person on Garden Street owned an automobile and it was already parked in the driveway that ran to a specially built garage on one side of a two-story wooden house a block and a half away.

"They're here," said Midwest.

The two men were all noise to us. Out they came growing greater and heavier like giants no more than five feet from where we lay stunned in the fragrance of flowering burdock. These men had keys to Casanova's garden. This was the mystery. The men walked by the path around Casanova's garden to the bocci path and went through the picket gate and the back yard of the house where Laura lived.

In the apartment below Laura's the lights were out. In her apartment the shaded light was on in the middle room of the three that opened east into the lots to overlook Casanova's garden. I knew that the back room was the bedroom of Laura's parents. The middle room was a dining room and the front room a living room. Hidden inside were other rooms, a kitchen, Laura's bedroom, a bathroom.

On Garden Street car doors banged shut. One quick look but I could see nothing through the weeds.

The two men who had been in Casanova's hut now very softly went up the steps to the lower porch, then up the next open flight of steps to Laura's porch. These porches were covered with morning glories but we could see the men moving. The strangers both stood, their straw hats bright with reflected light, outside the bedroom of Laura's parents. Something glittered in their hands. From Garden Street, suddenly, a police whistle sounded. Then a man's shrill whistle voice and the whole wild world of night exploded.

Now suddenly shouts, crashing wood, men's voices at war. Above on Laura's porch Boston yelled out like a raging storm of fury and smashed in the window of the bedroom. Blow after blow. Shout upon shout. The night blew up. The two men on the porch smashed their way into Laura's apartment. Inside, shouts and screams of anger in Italian.

Someone was screaming, "Antonio! Antonio!"

We were standing, ready to run. Laura's face had been blasted into the shock of terror and both of us saw first a chair come flying out of the middle dining room window, ripping the shade and glass with it so that the light was clear and the room bright, crowded with men in struggle and their shadows on the white ceiling like Saturday movies on 180th Street.

First the chair came through the window, tearing the shade and dragging it with it, and the shade fell like a kite. Then a man leaped out, flying through the air the way I had just a little while ago. This wild leap, this man in his shirt sleeves all white in the night, his gun glittering in his hand, flying out, hanging in air, until he hit the dry bocci ground, stumbling, a wrench of pain, but he was up. He ran toward the emptiness of the lot, toward the darkness and the secret of it, but it wasn't his lot, and Casanova's wire garden fence blocked him. He turned to Garden Street, but there were three men there with revolvers running down the path toward him. So this man in the white shirt came running around the south end of Casanova's garden toward us.

"Antonio!" cried a voice again from Laura's window. "Antonio!" Until the last part of the name was strangled for air. The sound of fighting, the buffeting of furniture, the house sounds wrenched and broken, fragmented above, while below Antonio fled into the forest of weeds, passing us not more than fifteen feet away, shoving his way through the burdock burs,

9

through the heavy stalks, thick, coarse, blocking him, holding him back in the tide of weeds. He fought his way through. Then suddenly the weeds were still and we heard his running steps. I knew he had found the transverse path that led up to Southern Boulevard and the Garden Street corner.

Up Garden Street figures ran along the pavement, leather shoes beating on asphalt, sharp toes plunging ahead. Sharp voices yelled out, "There he is!" From Laura's window a revolver fired, again and again.

Antonio stopped in the darkness and fire sparked as he blew two shots from his gun. We fell to the ground, clinging to it, trying to see and not see, trying to hear and not hear. Above in Laura's apartment a man leaned out of the broken window and raked the lot with six shots. We lay flat, the bullets cut like razors. Leaves fell, stems broke. Then the running again. Behind, the pursuers crushed through the burdock till they too hit the path.

"This way. That way."

"I see him."

"Fire."

Guns shot into the weeds. A gun flared out of the weeds. And at the corner of the boulevard and Garden Street, three bursts from a gun louder than any revolver. Heavy shots like the sound of a shotgun. There was a burst of silence now. In spite of the running sounds of feet and the running sounds of voices something silent had happened.

A voice called out in hot joy, "We got him!"

Laura and I crept through our hidden trails. Everywhere in the three attached houses on Garden Street and everywhere in the apartment house where I lived, the lights came on in the windows and faces and bodies appeared there and the voices of the people called out in bewilderment and curiosity, voices of people we knew but didn't know then for we had forgotten everything in the frightful violence of the night, in the destruction of the darkness and the secret of the lots.

"Police!" the voices called.

"Oh."

When we broke free at my street, coming out of the lots, we ran up a little incline to the sidewalk of my apartment house.

By now, of course, people had come out. There were lights in most apartments and the voices of excitement were everywhere.

Laura and I ran up three flights to my apartment. Each floor had four tenants. Ours faced south and east. "It would be better," my father said, "to face south and west. Then we'd also have the winter sun in all the rooms." In any event, here was where we had lived ever since we had sailed down on the night boat from Albany.

We met other tenants in the hallway, all coming down the stairs. A chatter of faces, all of them asking, "What's going on? Were those really shots?" These faces seemed very familiar to me. They had the same excitement of people going to the movies or the RKO Vaudeville on Tremont Avenue. We passed them as children, unseen.

I rang our doorbell and the door flew open as if everyone inside had been waiting for my arrival. The door closed quickly behind us. It was my Aunt Zenia who had opened the door. Then we were all in the dining room, which faced east and therefore had no view of Casanova's garden. My father was sitting at the dining table. There were cups and saucers and the smell of coffee. My mother was standing there and she asked, "What's happening?"

Zenia followed us in. "Does anybody know?" Zenia asked.

My father had placed his chin upon his hand, as if in deep thought, and there they all were ready to hear the answers if we had them. Laura's face was white and she stood there stiffly, listening not to the questions but to the war around Casanova's garden.

In the dining room with its overhead chandelier in the style of Tiffany, there we were with the heavy mahogany round table, the leather couch against the wall, the great chairs, the heavy sideboard with its cut-glass bowls and flower vases and every leg or arm, large or small, like the paw of a lion.

All the lights were on. My father asked, "Have the police been raiding the roadhouse again? Is that it?"

"No," I said. "Men with guns. They came in two cars. Also two men who went up the back to Laura's porch and broke the glass in the bedroom there. Then someone jumped out of the dining room window."

"Antonio," Laura said.

"Who is Antonio?" my father asked.

The faces now were no longer the faces of people just interested in an unusual event. They were the faces of people filled with alarm and concern for Laura and her parents.

"In your house?" Zenia asked. "Was it Antonio Galli?"

Laura was crying now. She hadn't cried during the whole affair, not even when the guns went off in her apartment. Not even when the man came flying out the window. But now she began to cry and shake, just standing there not knowing to whom she might run for comfort and relief from the terrible storm which had begun out in the dark fragrant lots and now blew in a fury in herself.

My aunt took her in her arms, soothing her while she looked at my father.

My mother sat down on the couch. "Well," she said. "They're Italian anarchists, aren't they? Isn't that what it is?"

This was a very long speech for my mother. But she also took Laura from Zenia and held her close, drew her on her lap, embraced and soothed and kissed her, all the while looking at my father and Aunt Zenia.

My father got up. "I think," he said, "we should go over there and see what happened to Laura's mother and father."

"Her mother isn't home," I said. "Only her father was home and Antonio and two other men. They were all in the dining room and these strangers came with the guns and went up the back porch steps."

Zenia said, with a kind of disbelief and fury, "It's a Palmer raid. It must be."

"Yes," my father said. He had put on a jacket, closed his shirt collar and knotted his tie. "I'm going to see what happened to Laura's father."

"Don't go," my mother said.

My father went over to Laura and touched her hair gently. "I think," he said, "we should go over there to find out what happened to your father."

Zenia said, "Of course we'll go. But we won't say that Laura's here. Remember that until we find out what's going on."

"If it's a Palmer raid," my mother said, "you mustn't go there. We too are immigrants."

My father looked at her with the sudden fury of someone who has for too long wondered that perhaps the life he had chosen was not the one he might have preferred to live.

"They don't arrest children. No one knows she's here." He raised his voice to my mother. "Only you and your fears know she's here."

My mother was obstinate. "People saw her come upstairs, with Ram."

My father looked at Zenia. He was asking her, Who was this woman he had married and why wasn't she like himself or Zenia? But Zenia comforted him with a touch of her hand and said, in her reasonable way, "There's nothing to be frightened about. I think we should find out what happened to Laura's parents, where her mother is, or if her grandmother is there."

"No," Laura said. "My grandmother isn't there. She's at her house."

"Where is that?" asked Zenia.

"On 189th Street," I said.

My aunt turned to me. "Did they shoot anybody?" Her face was flushed with indignation and excitement. She had arched eyebrows, strange beautiful arches of black, and below them eyes which at first you thought were brown, perhaps black,

13

if there are black eyes, but when she looked at you in daylight the eyes became deep purple. They had electric light in them at night that glowed in a kind of wet hardness in which the light of the Tiffany lamp dissolved. Her eyes were like strange places, very dark, hiding their radiance of gold. Her face, a little full, but coming together in a sudden chin like a heart, with a full mouth bigger than expected, and her hair very long, heavy, but a little crinkled, with tiny waves piled high on her head, whirled round and around in coils. She was a strong woman, graceful and beautiful, I suppose, and filled with authority which she exercised because of her lively spirit and general sense of commanding the universe to obey and show itself for what it was. For her, in those days, everything had a general answer.

My father, her brother, was slight, although not small. He had the same kind of hair, the same kind of warm or passionate eyes. He was good-looking but his face always seemed a little drawn. He was warm, temperamental, witty. He was a chemist by training, mainly a pharmacologist, and when he didn't own drugstores which he couldn't afford to keep, he used to work for Eimer and Amend, the chemical manufacturers downtown. Mostly, though, he seemed to be wanting to have a different profession entirely and often spoke of it as if it were still possible. Anyway he was clever and witty about it.

Now he and Zenia were at the door about to leave when the bell suddenly rang. My father said to my mother, "Take Laura into our bedroom and stay there with her."

My mother hesitated but my father's whole tone was now decisive and not to be argued with.

Zenia said to him, "Let's not talk too much. Let's just keep quiet. See what they want."

They were all taking it for granted that it was the police who had rung our bell to find Laura. My father opened the door.

And there was a policeman, after all. Only it wasn't a stranger. It was Farley, the policeman from the neighborhood whom everybody knew, and he said to my aunt, "Thank God, doctor.

14

You're here. Someone said you were visiting here. We have a man on Southern Boulevard and I think he's dying. He was just shot. Could you come down and help him?"

"Of course," Aunt Zenia said. My father brought her little medical bag that she was never without.

"What happened?" my father asked.

"The federal authorities have raided Johnny DiMarco's apartment. They said they were looking for bombs."

"Bombs!" My father's voice was sharp with disbelief.

"Well," Farley said, "they didn't find any. They arrested three men, one of whom was Johnny DiMarco, and meanwhile a fourth man got away. He ran through the lots. They were firing at each other. And this man, Antonio Galli, is shot very bad, believe me. I think he's dying."

Zenia was already leaving and my father said, "Were you there, too, Farley?"

"I was," said Farley. "They always have the local police around. But it was a federal raid. This way, doctor."

He was very polite to my aunt, and I joined her as she started to leave.

"Where are you going, Ram?" he said. "It's not for kids like you."

My father said, "Stay here."

"No," Zenia said. "Let the boy come." She had suddenly decided to continue my education for life and my father didn't want to argue but Farley was looking at him and my father nodded that it would be all right. Farley took the lead to show the way.

"Hurry," he said. "That man needs you now."

So there we were going down the stairs, my aunt, myself, the policeman leading the way. There were neighbors in the hall. They called to us. Everybody was so excited.

Downstairs there were two other policemen and the five of us hurried past Agnes's farmhouse and took to the path in the lots that ran directly to the corner of Garden Street and Southern Boulevard.

There was a small crowd of thirty or forty people there, policemen, automobiles. The men in ordinary suits with straw hats were the federal agents. My aunt ran, I ran, one policeman ran ahead of us and two behind us through the weedy forest that lined the path to Southern Boulevard.

Just then the boulevard streetcar, running south, came by. There were three passengers in it, all of them standing in the open streetcar. The motorman slowed down and stamped on his bell while the conductor held on, and they all looked out at the excitement until the car ran by in a blaze of light.

Antonio lay under a corner streetlight where they had carried him. Somebody had placed a blanket from one of the police cars on the ground. He lay there in his white shirt, full of blood, dark with blood, his face white, his black hair too black over his white face. There was pain and life still alive in him. He breathed very hard.

The police opened a wide circle for the doctor. Most of them, being strangers here, were surprised that this beautiful young woman in her pale blouse and summer skirt was the doctor, but of course the medical bag carried its own authority.

She knelt down beside Antonio and I stood close beside her. Her trained hands inquired everywhere. She opened her medical bag and took out a scissors and, with it, cut open the shirt which was dripping blood. She opened his belt and unbuttoned his fly. And there was the belly. He had been shot just above the navel. The flesh was gouged out and the blood seeped from it, coming up in luxurious spurts from its spring hidden deep in his body.

My aunt placed a heavy wad of gauze on the wound. She listened to his heart with her stethoscope. She counted his pulse. She asked, "Have you sent for an ambulance?"

"Yes, doctor," a voice said.

"Hold this gauze," she said to me. And I knelt down in the blood and held the gauze, hot with his blood, firmly against his abdomen. She replaced the gauze constantly.

Antonio now opened his eyes and saw the face of Zenia

close to his. "Am I dead?" he asked in Italian. His voice was broken and weak. "Are you an angel?"

She put her hand on his mouth to silence him.

It was only later as Zenia told the story again and again that I found out exactly what they had said to each other, and that was how I told it to Laura.

"What's he saying?" one of the federal agents asked. This was Boston. I recognized the voice.

"Will I live?" Antonio asked her in Italian.

Zenia answered in Italian, "If you keep quiet."

"No," said Antonio. This was all in Italian. "I feel I'm dying. Tell me the truth. I have to know if I'm dying."

Zenia said, "Keep quiet. Why do you have to know?"

"Because I don't want to die without knowing it. That's why."

The federal agents kept asking, "What's he saying?"

Zenia answered them. "He wants to know if he's dying." And she looked at Boston. "Did you shoot him?"

Boston said, "No. We don't know who shot him yet."

"He fired at me," said a strange agent's voice, his face hidden in the crowd of straw hats that encircled the body of Antonio. Beyond them were the neighbors.

Someone in the crowd cried out, "The ambulance is coming!" They could all hear the siren throbbing and calling as it came south on Southern Boulevard.

"Thank God," said Farley. "Here comes the ambulance."

Antonio murmured in Italian and Boston asked, "What's he saying?"

"He wants to know if you're sorry you killed him or are you happy."

To this there was no answer.

"They don't answer," my aunt told Antonio in Italian.

"They never answer." Antonio let out a long, slow, weary breath. "Well, when do I stand up? I suppose I'll never stand up again."

"Don't move," Zenia said. "You must fight to live."

17

"Too tired. I'm very tired. And now I feel a terrible pain." Antonio began to speak very rapidly in Italian. He suddenly took my hand, holding it tight, and pulled me toward him and said, in Italian, as I later found out, "You're the friend of Laura." He gave a long sigh and held my small hand in his rough, powerful ones with such force that I felt real pain. But I didn't say anything and suddenly his hands went limp.

Aunt Zenia said, "This man is dead." She kept working on him as the ambulance arrived and a young doctor whom I knew, an Irishman named Sweeney, came jumping out of the ambulance, carrying his black bag.

"Why, Zenia," he said. "You here? What happened?" She got up as he bent over the body and went through his tests. "He's very dead," said Sweeney. "There's nothing we can do."

"Yes," Zenia said. "He's dead."

Farley came close to her. "Thank you, doctor. Thank you, anyway. I sent for a priest. But he isn't here yet."

"Well," Zenia said, "my dear Officer Farley, only the priest can help him now, I'm afraid."

"Yes, doctor," he said.

Then Farley took her aside and I clung close too while Dr. Sweeney was busy with the law and reports and so on. Zenia asked Farley, "What have they done with Laura's father?"

"They arrested him. He's been taken off already."

"Where?" she asked.

"We can ask," he said.

"And Laura's mother."

"She wasn't home."

"Did they arrest her?"

"We can ask," Farley said.

He walked over and talked to the men. Then he came back. He was very confidential with her.

"No, they haven't arrested her. But where is Laura?" he asked. "She was playing in the street too."

He looked at me. Zenia said nothing, so I said nothing.

The policeman, after a long look, said nothing also.

Sweeney now came over to say he was going back to the hospital. He wanted to know if my aunt wanted a lift back. The body would be taken care of by the police.

"No," Zenia said. "I'm not on till morning and it's not morning."

"Well," said Sweeney, "I was just offering you the pleasure of my company. Can we ride you back to wherever you came from?"

"I'm right here where I came from," she said. "I can walk."

She took my hand and Sweeney said to me, "Take care of your aunt, Rammy." Then he got into the ambulance and off it went, still sounding its siren, for Sweeney on ambulance duty loved to hear the siren sound.

Farley came over to us and said, "I'll walk you home, doctor."

In silence we went through the lots. Other people were coming from 182nd Street to see what happened. They asked the policeman and those of them who recognized me called my name but we three walked on in silence.

Downstairs Farley shook Zenia's hand. "Thank you, doctor." He patted me on the head, then he was gone.

The two of us went back upstairs. The neighbors by now were mostly downstairs so we met no one all the way up. It was quiet in the hall and on the stairs. My father opened the door and we went inside.

Zenia said, "Whatever Antonio is, he's dead. The federal detectives shot and killed him." Then she sat down at the dining room table.

"Would you like some coffee?" my father asked her.

Suddenly she took me in her arms and held me very tight. To my father she added, "They arrested her father. Her mother isn't arrested but she isn't home."

Laura came out of my mother's bedroom with my mother in front of her.

Zenia said, "You'd better sleep here tonight, Laura. We'll tell your mother that you're here. I'm going back to the hospital. All of you better stay here."

My father said, "I'll be here."

And my mother said, "She can sleep in the other bed in Rammy's room. Would you like that, Laura?"

"Yes," said Laura. She was no longer crying that we could hear.

My father said to her, "If you like, you can sleep on the couch."

"I think," my aunt said, "that Laura would like it if she were with someone until her mother comes."

Zenia put on a light cotton jacket and took her bag.

"How will you get back to the hospital?" my father asked.

"I'll have the police drive me," she said. "I'll have to make some statements to them anyway about the dead man."

My father was facing all of us and suddenly he cried out, "I can't believe this!"

"Why not?" Zenia asked. "After all, in life, things are real, without any help from us." And then she left.

2

Laura lay in a fragile sleep of anxiety and fear. I couldn't hear her breathing for there she slept just beyond waking, in the realm of dreams.

In the dining room my parents and a few neighbors drank tea or coffee while they ate my mother's cookies. They discussed in a flow of whispering the dramatic events of the night.

Laura crouched beneath a sheet and light blanket, only her face showing in the tangled nest of her hair. She clung to the edge of forgetting because she wanted to, as I wanted her to, as my parents and the neighbors wanted her to, because it was safer to sleep, and better. Yet sleep like love is never real because it's better, only because its time has come. So she crouched at the edge of the next nightmare.

The door of my bedroom had been left slightly open. Although the dining room was a length of hallway away, they whispered. The voices ran on like the murmuring of the Bronx River just before it opened up into the lake, tinkling with spoons, with cup-and-saucer sounds, and now and then one voice would escape in a splash of excitement only to dip back again into the current of conspiracy. They were all repressed by the weight of the night and its happenings. And they were hiding the future from us. I could hear it in the secret of their voices.

I heard the midnight trolley. It was lonely that night as it came around the boulevard bend running past the Crotona gate of the zoo on its way to Fordham Road. I listened until its clicking faded, and long after it was gone the silence ticked the night away.

My mother's steps came carefully down the runner. She peeped in. Confident that we were both asleep for the night, she gently closed the door. Her steps retreated and she said something, for the voices relaxed and grew louder.

Mrs. Townsend was a neighbor whose husband had a store on Tremont Avenue under the elevated tracks of the subway. She had two small daughters. She asked again what they had been asking about all night. "But what do you do with the girl?"

I was out of the bed and at the door, edging it open, perhaps an inch, so I could hear better.

It was restless fear that kept me awake. I listened and I wondered and I was afraid to miss what they were saying to each other.

I trusted my parents but I also was afraid of their decisions. They had reasons, but so has the weather. I can remember being in my mother's arms in what must have been a movie theater. There I opened my eyes out of sleep before sleeping again. She rocked me. I was there in the rocking in her embrace and holding. I could see floating in great beams a drift of dust motes rising through the eerie sun of the projector's beam. And there was music, a piano so excited I could feel its excitement in my mother's arms. She held me loosely, but like a monkey riding its mother's belly through wild jumps of flight, I knew I was with her while she at that moment was in a mad flight of feeling. The dust motes floated serenely as the dark and light of the images altered, undisturbed by the passion of the unseen screen. I rode in my mother's arms safely there in her embrace and her rocking, rocking me away in the dream-remembered sleep of movie houses.

I felt no such safety this night in the embrace of their whispering. Yet there was something daring about my fear. It left me ready to jump again even if I was afraid to jump.

Another neighbor, she lived on the third floor in the back, spoke with great knowledge. "The way it is. The police will come early in the morning. That's when the police come, while people are asleep." Her German accent had all history behind it that night. "They'll come and get Laura. After all, they have her mother and her father."

"Not her mother," my father said.

"It's only a question of time." This woman knew, and around the murmurs of agreement, and always along with this, went a doubtful note because they were frightened for themselves, since nearly all of them were immigrants.

My mother finally spoke. "The police will want to know why we are the ones who took her in and what do we know. Isn't that their way?"

"What do we know?" my father asked.

Now they all went at it, how it didn't matter, and besides it was just an accident and so on. In their common fear, the voices fell into a hiss of whispering and I closed the door. I was cold with danger and their fear of it.

The conspiracy of whispers, of murmuring, of voices went on and on. I crawled back into my bed and hid there. In the darkness which was touched with light from the open window and the streetlamp a few stories below, I watched Laura's sleeping face.

She hadn't moved in all that time.

3

I first met Laura when it came time to move from an old school to a new and modern one on Crotona Boulevard and East 180th Street.

Our class set out for its new home carrying whatever could be carried along Crotona Boulevard: pictures, vases for flowers, maps, some books, supplies like pencils, erasers, chalk. The tallest boy, who was Ronny, carried the American flag. We made a procession of laughing and playful students led by our teacher along the distant border of our neighborhood. Everybody was delighted to watch as we went by. Here we were, the children of their neighborhood, marching loosely and with laughter on our way to a brand new school.

After we moved into a new classroom it turned out the new school wasn't really ready and the old school already had new pupils from a different neighborhood. What they did was to rent a one-story new building divided into four large stores and turned them into four temporary classrooms.

Once again we marched but this time we felt like exiles in our new school.

The teacher asked me to carry some books to another classroom, which I did, and there I met Laura just before she moved to Garden Street. She had brown thin forearms, brown hands, tanned but dark anyway. She was dark, with tawny blond hair, hanging in two tails.

"Here," she said with authority. "I'll take them."

I gave her the books. We didn't look at each other.

After she moved to our neighborhood we became friends. I reminded her of our first meeting.

"I don't remember it," she said without regret.

Laura played many games with the boys, games of running mostly, but she didn't play ball with them, usually. She skated with them and played skate hockey. She even played touch football. But she didn't play Ride the Pony. Nor did she lie with the boys in the darkness in the weedy lots talking about what everybody knew about sex, including jokes, myths, fables and gossip. This she did with the girls. But otherwise she was one of the boys, especially in running, skating, climbing into the zoo and the long adventures in the Botanical Gardens or down on the Bronx Lake. She lived in a divided world. In general, in those days, boys and girls shared just a few common games, such as listening to ghost stories told by Agnes Helder, who lived in the farmhouse next to the apartment house in which I lived. But these ghost story tales included even younger children.

Between Laura and me there was a personal intimacy and friendship in that she would go to my house on rainy afternoons, or I to hers. In that sense we were more intimate with each other than I with the other boys, and she with the other girls. The boys from nine to eleven were a whole world apart from the world of the girls, with the exception of Laura, who was eleven. I knew her lean, hard body quite well, better than my own in some ways, because I was more interested in it. I admired her extravagantly as someone who, like my Aunt Zenia, was filled with the mystery of a different kind of physical destiny. But in my house as in hers, many of these sexual matters were open rather than closed, as they were among the chattering, laughing boys. All the other children seemed stupid and backward. The word "backward" here came from my father and my aunt, who in general, like most Russians of their time, classified almost everybody in our neighborhood as backward people. They were people who didn't inhabit our intimate world. In fact, all the children, with the exception of Siney, who went to a Catholic school on top of the hill above Crotona Boulevard, attended the same public school, and had the same education. The difference was, the other children came from the homes of people who never read books, who knew nothing of the existence of the great subject that was called, in our house, "Humanity." They were backward, as my Aunt Zenia described them when she talked of the duty of humanity to lead them out of the backwardness by political events and education.

Laura's family was special also. First, they were Italians, although her mother was from Minnesota and had for some reason come to New York to work or go to school. I wasn't sure. But she had ended up in Greenwich Village, where she met and married an Italian seaman who had deserted his ship. My Aunt Zenia said that Laura's father was an anarchist.

"At least," my father said, "if you must be mad about politics, that way is logical."

"Logical, of course." Zenia shook her head in loving exasperation with humanity. "Logical, but not reasonable."

Laura's father was short, but young and powerful, with heavy, dark hair and mustache. His teeth were large, very white and strong. It was a pleasure to watch him eat. He could crush beef bones with his teeth. He could eat fish bones, and when he was in the mood he would drink a wineglass of the local wine made in those Prohibition days in the Italian neighborhood so that the whole world reeked of it for weeks. He would drink down the wine and then chew up the glass, spitting it out without ever cutting his lips or tongue. I admired that immensely. There was such strength in him and in her thin mother. She was almost emaciated, bony, with a breastless body, but a face of extraordinary beauty and clarity. The bones and lines of it intrigued me endlessly. Her face was violently pale and her blond hair thick, long, heaped and heaped upon her head. Laura was like her physically except that she had tawny blond hair. Laura's mother had one of those midwestern accents and a coolness of manner, never raising her voice, a woman of leanness, blondness, and strong will. Between her and her husband, for we discussed these things on those rainy afternoons, there was a very deep passion. And Laura had, from time to time, secretly observed, in the darkness of the dark, the motion and the passion of their lovemaking. Somehow, this had brought into her life an exquisite tenderness toward her father and a gentleness toward her mother. And she responded to their every wish without rebellion, with a kind of happy willingness which, mixed with their passion and the warmth in that house, made it a pleasant place to be whenever it rained.

If her parents were both out, which they were a lot, especially at night, then her father's mother came to be with Laura. The grandmother barely spoke any English. She was rough in her ways, but willing to feed children and oblige, talking Italian to Laura. Laura spoke the language in a childlike way, not as she did English. Her mother spoke a schooled Italian and her father spoke with great passion and clarity, a man of intellectual power who read books too. In Laura's house, there were books, some of which were in my house also. But there were other books in Italian. My Aunt Zenia had treated Laura's mother at Fordham Hospital and so got to know her. From time to time Zenia would visit Laura's house, sometimes to have dinner there, and I was happy to be along, although the conversations were mainly in Italian, mostly political and argumentative on many unknown questions. It seemed, when I sat at the table in their house with Laura, and all the adults there, strange men and women, talking all the time, that we children lay in a bower of conversation whose flowers were arguments and whose notions were a perfume we breathed, unlike the rest of the children in the neighborhood.

4

Zenia used to invite to Sunday dinners interns and residents from the hospital, including Dr. Sweeney, who was in his joking way in love with my aunt.

"Imagine," my father said. "Imagine yourself married to Sweeney. What does that make you think of?"

"Nothing," Zenia replied. "I like him. But he never thinks of the Russian Revolution. When I asked him, Well, what about Ireland and the Black and Tans, he said to me—he can be very passionate and sincere, although he prefers jokes—he said, 'Zenia, it's very hard to be an Irishman. I try to think of Ireland as a foreign country. If I were you, I'd do the same with Russia.' "

"He's right," my mother said.

"What did you say, Zenia?" my father asked.

"I said it was the Soviet Union, not Russia, and that someday I would go back there where they needed doctors to help them survive. Then Sweeney got very sad and we went to a speakeasy near the hospital and drank what he called 'spiked beer.' 'I would like you to love me,' he said in all sincerity. I told him that I didn't love him but I admired him and considered him a friend. 'You must be waiting for love then,' he said."

"Are you?" my father asked.

"Would I wait for love?" She was laughing now in great gaiety and confidence. "I told him I wasn't even waiting for marriage. He kissed my hand, for he's gallant and charming. 'No,' he told me, 'you'll never marry. You'll be so busy explaining the nature of marriage in the dialectic of social institutions that you'll be an old maid by the time you get to your last contradiction.' Then he stopped himself and said—he's really a man who doesn't despise truth, he's just afraid of it—'No,' he told me, 'you'll never be an old maid. You'll die like Joan of Arc, married to some illusion in history.' But he was very drunk by then. Do you believe"—and now she had a worried frown on her face that made her eyebrows arch and fall like little black caterpillars—"do you believe I'm such a fool as that? Is that what I seem to be?"

My mother had long since left the room and I lay on the leather couch in the dining room, listening, half asleep, as the brother and sister talked in this intimate way to each other as if the blood in their bodies flowed from a single heart. But they were really quite different from each other.

My father said, "I hope that was one of your Sweeney jokes about wanting to go back to Russia."

"Sweeney's jokes are not so far from Sweeney's truth," she said.

Many men admired my aunt and tried to marry her. The oddest was a doctor who had studied psychoanalysis with Freud in Vienna. He was a cheerful man who lived at ease with the horrors of the human spirit. Of him, my aunt said, "He can interpret anything. He can explain anything. His predictions are common sense which I respect deeply. I like his bedside manner."

He came pretty steadily for three months, then dropped out of sight. My mother liked him. My father laughed at him. I think my aunt was intrigued by his nature. He was a plump, hard man without a neck, partly bald and shorter than Zenia. His English was interesting because every word was distinctly pronounced according to the directions in the dictionary. This was when he interpreted something or explained or predicted it. Sometimes for relief he would laugh and throw his hands up as if releasing a pigeon into the air and cry out to everyone, "Let's be gay!" He would then make cheerful remarks using slang expressions which he had studied for such occasions.

I liked him too. He was patient with everyone, but in the end he gave up trying to marry Zenia and became a resident psychiatrist at Rockland State Hospital.

"What in the world did you see in him?" My father often pressed this question on Zenia.

"Oh," she said at last, "if you must know, I think he was naturally a kind man."

But the admirer of my aunt who appeared and disappeared the fastest was a relative. I think he was the one she should have married.

One summer afternoon not too long after the end of the war a second cousin of my mother came back from overseas. He visited all the relatives and when he came to our house took me down to the Bronx Lake. "I would like to row a boat," he said.

He was a stocky young man from Tennessee. I still don't know what a man just back from France and the war was doing with a young boy on a summer afternoon in New York.

I found him admirable, someone to be respected. Of course I was fully up on World War I by way of movies but mostly because of the little cards we gambled with. They had pictures of the important people who carried on the war, most of them in uniform but some in civilian clothes, and they were all old men.

Whenever I think of Victor, he's rowing with powerful shoulders, sweat on his broad temples, pulling the flat dumpy boat with strong regular strokes. Finally, when we were halfway up the lake in the center between the shores, he stopped and smoked. The boat barely drifted in the slow current of the lake, which reflected the sounds of the few other rowers dotted here and there or lost beyond the curve where the water fell across a dam into the waterfall. Past the dam the lake became a river again. It flowed under the bridge that supported a road and you could always catch crayfish if you were fast enough. Farther down, the river ran narrower and deeper until small factories began and the water became luminous with waste. At any time during summer some nude boys would be swimming beneath the bridge.

There were large boulders in the river left over from the glacial past as well as rocks that had just been dumped there. My aunt often pointed out a pothole in a boulder and then she would say, "A glacier left that."

"What glacier?"

"Why, the Wisconsin, I believe," she said. "Just like the rocking stone it left in the zoo."

She would also point out the scratch of the glacier on the Manhattan schist when we walked in the Botanical Gardens.

"Would you like to row?" the soldier asked me.

I shook my head. "My Aunt Zenia likes to walk around this lake."

"That's a remarkable woman," he said. "I never quite saw anyone like her before."

I was happy to hear this. Zenia was remarkable in many ways, but the most remarkable to me was that in any wild place very soon she could find and catch a garter snake or green snake, and on our trips to Westchester she would find puff adders, which frightened me by blowing up their heads and hissing as if they were poisonous.

"Are there many men trying to marry her?" Victor asked.

"Plenty."

"Anyone in particular?"

"It's hard to tell."

He said, "It would be. You know what? If I thought I could make your Aunt Zenia fall in love with me, I would marry her and take her to Tennessee and then to California, for that's where I'm going after I visit home."

I was amazed.

"There was a fellow in my squad from California, southern California," Victor said. "For that's where I'm talking about. He was unusual. He came from a large family with sisters and brothers. They live somewhere around Los Angeles. I figure if any of his sisters are like him, I'll marry her and live there in California with her."

He made me laugh. "Don't you care who you marry?"

"Very much," he said. "That's one thing I care a lot about. My plan all during the war was to come back alive and marry someone like my friend."

"Is your friend back in California now?" I asked him. "What's it like there?"

"My friend's dead," he said. "I don't know what it's like there. He told me it was summer all the time mostly plus palm trees and oranges like the Garden of Eden. And I asked him what he did for excitement. He said, 'We have earthquakes.' "

"Suppose your friend's sister doesn't want to marry you."

"Suppose you were his sister, would you turn me down?"

"No," I said.

"Well, that's why I'm confident. I'm hopeful."

"Was your friend shot by the Germans?"

"He died for his country." He thought for some time. "There's more than one way to die for your country. But there's only one way to die and that's the wrong way."

He began to row again with fury and power around and around until he was hot and exhausted. Then we had ice-cream sodas at the boathouse while the sun began to sink into late afternoon.

When he left, he gave me his helmet which he had brought back with him as a trinket of the war. My mother, like the soldiers' mothers in the neighborhood and probably all over America, turned it into a hanging pot for a plant. I used to see it every day until finally we moved, and by then it was no longer important to me and so it was lost.

The night Zenia and my father talked about Sweeney, the lover, was not the only time she joked about going to Russia. The last winter was hardly over when I first heard it. They were talking about vacation time and what they might do. Sometimes we went up to visit my mother's sister, who lived in Highland Falls, where her husband was a dentist.

There was the excitement of West Point, where I had seen my first moving picture. On Saturday nights the whole town came and sat in rows on temporary folding chairs while the army band played. Moths flew in front of the projector and cast their giant shadows on the cloth screen.

After it was over we walked home, first through the gate with its regular army guards, then on to Main Street, where a few blocks away from the Point my uncle lived in a white clapboard corner house where he also had his dental offices. My father was in Albany most of that vacation, trying to find a drugstore, and he did in the end, for we moved up there for a few years.

We also took vacations occasionally in the Catskill Mountains, so when Zenia began the discussion on this night it was no surprise. "I was thinking," she said, "I might take a vacation."

They all agreed. She had worked so hard. She was finishing her internship and she was ready to begin her career as a physician herself someplace. No one had ever discussed it with her, or she with us.

"A vacation! Where?" Everybody wanted to know. "Where?"

Names fell out. The Catskill Mountains. A trip west. This charmed everyone. She laughed, her brilliantly white teeth suddenly apart, and there was her red mouth. Her mouth was fleshred. Inside her mouth, the secret organ of her tongue, her gums, the brilliant secret way she had of laughing and of seduction. She cried out, "Why? Why not the West? Hollywood!"

This dumbfounded them all. It was then a name that had no name, but she had seen it somewhere. She knew a doctor from there, a young man who had studied with her at the College of Physicians and Surgeons, and he had written that he was in a movie.

My father was amused, perhaps delighted, it was hard to tell. "Where else could you go?" he asked.

"I know where there are mountains that are higher and more mysterious," said Zenia.

"Where? Where?" They ran off the names. The Rockies. Not possible to be higher than the Rockies. The Andes. Certainly higher than the Rockies.

"Europe," Zenia said.

"Switzerland." They all said the name at the same time.

"Russia," she said.

She drifted about, looking without surprise at their surprise, but full of the expectation and magic of the word she had set free among them. Surprises like that are like wild birds caught in a house, beating like mad against invisible windows.

"Russia!"

"Why not?" she asked. "It's ours now. There are no tsars to stop us if I want to look, to go there just to see."

My father was shouting. "No one can go there. There's a war. There's misery. They're starving to death. What kind of a vacation is that? There's no way to get there."

"Well," she said, caressing my hair—I loved for her to do that and eased myself against her, half in her lap, where the warmth of her flesh flowed in waves of blood against my body—"Lenin did it. Of course, it's just a dream. Don't you want to see it yourself?" she asked my father.

"I wish them well," he said, "but I'm here forever."

"I'm nowhere forever," Zenia said.

"No!" My father was angry now. "That's silly. That's ridiculous."

Zenia pulled my hair and got up, and he took her hand and kissed it like the Russian he still was. She perched momentarily on his lap, looked at my mother with her great eyes inviting confidence and confession. "What do you think?" she asked my mother.

My mother thought for some time while they waited to hear. "If I had only one thing in the world to forget," she said finally, "I'd forget the Old World. Now and forever."

A few weeks later a spring rain was falling on the brittle weeds of our lots when my father announced, "I'm bringing a friend home for dinner Sunday. I hope you'll be here."

"Why?" Zenia asked.

"Because," my father said, "I'm bringing him home for you to meet him. He's an extraordinary man."

"In what way?" Zenia wanted to know.

"What does he do?" my mother asked.

My father said, "He's a drug salesman."

Everyone laughed. We were used to his bringing home funny stories about drug salesmen but never the salesmen themselves. "He's really a chemist with a great desire to be rich. So he became a drug salesman for McKesson and Robbins. I don't think that will make him rich, but then, let him tell his own story."

Harry Rivers was a man of surprises. After dinner, the big round table cleared of everything but the linen cloth and the stiff linen napkins, Harry leaned toward me. He was much taller than six feet, a thin wiry man with a lean long face and green eyes, always touched with excitement. He had very big hands, not fat but large, powerful, full of feeling. He used them a lot when he spoke, and he spoke a lot in a voice that thrilled me with strangeness, since he came from Oklahoma. "Would you like to see some magic?"

We all did.

"Now take your napkins and make them stand up like a wigwam," Harry said, showing us, and we did that. Now each of us sat at the table behind a linen wigwam.

"Tell me," he said, "are you sure there's nothing under that little tent in front of you?"

"A few crumbs of rye bread," my father said.

There was nothing, of course. Harry took some coins from his pocket and selected a quarter and put the rest of the money away. He passed the quarter around. "Look at it," he instructed us. "You see, it's 1914. A silver quarter." Like all the rest I looked at it, and as we passed it around everything became more exciting, just because no one knew what was about to happen, and at the same time everyone expected something marvelous.

My father was smiling, just as if he had done something magical by bringing Harry there.

"Now we're ready," Harry said. "Keep your eyes on this quarter." He raised his napkin and placed the quarter there and covered it with his linen wigwam. He stood up. He was so tall that his head and shoulders were in the darker part of the room above the Tiffany-style lamp. There his green eyes glittered black. He held a hand about a foot above his napkin and in his Oklahoma voice began to talk to it. "Come along now, little birdie. Come along with me."

He coaxed the invisible coin between his napkin and my mother's. "Now see!" he cried out and, with a swoop, swept up her napkin and there lay the quarter.

We gasped with pleasure. Laughing all the while, he asked Zenia, "I need an assistant. Who would you suggest?"

"Why, who would you think?"

"Naturally," he said, "Ram. You pick up my napkin and tell me what you see there." I was ready to see anything that would surprise and shock me, that would delight me. I raised his napkin and there was no quarter.

Harry replaced my mother's linen wigwam over the quarter and now in the same way moved on around the table from one to another, and each time the quarter moved magically on with him. Zenia was the last. She looked up at him, her eyes shining with appreciation and warmth. He had one of those easy grins that wander around like native American animals.

In the end the quarter was back where it started. And I was back in my seat and all the linen wigwams stood in front of us around the table.

"You've all been so pleasant and helpful to me," Harry said. "Therefore when I count three, all of you raise your napkins at the same time." He counted to three and we did and everybody had a quarter under the napkin.

Zenia roared with delight. "What a wonderful man you are. Indeed you are. It must take as much practice as it does to play Mozart."

His face clouded. "It does. When I was young, I wanted to be a magician, not a musician."

"Oh!" Zenia took his hand, squeezed it warmly with assurance and sympathy. "I didn't mean to make less of what you did! Why should I? You delight me. I just wanted a young boy to realize that hard work leads to magic."

The way she took his hand and pressed it made him smile again. It was of course her natural bedside manner carried over into everyday life. Beneath it was the generosity and enthusiasm of her spirit, personal and magnetic. How could you tell when the same face, the same gestures, the way she suddenly leaned forward and touched your hand, shoulder, your face, was the expression of what she felt or of what she wanted you to feel? She insisted there was no difference. "That's the difference," my father insisted. "You don't think so."

"You must understand me," Harry said to Zenia. "Although I'm nothing but an amateur, like someone who plays Mozart well enough for themselves on the piano, at heart I'm a man who wanted to be a real magician. I wanted to stand on the stage and amaze the world with what they seem to see."

"Amaze me," she said. She faced him squarely with her elbows on the dining table.

He thought for a while while my father gave my mother one of their quick intimate looks in which they exchanged hope. This was a man Zenia would have to reckon with if she came to like him at all. I already was devoted to him.

He put his hand in his jacket pocket and took out a shining metal puzzle. There were two large nails so bent that they fitted in a ring within each other and the idea was to get them apart. "Try that," he said to me, "if you haven't seen it already."

I said nothing but opened it up at once.

"I thought so," he said. He took it back and then handed me three rings, one within the other. "Try this."

I took this apart also, for I had done these little puzzles many times.

"Well," he said, "if you know those hard ones, try this easy one." He took out a small block of wood and put it on the table. It was polished and shining. He pulled it apart deftly and there lay about a dozen geometric shapes of different lengths, sizes, with different angles, some thicker, some thinner. "Put that together if you can."

I looked at it for some time.

"You see," he said, "if there isn't one thing, there's another."

I started to work on it while he went on talking, this time looking at my father and mother and finally at Zenia.

"Have you ever heard of the Green Corn Rebellion?"

"No," my father said. "It sounds like the Boston Massacre. Was it a long time ago?"

"Tell us about it, Harry," Zenia said.

"Well"—Harry Rivers now turned to all of us—"it was like the Boston Massacre in a way, although it happened just a few years ago. That wasn't much of a massacre and this wasn't much of a rebellion but they were both something, after all. It was in 1917," Harry said. "My brother was a farmer in Oklahoma. He wasn't like me. I'm tall. He was short, packed tight, like a summer drought. He was also older and had a family. He was what you'd call, I suppose, a Christian socialist. He was a Christian in what he believed and a socialist in what he hoped for. They were drafting people into the war. Of course, he was a farmer and he didn't have to go but he was against the draft and he was against the war."

My father said to us, "Harry was in the war."

"Yes," Harry said. "I was in it. Would you like to see my wound?" He held up the pinky of his left hand where the last joint was a little bent to one side. "I broke it playing baseball in a small town outside of Verdun. You've heard of Verdun? That's where Harry Rivers broke his pinky catching a fast ball." Having said this, he suddenly found himself looking around the table from face to face and suddenly I saw he was not seeing anyone. "I walked away from it, as you can see by this little pinky of mine. My brother walked right into it without leaving

Oklahoma. It was a sunny day on his farm and I was helping him before I left for the war and he came over to me. 'Harry,' he wanted to know, 'are you going to march to Washington?'

" 'Not all the way,' I said, 'but I'll walk along awhile.'

" 'Then come on,' my brother Fremont said, 'or they'll get there before we start out.'

"My sister-in-law left the children playing in the yard. She walked a couple hundred feet along with us and then stopped and watched us go on. He waved to her. Earlier she had asked me to see if I could get my brother out of going all the way. 'All the way is too far,' she said. 'I'll never live through it.'

"My brother was a farmer down there, although you couldn't call it real good farmland, but mostly scrub oak and sand hills in that county. Sasakwa was the town, if you could call it that. And the road, if you could call it a road, was really a kind of dirt trail. If you followed it, you came to a place called Spear Hill. It was night when we arrived there, my brother and myself. There were only a hundred men camped there. They all had hunting guns, shotguns. Some had revolvers. And they were getting ready to join up with some other tenant farmers, black and white. There were some Choctaw Indian farmers too. There were red men, black men and white men there. They called themselves the Working Class Union and they were on their way to Washington to stop the war. Now who were these men? Why, they were all our neighbors. They had lived around there a long time and they were all the children of immigrants. The white ones had come over from Europe and the black ones had come from Africa and the red ones from Asia, at different times, of course, just like the rest of the immigrants in this country, and in fact, as I believe, just like people everywhere. No matter where you live, a long time ago, there was somebody who was just an immigrant. What am I talking about?" he asked himself. He stopped and looked around at us.

"Evolution," Zenia said.

"Revolution or evolution," Harry said. "It's the same thing. It depends on where you stand when you look at it. We went through Sasakwa and then we took the dirt road to Spear Hill. Miles away in the darkness you could see the sparks of the campfires flying up into the sky where the men on Spear Hill were barbecuing beef and making green corn in the Choctaw way. They call that tom fuller. If instead of walking up that road then we had been walking up that road two hundred years before, the Choctaws would have been dancing the green corn dance, and if you had walked up Spear Hill thirty thousand years ago there wouldn't have been any Indians at all. I don't think they arrived here yet, or maybe it's a million years. I don't know. If you pick the right time, somebody's not there yet."

"Can you say," my father asked in general, "that there was a time when nothing was everywhere?"

"Why not?" Zenia was clear about this. "If you say something was always there, you have a mystery. Or if you say suddenly it all began, you have a mystery. It's just a question of how it works out in the language of mathematics until something better turns up."

"Forward, march," my father said. "We're on the dirt road to Spear Hill, Harry, for better or worse."

Harry went on. "It was in August and everybody was mad about this imperialist war and nobody wanted to be drafted and go off and fight. So they said. That's why they had joined the Working Class Union, which had been around Oklahoma and Arkansas for some time. I had a meal with them. They were talking a lot about marching on Washington and some hotheads had blown up a few railroad ties and cut down some telephone poles and whatnot. They had this dream they were talking about. They saw themselves on their way to Washington, hundreds of them becoming thousands, becoming in the end hundreds of thousands, all farmers and working men. And they dreamed they would get into Washington and stop the stupid war and not have to go to it. Why, they were going to take over the whole government once and for all and get everything running right.

"They had been living out here around Spear Hill for a

week or more, eating that same barbecued beef and that old Indian dish of green corn. They had wagonloads of ears to live on and of course, being farmers, they had the beef. It was a strange thing sitting out there with them in the night. It was an army. It wasn't organized much like an army. They sat around campfires with their guns ready. 'Ready for anything,' they said. They never seemed to think of the rest of the country as a real thing, with soldiers and police and armed citizens mad as hell at anybody who wanted to stop the war. They got themselves into a riot of talk about the future. The stars were out and the men were out and the wind was out and they were out. It was nature and them against the wickedness of the world.

"I got the hell out before I would find myself in Washington with them. I left my brother there, talking away with them, and walked down that dirt road. I see it now as the loneliest road in the world. I was walking out of a dream of life into a world of war and death which was the real world, and behind me, sitting around the fires, eating beef and tom fuller and drinking booze and coffee, were a hundred dreamers counting up their dreams into hundreds and then hundreds of thousands. They had never seen anything but pictures of Washington, D.C. They had never seen anything but pictures of President Wilson. Let me tell you about the loneliness of the road that night back there in 1917. August, it was. Scrub oak in the fall always looks as much like trees dying as living trees can. There was dust in the road and darkness under the trees.

"I can't tell you why I left them, only I knew what they were doing wouldn't happen. I can't tell you why I walked back, because I knew I was going off to the war in Europe and we all knew then how that war was a killer of men. The war sat in Europe like a bottomless grave. No matter how many men you shoved in, it never filled up. It just took all you had and waited there for more. And this was the road between that bottomless pit and the bottomless dream on Spear Hill. Between them was the loneliness of the road."

By then, no one was doing anything but listening. We

looked at him, although he didn't seem to look at us any more. He was far away on the road. Then he shook himself, and all of a sudden the story was over. He went on, factually.

"A few men got killed and all the rest were arrested. They sent eighty-six or so to jail, and my brother was one of them. He had violated the draft laws and all that stuff."

"Is your brother still in jail?" my father asked.

"No," Harry said. "My brother wasn't in jail very long. He went in one week and came out the next in a coffin. There was a real American patriot in the jail. He was serving a life sentence for killing his wife and child. And he and my brother had a fight about the war. And he hit my brother with a wrench and killed him. Well, of course, that was the end of the Working Class Union and my brother too. It wasn't the end of the war. I never felt one ounce of patriotism about the war, but there's a funny thing about it: good or bad, the war is yours and belongs to you and the other soldiers who fight in it. It's your war and it has everything you are that's good in you. It becomes sacred to you. Well, that was the end of it all. That was the Green Corn Rebellion."

What is there to say after hearing a story as sad and terrible as the one Harry told about the Green Corn Rebellion? My aunt asked, "How do they make tom fuller, that corn food they were eating?"

He told her.

"And why do they call it tom fuller?"

"You've got me," he said.

"Did you ever go back home?"

"No," he said. "I promised myself never to go back there until they raised a statue to my brother on top of Spear Hill. On it I want them to put a notice in marble and gold: 'Here stands the man who won the war.' " He smiled at us. His voice was back in the room instead of in the scrub oak woods and sand hills of Oklahoma. "Of course nobody won the war, but if anyone deserved to win it, it was my brother."

"What did his family do?" Zenia asked.

"Why, life goes on. People just pretend it didn't happen. Life is the same."

"Except for one thing," Zenia said.

"What's that?"

"That war did some other things. Now we have the Soviet Union where Russia used to be."

"Is it better that way, you think?" he asked.

"It's different," she said.

I told them about the other soldier and how he rowed me in the boat on the Bronx Lake. I told them what he said, how there were different ways of dying for your country, but there was only one way to die and that was the wrong way. I told them everything.

Harry said, "I'd like to meet that man."

"You can," I told him. "He's in California and he's married to his friend's sister."

"How do you know?" my mother asked.

"Because he said he would."

Harry laughed. "I admire that man. That man I could be friends with."

"That was a man in a hurry," Zenia said.

"Naturally."

"Why do you say 'naturally'?"

"If you have lived through a war, then you're in a hurry to get back and, once back, to get on with everything you've seen dying in the war. Did he ask you to marry him two minutes after you met?"

She didn't answer him.

"I don't blame him," he said.

"Are you in a hurry too?" she asked.

"Will you marry me?" He asked her this in front of all of us. "Don't be angry. You're the kind of person that makes everyone feel it's time to be in a hurry before you're gone and lost to them. Is that something to be angry about?"

My father said, "Harry, you'll have to go to the bottom of the list."

"How long is it?" Harry asked.

"Endless," my father said.

Harry was laughing. "At least I'm on the list."

"Don't be too sure," Zenia said. "You drink too much."

"Not usually," he answered. "Only tonight." He faced her the way she had faced him earlier, when he had decided to amaze her. "Because you make me nervous. It makes me dizzy to sit here with you. I've no reason to be dizzy. After all, why should you make me dizzy just because you're here? I'm drinking a lot. That I know makes me dizzy. Now I'll have a good reason for it. And being dizzy won't be a mystery any more."

They went on talking. When I awoke in the morning, the puzzle was still apart. By late that afternoon, after it had stopped raining, I finally fitted the box together. Then I went over to Laura's house and let her try. After we took it apart, we couldn't put it together again. I told them all about Harry Rivers.

"Where did you say," her mother asked, "where did you say he was from?"

"Oklahoma," I said.

5

There was no music in our doorbell. It just rang and was already silent when I found myself awake. Deep night was everywhere.

I heard now the soft voices of my parents fragmented with the puzzle and anxiety of it. Someone had rung the doorbell, but whoever it was was not ringing it again.

My father ran by my door on slippered feet. His dressing gown brushed against the doorknob. His voice questioned the silence. By then my mother was there with him and the apartment door opened and closed, the spring lock clicking safely into its metal slot.

I was out of bed and listening from my own bedroom door, which I gently opened to hear better. Laura lay on her back now. I could see her slow breathing. Great dark wings carried her far into the world of sleep.

The light in the foyer was slightly touched with pink because of our hanging hall lamp from Vienna. It had hunting figures from Greek mythology etched in tinted glass panels. I heard Mrs. Townsend's voice. She who knew everything was now back with prickly whisperings of great danger.

"What did they say?"

Mrs. Townsend's guarded words kept them close to her. "I'm just telling you what I heard. Art Burrows, he's the one. Being the janitor, of course, he knows everything, and he was talking to the federal people when they came here to ask lots of questions, like who knew Laura's parents, things like that. They asked everyone."

"They didn't ask us," my mother said.

"Why should they? They knew Laura was with you."

"How?" my father wanted to know.

"Because Art Burrows told them. He told them everything."

"What do you mean, everything?" My father was indignant but he was also afraid. He became indignant because indignant was brave.

"He told them about Zenia knowing Laura's parents and how she went to visit them and had dinner there and he told them that Laura was here with you, which they knew anyway, they said. Art also said that he would tell them if anything strange happened here if they wanted him to and they said they wanted him to."

"What do you mean, strange?" There was strangeness now in my father's voice. "Nothing strange goes on here. It's all out there with them."

"Why, yes. That's true. He said he would keep an eye on you and call them, say, if you left or moved away or anything strange like that."

"How could you hear all that?"

She said, "I just went down to ask him if he knew anything. You know he knows everything. He sees everybody. He makes jokes. Everybody likes him and tells him everything."

My father said, "He's a spy in this house."

"That may be. But I went down and they were talking outside his door. That's how I heard them. You know how the basement is. I went out and down by the side steps."

There were steel steps that led from the ground floor out and down into the yard on that side of the house. Here the lots were much higher than the yard and a stone wall kept the earth from falling in. Art Burrows and his wife lived in a basement apartment whose windows opened on the yard. They were the janitors. They collected garbage and waste through dumbwaiters that rose through every apartment and they cleaned the apartment house. There was a public telephone downstairs in their

46

hallway, and the Burrowses would ring your downstairs bell three times when a call came through asking for you. They were happy to do this, they said. Art was a merry man, biggish, plump and fatty, not fat and muscular like the friends of Laura's father. Mrs. Burrows was the strong one in that family and did a lot of the carrying. She was a suspicious woman, not friendly to children, while he was everybody's friend. It seemed now he was also everybody's enemy.

"I think," Mrs. Townsend said, "he has been seeing these federal people and talked with them before what happened tonight. That's the way it sounded to me. When I came down the steps into the yard, I opened the door there to go inside and looked down the corridor to where he lives. But I stopped because I heard them talking down there. It was dark except for that one electric light bulb they have in the hall but I could hear everything they said." She paused and nothing was said. Suddenly there was urgency in her voice. "You have to send the girl away. They'll watch you as long as she's here."

"But where can I send her?" my father asked. "I don't know where Laura's mother is."

"Her mother must be in jail also. They never tell."

There was a long silence that I couldn't understand.

"Thanks for telling us," my father said.

"Don't say I told you."

"No," my father said. "Thank you." The door opened and closed behind her softly. By then I was back in bed pretending to sleep, and when they opened the door to look in nothing moved in our room. The door closed with a sigh. It was my father sighing.

As they went back to their bedroom I was up again, and I stood in the dark of the hall listening.

My father said, "I don't trust her."

"Then why did she tell us?"

"To frighten us. What does Art Burrows know about anarchists? He knows about garbage and dumbwaiters. He reads the newspapers we throw away. He reads old letters and matchboxes. He makes lists of banana skins and chicken bones. She comes to warn us about Burrows. But she's the one. Then we do something and become part of this whole thing. She's a provocateur, not a friend." His voice went higher in his anger. "Does she look like a friend to you, with her fake socialism? I wasn't born, I didn't live in tsarist Russia for nothing. I know the ways of the Cheka. I know them all. They are everywhere. They're part of all governments. I'll tell you something else. You can be sure one of Laura's father's friends, one of those anarchist friends of his, was a provocateur. Why not? It's always that way."

My mother said something I couldn't hear, but the tone of her voice was soothing.

He exploded. "I won't live here in fear like that. Never! I'll go back to Russia too, with Zenia. You should see the spies the Treasury Department has everywhere because of this idiot Prohibition. Imagine selling liquor in drugstores on doctors' prescriptions! The doctors sell their prescriptions to bootleggers and the druggists sell their liquor to the same men and get the doctors' prescriptions to cover it. We're drowning in rubbing alcohol. That means they make more pure alcohol which they sell to gangsters. One thing covers the other and everybody pays the agents of the government. Meanwhile, Attorney General Palmer chases immigrants. People come here for freedom and liberty and a chance to escape those terrible old places where misery is history. I won't stay here. I wish they had sent me back on that Soviet Ark with Rosa Luxemburg. What about this child Laura whose parents are in jail? What about her? Do they have a jail for children too? They do. Only they call these jails asylums. Lunatic asylums for the crazy and children's asylums for the young and innocent. Damn them and their hypocrisy!"

She stopped him. She must have put her hand across his mouth.

Somewhere in the zoo a lion raised his voice and then one by one the great cats began to roar. Out of the dark refuge of their prisons their voices sounded through the night, calling out across the Atlantic for their African homes.

My mother said, "What are you going to do in the morning?"

She and my father whispered so quietly all I could hear was the hiss of their breaths. But I heard the lions. After a great crescendo, one by one the beasts let their voices collapse into their bodies with gasping rumbles like a passing Catskill thunderstorm. Their lion voices dissolved back into the Africa of their dreams.

Now my parents stirred comfortably in bed. Their movements had the sound of agreement.

Back in my room I closed the door. When I turned, I was surprised to see Laura sitting up, her eyes wide open. In the eerie light reflected from the streetlamp below and seeping through the thick chestnut trees, Laura's face was white, her eyes were black, although I knew they were really gray or green.

I sat down beside her. "Let's get dressed."

She didn't ask a single question. We both dressed. We both kept absolutely quiet. We each took one of my heavy sweaters and I gave her a pale, silvery scarf which Zenia had left in my bedroom.

"They mustn't hear us," I said, "or they'll stop us."

We were quick, we were silent, and we were gone.

Outside the night waited for us.

Laura and I ran into the lots on the other side of Agnes Helder's farmhouse. Here the lots tipped down, leveled out, and for some reason the burdock didn't grow. It became bare earth and tattered grass where we played baseball just behind the Greeks. Then the burdock insisted again, except for the beaten path that led to Garden Street and Southern Boulevard. It was that same path which Zenia and I, accompanied by the policeman, had taken. We knelt beneath the burdock and could see the boulevard streetlamp where Antonio had died.

No one could see us there, but then there was no one to see us. There was nothing, no automobile, no trolley, no horse and wagon, no cat, no dog, only the boulevard running north along the park to Fordham Road or curving south at 182nd Street, where it ran on and on with its trolley tracks until it joined Westchester Avenue. There the subway which had come out of the earth after crossing under the North River rose into the night and ran as an elevated line until it too came to the south end of the zoo.

I longed to hear and see a streetcar but none came along. The steel tracks glittered under the live wires overhead.

"Where shall we go?" Laura asked.

I didn't know.

"We could go back upstairs."

"We can't."

"Why are we down here?" she asked. It was scary out there in the midnight emptiness with nothing moving, only the night lying on everything. One by one the streetlights stood alone. This midnight universe on whose edge we waited didn't care much about us. It belonged to Jack-the-Ripper.

"Is this where Antonio died?"

"Who told you?"

"I listened when everybody talked."

"There by that streetlamp." I pointed to the corner streetlight where he had been carried and put down on a police blanket. It was really a brown horse blanket but the policeman had brought it over. In the end they had covered him with yet another one so he lay like someone sleeping with the blanket over his head.

Laura stood up to see clearly. "Is that his blood on the ground there?"

"Yes."

She was down again beside me, crouching close, our bodies touching while I wondered what to do or even what to say to her.

"My father told Antonio not to carry a gun. He told him, 'If you carry a gun, you'll shoot it and then someone in the end will shoot you.' But Antonio wouldn't give it up. He said they wouldn't take him and throw him out of a window downtown like they did with Salsedo."

What had happened to Salsedo had been discussed with passionate indignation in our house. Everybody felt it was a terrible thing although the government said he had accidentally fallen out of the window. "The government says nothing," Zenia reported after going to a meeting in which a committee of five, including herself, had met with the federal attorney in the federal building. "They denied, of course, they had pushed him out. They also said that those of us who weren't born here didn't have to stay. If we didn't like America, we could go back where we came from. There's a certain truth in that." She looked at the shocked faces around our dining room table. "On the other hand," she said, "here we are, after all. Let them change, and not throw immigrants from the window as if they were barbarians invading a foreign country."

This night lay there like a foreign country.

Laura said, "We just can't stay here like this. What do you want to do?"

I told her that we must find Zenia at the hospital but we couldn't go there until it got to be morning. The hospital was far away, as she knew, having been there with her mother.

"Then why couldn't we wait for morning in your room?"

I told her about Mrs. Townsend and what she had said. I didn't tell her everything. But I told her enough and she began to tremble because she felt the police would come and take her away from her father and mother and she would never see them again. I comforted her and myself by telling her that Zenia would take care of everything.

"We must find a place to hide," I told her, and she stopped crying because this was something to do.

"Where?"

"Where no one can find us."

I held her by the hand and we stood up and looked up and down the length of the boulevard. Nothing moved. Far off an apartment house showed a few lights like ships at sea. The wide boulevard stretched ahead.

"Run."

We ran across the dangerous emptiness of the boulevard into the shadow of the zoo, whose trees and brush pressed up against the high page-wire fence that separated the inside from the world outside. Maple trees planted one by one in a long line marched away to the distant Fordham Road. We stood under the one everybody called the Umbrella Tree. It was our way to get into the zoo after closing hours. There were two long branches from this maple which, unlike the others, extended across the sidewalk and just barely over the top of the page-wire fence and its flesh-tearing triple strands of barbed wire that leaned rigidly inward to discourage fence climbers. There was usually no reason to get into the zoo over the fence since there were entrances and gates, but the zoo closed at four thirty and everybody was asked to leave. Then it was that we went over into it by way of the Umbrella Tree. Inside the zoo was the place where we could both feel the safest. It was a favorite place to play after closing hours. We used to play baseball in the wapiti pastures until night fell while the animals huddled in a far corner and watched us with inhuman eyes that told us nothing. A crab apple tree grew in the center of the field there. These horned animals were shy enough yet there was something wild and daring for us in playing there, ready at any moment to run for safety and climb the fence if the formidable wapiti moved toward us.

"Where shall we go in the zoo?" Laura wanted to know.

"To the farm," I told her. "There'll be nobody there all night and tomorrow's Sunday. After the people come into the zoo, why, we'll just go along with the other visitors and go out by the Fordham Gate and walk to the hospital."

She was suddenly full of excitement and life. We both felt this park of wild beasts was safer than the world, which had come apart during the raid. We knew the zoo as we knew our own lots. We had spent years wandering through it, behaving as tourists by day or adventurers after closing time. We knew no one was there, only the few zookeepers on guard and the wild animals who lived there.

This was our way of getting in. We used to climb up the fence, reach out to the double branches that overhung it and haul ourselves up so that we finally stood on one branch while we held on to the other about three feet above it. Now I did that and Laura followed me. There we swayed, holding on, while she crossed finally over the wire fence into the zoo. As the branches grew thinner and branched out as branches do into many small and flexible twigs, her weight made the lower branchlets arch down to the ground. I clung to the upper branch so that when she dropped off inside the zoo the whiplike return of the lower branch wouldn't throw me.

It was my turn now to come down out of the Umbrella Tree and I took one last look through its cloud of leaves back over the boulevard, Antonio's lamppost, the lots and our apartment house, standing there so far away. There was a lighted window on the fourth floor. It was Mrs. Townsend's kitchen window. She was still up, then. I wondered if the federal agents might be in her apartment watching ours.

I held the upper branch and balanced along the lower one over the zoo fence, over the three strands of barbed wire. Now as the branches thinned in wider and wider clusters of leaves looking for sunlight and space, my weight slowly brought the end of the branch down, and when I was about six feet from the ground, both big branches rested on the zoo fence and bent like two great bows. I dropped to the grass and was into the brush with Laura as the tree snapped back into place.

Inside the wild night flew away. All the terror and death of the raid were outside at last.

We both knew the best way to the farm at the northeast corner of the zoo and we moved together, making our way around the enclosed pastures of the deer until we came up behind the heavy steel bar fences of the wolf dens. They heard us and were soon out, their eyes bright in the darkness. We had no fear of them, having on many long afternoons sat in the brush and watched them after the zoo closed. The marvel of these animals that had become part of our knowing them was that they were creatures you never really got to know. You never knew them. You never knew any of the animals in the zoo but you were always outside of them, watching them, not like people or dogs or cats or even tame canaries and such things. There were the wild animals in their cages and here was some unknown world full of fear and belonging. They were wild. The way they lived in their prisons, they still were wild. I never believed the zookeepers who fed the animals, throwing them chunks of meat; even in the house of lions, the keeper scratching a maned shoulder through the bars was only pretending. There were stories of children and even grown-ups, foolish enough to step over the low wire fence and put a hand inside a cage to pat or feed only to receive a flash of claw or tooth. We knew the zoo better than all of them and knew these were the wild. We were out of the wild and the animals were in the wild. They had been kidnapped and brought from their homes in the forests and plains of the world, out of deserts and mountains, and here they were for us to look at. But what did they see as they looked out of their cages at us, posing on their ridges of Manhattan schist or grouped in the wide pastures or in the empty cells waiting for food and water? Here they lay or walked or jumped or flew and nothing they did made any sense. My Aunt Zenia said, "Their job is to earn their living in the wild and here they can't. So what are they, poor things?" But they entranced me with their differences, which were so many, yet all had eyes and legs and living bodies.

We looked at the wolves watching us out of the darkness. Their eyes glittered with red.

"What do they think of us?" Laura asked.

"I don't know. What do we think of them?"

"I'm afraid of them," she said.

So was I. But not the way I was afraid of what this night had done to all of us. "The wild has gone its way and we have gone ours," Zenia said. "And now, when we meet, we see from far off a past we can't remember, but it's there. You," my aunt said, "will soon be old enough to read that most readable of all men, Charles Darwin. But I don't see why you can't read his journey." And she brought me a copy of the *Voyage of the Beagle*. It had many line drawings but I just dipped into it here and there. What I imagined was the old man with his dignified face and beard like Karl Marx wandering around in the wilds of Patagonia, but of course he was a young man then, out to study the world for its secrets.

"We know the answer," Zenia said. "He put his finger on it. Time, chance, big numbers."

"You call that an answer?" my father said.

"It'll have to do, but we can pick our own way."

My father clapped his hands with laughter at the folly of it all. "Imagine," he said to the whole table, for Harry was there that night, and Sweeney also. "Imagine, the universe has no choice, but we do."

Laura and I were just hiding among Darwin's secrets.

We crossed the little meadowed hill and came out on the far side of the wild duck pond and then ran along in the darkness which from time to time had one zoo lamp standing alone in the night. Ours were the only steps in the dark cold air. The summer night was rich with scent here. The zoo had its own wild fragrance laced with the acid perfume of animals.

Sometimes running, sometimes walking swiftly, always in the safety of shadows, we fled around the wild duck pond, avoided the reptile house and very soon were running free toward the northeast of the zoo where the woods began, crossing over the creek and the rhododendron forest with its wooden walk and finally over the low single-wire fence into the dense trees, open brush and finally the meadow.

We waited there, breathing hard but free, feeling the safety of this open field. There were some outhouses and a barn and a few hundred yards away a half-dozen Holsteins feeding in the starlight.

The sky was black here without any mirrored glow of

downtown and streetlights. We looked up at the Milky Way. We knew the usual names that really meant nothing in that ever-increasing darkness.

We ran freely across the meadow to the barn and the Holsteins raised their heads and after a long chewy look returned to their night feeding.

The barn doors were open and the inside packed high with bales of hay.

There were canvas covers neatly stacked against one wall among the hanging tools and a small tractor. We took two canvas haystack covers and pulled them across a mound of loosely piled hay. There we spread one as a sheet and one as a cover and sat so we could look out the open doors into the starlight and the comfort of the feeding Holsteins.

"What's going to happen?" Laura asked. She asked the night rather than me but I answered for all of us.

"We'll see Zenia."

Then we lay back there, lying side by side. We never said another word and the night rolled on.

I lay there thinking, not of what had happened but of the night rolling on and on wherever it was and how, as my Aunt Zenia had told me, beyond the sun the night rolled on and on. Once we had stood on a mountain clearing in the Catskills above Big Indian and looked off on a moonless night into the universe. "There," she said, sweeping her hand over it all, "time and space are one thing. And each one of us is one thing too. It would be there if we didn't know it, but if we didn't know it, how could it matter if it were there or not?"

We two beneath the canvas in the barn had shifted naturally over to each other for warmth and comfort against whatever it meant that space and time were one.

6

When I awoke the sun had already betrayed the secrets of the night and they were gone.

Laura smiled across her hunched knees. She smiled out of the tangle of her uncombed hair. Then she jumped up and ran out into the field, which dazzled with daisies and black-eyed Susans. Sunday visitors strolled around in peace, the women with parasols against the bright rays, the men now and then taking off their hats and touching their foreheads with blazing white handkerchiefs. The Holsteins munched away and the people walked past or stopped to look, all friendly and filled with the sweet warmth and easiness of Sundays in the zoo.

They all seemed to be going off behind the barn to the dirt road which led past an open wooden fence gate to the regular zoo path that would take them to the Grand Concourse and the Pelham Entrance. There were ducks in Lake Agassiz. North lay the Botanical Gardens, and Laura and I talked about going there also. We strolled because the others did.

It was Sunday in the zoo and the visitors had come from distant parts of the city, come by subway and streetcar. In the open concourse, lying there in its formal circle beneath the steps that led up into Baird Court and the great houses of lions, primates and birds, a few automobiles drove in and parked in a circle. There were also some carriages.

Now everything was as it had been and we were with them, strolling.

We stopped at the goldfish pools and watched the cod

mouths open to beg crumbs from the children. Everywhere the sun grew hotter and more serene. The pavement was designed geometrically with red and white stones.

But everybody was going up the steps and when the lions began to roar, then people hurried a little, wanting to get there to stand close and feel the great beasts, who, in their cages, picked up the rhythm of the roar from their neighbors. On hot days, even though the doors were wide open and the slow winds stirred through the great hall of lions, its acrid smell drove people out into the open again. Outside in the semicircular end cages, a tiger patrolled the wire, but the lion sat where it had finished roaring, his shaggy mane, his neat shining body, his air of having nothing to do, as if it were Sunday all his life, betraying no curiosity. They never seemed to see us. "Why should they?" Zenia asked. "We no longer mean anything. After a while, even if you let them out, they'd want to go back in again."

"Suppose you put them back on the plains of Africa?"

"Who knows," she said. "They might die of starvation. It takes great skill and practice to make a living in nature. It's the survival of the fittest."

But now it was Sunday and we walked with the others.

We stood outside the bird house and watched the toucans and their enormous colored beaks, we watched the parrots and all kinds of different birds. There were birds of paradise with extravagant Victorian tails. There were little birds like those I saw on my walks with Zenia. She knew them by name. It is a kind of habit you get into, noticing them. We didn't go into the house of primates but just wandered with the strollers so much at peace, and we in our peace too.

Of course I knew I was dreaming, I knew I was in a dream, so happy and content I didn't want to wake up. I knew I was in a dream because I was waking up all the while and I struggled with all the will I had to keep on strolling with Laura and all the Sunday visitors. The children ran around us playing and the grown-ups strolled and Laura and I were with them all the while as I woke up. We held hands. Laura's hands were like Zenia's. They were dry and warm and full of life and confidence.

Suddenly everybody began to gather around the sea lion pool and we hurried to join them. The growing excitement helped me find my way back into the dream. I pushed through the crowd of expectant faces, of bodies gathering, until Laura and I found ourselves against the steel fence which circled the sea lion pool.

I thought the keepers were feeding them. People loved to gather about the different animal houses to watch the zookeepers feed the animals. But only the sea lions played the game of hunger with them. The lions just let the chunks of meat be thrown in and made no move. They knew it would be there. Their hunger was mechanical and no joy to them. Monkeys always misbehaved while they quarreled with each other. But the great apes so often alone in their cages would indolently lie there and stretch out a fingered foot or hand and just touch the bananas, apples and vegetables, sometimes gathering them in indifferent clumps beside their bodies. They ate as if it were at least something else to do. Birds of course ate all the time, flying about and never losing their quick dashes of caution, ready to escape even as they settled down to peck away, never at ease. Only the sea lions played with the joy of eating when a zookeeper threw a dead fish into the water or even into the air and the one sea lion on top of the smooth mound of rounded rock would fly into the air to catch it while others rose from the waters like mermaids around the island of Aeaea. Watching the sea lions eat was always a pleasure to everyone, including the graceful mammals themselves.

But this was not the case in my dream.

The molded shape of man-made rock wasn't like natural rocks at all, but smooth, carved, undulating in shape, rising to a rounded height, and there it was arrested like a statue. The sea lions made their way up, rocking back and forth as they climbed, forcing themselves on legs which had become powerful flippers until they reached the top, and there briefly the sea lions waited, swaying endlessly. Many animals in the cages did this. The polar bear often marched without stopping, rocking forward and backward, up and down, along the bars of its cage, swaying its head endlessly from side to side like a blind singer hearing what we just saw. Captive humans in the asylums of the lost stood and swayed, looking inside to their own arctic dreams in the same way. First one and then another sea lion climbing, waiting, swaying, dived down while the crowd laughed with pleasure, pointing, and children sometimes clapped their hands.

I was by then desperately trying to stay in my dream. As the sea lions mounted, I too mounted an undulating and smooth sculpture of waking. I fought desperately against it. I concentrated all my will not to awaken, to dive down as did the sea lions into the soft and happy waters of my dream which kept coming apart. I let go of Laura's hand and clung to the fence, tightening my grip, for I was like a dreamer under the waters of sleep, rising against my will to the surface of waking, and I held my dreamer's breath and tried to stay below. I held on and now I knew it was going, that in the very next moment it would be gone. It was like the last ray of the Catskill Mountain sun when one of the wild and fleeing clouds that so often raced across the mountain obscured the sunlight of the dream.

Then I saw my Aunt Zenia. She walked slowly and gracefully up the sculptured rock and, where it was too steep, bent gracefully down and used her hands to steady herself. Her hair hung loose and she was at the top, where she stood for a moment, then raised her arms high above her head and began to bring her hands together. She was nude and beautiful as I had seen her on the high rock side of our Catskill creek pool.

Then there were butterflies and birds. Then there were blue skies and far away a mountain cumulus rising in endless mounting, billowing turrets, absolutely still, posed like an alpine height of snow, bristling with sunlight. The hot sun had warmed the air without breaking into the deeper shadows or the rock hideouts in the pool where the fat trout waited. The brook was alive with its perpetual monologue and Zenia leaped and with the leap, in a blaze of sundrops, demolished my dream, and I let go of it for another.

The starlight was cold outside the open barn doors and empty.

All of a sudden I was sitting up in a night empty of dreams for Laura was gone.

"Laura."

First fearing, then not caring, I called her name and ran out into the pasture.

"Laura!"

Clumsily the Holsteins got up and hustled away, bumping awkwardly into each other. One broke into a slow trot. The rest in sudden alarm followed until they were in a distant corner of the pasture under the trees which hid the fence at the Boston Road.

I stood alone there.

"Laura!"

I yelled her name against the aloneness of standing there.

Insects throbbed as they always do. I listened for her voice, her call in the silence of the night which is never silent, hoping as I yelled her name to hear her call, and I knew all the while as I trembled with the shouting which frightened me more than the emptiness that she had never slept at all but just waited in the secret of her fear and then fled into the vastness of the zoo, running, running until she could escape by the Crotona Gate, across the boulevard and back to her apartment where at least the very men who had arrested her father and killed Antonio would be waiting in the electric light out of the night. She hoped her mother would be there. She wanted it. There were too many hours until the next day for her to hide in the zoo where now I stood alone, crying out her name although I knew there would be no answer.

The voiceless silence around me vibrated with the humming of the insects making their mad and monotonous love sounds. It stuck like a tuning fork inside my head. I took a step into the cropped and scratchy grasses. I stepped into a sea of sound which emptied briefly beneath my feet only to flood in again as the insects carried on their endless strumming. The whole night of stars shook with their sound. It was either that or my own blood pounding fear into my head. I was alone here. I alone was myself while the enemy night was everywhere.

I ran behind the barn, wanting to catch up but knowing it was too late, yet running. While I ran, the fear which had been hovering in me began to fly. Just running did that.

The wooden gate at the end of the dirt road was closed but I went over, climbing, leaping to hit the zoo path that led by way of Lake Agassiz to the Concourse. I called her name again.

"Laura!"

Her name flew across the lake. There were no ducks in sight. Nothing. Blank water under the starlight and the little rush of the waterfall where it tumbled into the Bronx Lake.

In the circle of the Concourse the starlight was ominous. Like ornamental candles tucked around its edges, the zoo lamps in their elegant iron stands glowed, each one alone in its isolated brightness. The road flowed in from the Pelham Entrance. It made its circle, empty of anything. The goldfish pools lay motionless, with the stone steps leading up into Baird Court between them. This dull light was everywhere. It had no crispness like the happy country nights of Big Indian but was dull as if tarnished and withdrawn, yet light enough to see the white paving stones and the red design now black in the walks.

I ran across the Concourse and up the steps and stopped. Baird Court was too empty. It was enormous in its emptiness and I suddenly felt it was dangerous to run across it between the great houses of birds and lions to my right, the house of primates to my left, the "monkey house," we called it. Beyond the central lawn to the right the elephant house stood whitely among the trees. Starlight shadows don't have the clarity of moon shadow. They lurk. They wait there for you, soft and embracing to drop you into a pit, into holes and swamps of fear.

I crouched close to the stone balustrade, searching for some movement anywhere. But there was none. The cages were empty. The animals had withdrawn from the cold night.

I knew there must be a zookeeper here but then I thought I could run faster than any one of them. They often chased us away after hours. But they never bothered to catch us. "Goddamn kids," they yelled, laughing out of their pipes and mustaches.

The zookeepers were in fact not real creatures of fear for they were like the animals they took care of, just part of the zoo. The zookeepers picked up pieces of paper. They fed the animals. They swept up after the Sunday visitors. They answered questions and tipped their peaked caps. Sometimes you saw them idly scratching a chimpanzee's back. They were all part of the same zoo I knew so well.

I could have gone around behind the houses but I began a mad run across Baird Court. The pavement seemed so loud under my feet I swerved onto the main grass center, running more silently there. Somewhere an animal flung out a racing growl. One wild roving glance and looking back I saw a big dog break out of the shadow of the lion house and take after me. There are no dogs permitted in the zoo. I had never seen a dog there. It was big, short-haired, with a boxer face and it came speeding after me, snarling wildly. The shock of it ripped loose my fears, which then outran my breath.

It was no use anyway. I stopped dead and turned around.

The dog was just a big mutt and he ran up, mouth wide, tongue lolling, panting and laughing with a dog's tame face. So we faced each other, our breaths heavy, then with a yelp he ran off the way he had come.

I walked off the way I had been running. The fears of the night were like Hudson williwaws.

When I reached the end of the court I started to run again. I ran past the thick steel bars of the empty elephant yards. Now I was free, running clear again. I only looked ahead, my eyes straining along the path as I passed empty benches running between the single-strand wire fences that marked the side of the walk from the lawns and shrubbery forbidden to visitors. The wire stretched out. It shone dully or caught brightness from the occasional zoo lamp. I could smell the elephant house. Each of the houses had the smell of their animals that nothing washed clean. They were all touched with the excrement and urine and this with the cold of night clung in pools of scent around each house or field or den.

I ran past the walk which led to the public toilets. There was a slight smell of lion in the air. His arm came out and caught me roughly, stopping me dead in my tracks in a hard, alien embrace. My terror broke free. I screamed once, then went stiff with death.

He was big. He wore a sweater instead of the zookeeper's jacket but he had on a zookeeper's hat and a big mustache. Heavy eyebrows and a loose mouth that reeked of tobacco, alcohol, wet and red, smiling with animal power.

"Where did you escape from?" he said. "We don't let the animals out at night."

There was amusement in his voice although it was harsh and heavy with authority and strength.

I went crazy to escape, to be free, kicking and poking, twisting, turning, but he only tightened his grip until I choked, gasping.

"Don't try it," he said.

I stopped, helpless. After that first look, I couldn't face him. Those colorless eyes were shadows in his face. He smiled without smiling, the lips pulled back in the motion of a smile. He held my left arm with one of his hands and held me by my bunched sweater at the back of my neck. No grown-up had ever held me this way. Boys had tried and failed. It was completely different. I was helpless. This was a true helplessness.

"Runaway?"

I nodded.

"Where's the other one?"

I was silent.

"That was my dog."

I didn't say anything.

"Where do you think you're running?"

"I'm going home," I said.

"Where's home?"

"Out the Crotona Gate," I said.

"Well," he said, "I'm going to keep you here and call the police but they won't come around till morning. Did you stay in after the park closed?"

I nodded. I said, "I'm going home now. Just let me go."

"I'm told to hand you over to the police."

He pulled me along toward Baird Court and the dog ran up and began to bark at both of us.

"Shut up," he yelled at the dog, who cringed and ran behind us then, sniffing at my heels and staying behind, eager but docile and afraid.

The zookeeper pushed and pulled me along, up the steps into the lion house. There the keepers had little offices at each end of the double line of cages under the domed roof. The dim lights of the lion house concealed in shadows the dark cages and the silence of the giant creatures within them.

He opened the office door and pushed me in. Inside was a lighted room. It also faced a cage hidden from the public where the zookeepers sometimes kept a sick creature or a new prisoner of the zoo. It was all rank with lion smell and in the cage was a young female lion, sleek and awake. She was playful and came rubbing up against the cage, and the keeper, still holding me by one hand, reached through and fondled her head. She moved like a domestic cat against his hand, which caressed her long body and flank.

There was a plank wooden table in the small office room and the walls had shelves with bottles and medicines. There was a hanger there with the zookeeper's jacket on it. There was a thermos bottle and a black lunch box.

I watched him in silence.

"You might as well settle down here," he said, "because you're going to be here till morning."

"Why can't I leave?" I asked.

"Because you're not going to." He poured out some hot coffee for himself. He didn't offer me anything. There was nothing friendly in anything he did. I was just something the hunter had caught and there at the hunter's pleasure. I sat huddled in the wooden chair.

Then I saw Zenia's scarf on a shelf, loose, silvery, fragile.

I don't know why I suddenly felt it, I thought Laura was dead.

He said, "You sure there was only one of you?"

"Yes," I said, "just me."

"I heard someone earlier."

"I was just looking around. It was cold. I didn't know where to go. I thought I'd come into one of the houses."

"Well, you're in one now." He picked up the scarf. "This is silk," he said. "I found it on the walk when I heard you walking around before."

I didn't say anything.

"It's a woman's scarf. Pure silk," he said. He fluffed it in his hand and the scarf floated off and settled down on the table. He leaned against the cage, his back to the lion, who leaned against him through it while he drank his hot coffee. "Why did you run away?"

"I was just mad," I said.

"I ran away," he said. "That's always wrong. You learn too much."

I tried to be friendly. "Did you become a zookeeper because you like animals?"

He shrugged me off as irrelevant.

The reek of the lions was thick here. The zookeeper himself smelled of it. It had been the first sign that he was near, but I hadn't known what it meant as I ran past him.

He said, "Are you afraid of the animals?"

I didn't answer.

He put his hand in the cage, which here was nothing but vertical parallel iron bars from the raised platform to the ceiling.

He tugged at the lion's ears, pulled them. "This," he said, "is just a young pussycat." She was nearly full grown and her fur was silky and shining in the naked electric bulb of the zookeeper's office. "It's boring here at night, working every night. I guess," he considered, "I should ask for a change, but then I wouldn't be here alone with these pussycats of mine. Take this one. Isn't she beautiful?"

I nodded.

It frightened me to see him put his hand in there while he scratched the lioness. Suddenly he unlatched the cage door. The latch was simply a length of steel attached to the door by a wire chain. Then he opened the cage door.

The lion flowed around in its effortless way without coming out. He put his hand in and grabbed her tail and she whirled with incredible swiftness on him. She was around and his hand was still trying to let go but she simply pawed him without her claws and faced him and then leaped past out of the cage. It was about five feet to the table and she landed there easily with the grace of limitless power and stood there, her tail making abrupt waves this way and that. She yawned. Her giant mouth opened wide and I could smell the decaying odor in it. Her fangs were perfect to rip a world of living bones and flesh apart. He came up behind her, looking at me from his end of the lion's back. Her tail struck him as she swished it jerkily back and forth.

I was absolutely still in my chair, held there by the awful fear of the lion.

"Now you can feel like a lion tamer," he said. "Only this is no tame lion. We've had her just a month, that's all. Don't you want to say anything?"

I shook my head.

"Are you afraid?"

I nodded.

"Why? She's friendly, powerful. She's strong, she's well-fed, she's beautiful. And she doesn't eat little boys who run away from home."

He began to caress her flanks, rubbing his hand along the

giant muscles that lived within her skin. The smell of lion was like poison and fear in me. I knew he wasn't afraid. I knew he knew I was.

I was so afraid that I didn't know anything but the smell of lion.

He felt her belly. He ran his hands along her great and powerful thighs. She growled softly and arched her back against him. Her weight shoved him back, and all the while he kept caressing her he cooed to her, using baby words.

In the electric light his eyes were bronze and shining with feeling but her giant eyes were impersonal. They gave me no hint of what she thought, only danger. He put his face against her great thigh, his mustache amongst her hair. I had never felt fear like this before. This fear was nothing like the risky darkness of our lots or movies or the fears and dreams which always made some sense even as you dream them. This fear was just there, choked hard like a scream that couldn't come out.

The lion stood easily on the table, one foot resting on Zenia's scarf. She kept arching her back. When he ran his hand up the back of her legs toward her tail, she stretched out and her arching tail with its tuft of hair at the end flicked his face.

I felt it coming on the way nausea comes, only it was fear. My head was hot with it. My chest was tight with it. My heart raced with it. My breath was breathless with it. I knew I was going to scream, and I knew I couldn't. I knew if I screamed, something horrible and unbearable would happen, and all the while he stroked her smoothly, cooing at her, his voice rumbling as her roar rumbled within her. Her rumbling voice came out of some interminable cavern of echoing sound.

Out in the great dark lion house a lion began to roar.

"They're calling you there," he said to her. "Thet're asking for you, those big lions. But you're here with me, aren't you?" He reached his arms around her loins, embracing her, and she crouched down, her left front paw raised, and the claws came out, shining like ivory and pointed like death.

The lion on the table let out a great sound, so close I closed my eyes against it and saw it.

"Come on, you little bitch," he yelled at her. And suddenly the lion wheeled on him and her right paw, claws out, struck him as the cat flung herself against him and they both went down screaming in the roaring on the floor.

I jumped from my chair, grabbed Zenia's scarf from the table and was out of the room, slamming the office door behind me. I felt the lion hit the door with all her weight but I was a door away. I opened and closed the lobby doors and then the outside lion-house door.

I was out in the dark cold night air, running from the storm of roaring in the lion house, just running like mad. I ran past the elephant house. I ran past the fox dens. I ran past the deer cages. I ran past the llama cages, the dromedaries, the camels, and whirled through the Crotona Gate, the heavy revolving gate bars screeching behind me.

A streetcar rattled by, one of those summer streetcars flashing its electric tentacle to snap firelight like great fireflies above it from the live wires that gave it motion. The motorman stood there inside the open summer streetcar with one passenger, and beside him, sitting there relaxed, was the conductor. It ran by without stopping through the empty streets, taking the great turn on its way south.

I fled across the boulevard into the lots. There I hid in the non-feral sweetness of the dark burdock. I still had Zenia's scarf.

There were no lights in our apartment house, not even one, just darkness everywhere. I made my way to Casanova's garden and looked across it at the electric lights still on in Laura's apartment. A stranger passed the living room window. He was speaking as they do in silent movies. All I heard were insects and one dog barking on Mapes Avenue. Then I saw Laura. She came to the window. She looked out. There was a smile on her face. She began to wave to me.

"Laura, Laura!" I screamed her name again and again

with relief, with fear, with exhaustion and with, in the end, a good-bye sorrow. "Laura."

I woke up in the dawn.

Laura, pale and cold, was watching me with an intent silence. "You were calling me," she said.

"Why didn't you answer?"

7

As soon as the Sunday visitors began to move through the zoo, we left by the Fordham Gate. It was a long hot walk to the hospital. We took off our sweaters and I carried them along with Zenia's scarf.

"Are you hungry?" I asked Laura.

"Yes, I am. But I don't care."

We were so impatient to arrive, nothing but hurrying there made any difference. And every streetcar that passed our way made every block we walked emptier, longer, more annoying. Then, as in every arrival at a familiar place, the early signs appeared and we began to run again, knowing the hospital would show up at any moment, and so it did and we were there.

Here, I knew where to go and led Laura to the emergency entrance, where two ambulances waited in the driveway. The nurse on duty knew me and her face became a smile as she saw us. Before I could ask for my Aunt Zenia, the nurse said, "Doctor Mont's waiting for you."

She took us up the stairs to a wide hallway outside one of the wards and we waited there until Zenia came out in a rush. She kissed us but otherwise her manner was very matter-of-fact.

"Your mother's waiting home for you," she said to Laura. "I'll take you there right now. And you," she said to me, "I told them you'd be here soon. What time did you leave the house this morning?"

I said, "Early."

Harry Rivers was there with his automobile on which the

name of McKesson and Robbins was painted neatly on the door. He had been waiting downstairs in the doctors' lounge talking with Dr. Sweeney and having some coffee. Sweeney came out to Harry's car with us, and after we all got in he handed out doughnuts, one for me and one for Laura. She didn't want hers. So I ate both of them.

There was a happy air in the automobile because we were going back home, and at the same time a sense of bad things going on, because nobody knew where Laura's father was being held by the federal agents. Two lawyers were now looking for him, and the words "habeas corpus" kept turning up. One of the lawyers taught at Columbia.

"How did you ever get to him?" Harry asked my aunt while we drove swiftly down Southern Boulevard.

"How do you get to anyone?" my aunt said. "I went to him. I explained the case and I asked for his advice and help."

"He's pretty old, isn't he?"

"Yes. Old enough to remember the Civil War. He showed me a copy of *Uncle Tom's Cabin* given to him by the author and signed by her." She nudged me. "Would you like to see that?"

"Of course I'd like to see it," I said.

She said, "He also could show you his father's formal sword given to him by his regiment at the end of the war."

"I have a German general's sword," Harry said, "but I stole it when we captured him. He complained bitterly about losing his sword, not about losing the war. But it didn't matter. One was over, and I had disappeared with the other."

We turned down Garden Street, and even before the car stopped in front of Laura's house she was out and up the stoop and inside. When Zenia got out of the automobile, I handed her her own scarf and she asked me, "Shall we give it to her?" I nodded. Zenia followed Laura upstairs while we waited below. But it wasn't long before she was down again. She gave me a long astonished look but didn't say anything. We drove around the block to my apartment house, and there Harry waited downstairs while Zenia and I went up together.

My father was still home. Even though he was smiling as he embraced and kissed me, there remained on his face one of those worried looks that never, once they cross the face, seem to disappear altogether. My mother gave me a rough hug and kissed me.

"So here you are," my father said while we just stood around, everybody looking at me.

"And very dirty," my mother added.

"Home at last," my father went on cheerfully. "And welcome back. I've got to go downtown to relieve my clerk, but I'll be here for dinner. Expect me."

He was ready to leave and still didn't go, and Zenia had to get back to the hospital but she didn't go either, and they all just waited, looking at me.

Zenia said, "Laura's mother is taking her to her grandfather's farm in Minnesota."

"When?" my father asked.

"Tonight. They'll take the train to Chicago and from there to Minnesota. There's going to be a lot going on here and she wants Laura out of it."

I said, "Oh."

"This isn't the end of it all," Zenia said. "She wants Laura where she'll be safe, just as you do."

Then I knew Laura had told her and her mother where we had spent the night.

"Did she like the scarf?" I asked.

"Who wouldn't?" Zenia said. "It's my best."

Then she and my father left together and I got undressed and took a hot bath. This was supposed to prevent a cold.

While I was in the tub my mother came into the bathroom. "I'm glad you're back," she said. Before she went out again, she suddenly got very angry. She leaned over and slapped my face. "You think," she cried out, her eyes shining with sudden fears, "there's any place in the world safer than your own house with your own father and mother?" She left the room, slamming the door behind her. I held my nose and forced my whole body, head and all, under the water. There I looked up into the world like a sea lion holding my breath until I gasped and came up for air.

I stayed home the rest of the day. Every once in a while my mother would appear and take a long look at me as if I were a beloved stranger.

"Pretend," she said, "just pretend you're getting a cold."

"But I'm not."

"Then maybe you are getting one."

"It's all right," I said. "I'm just glad I'm here." But her affectionate smile remained suspicious.

It was a day of waiting although no one knew what for.

For a long time I sat around and did nothing at all. I looked out of the open windows at the dusty wheels of chestnut leaflets and the clusters of thorny husks. By the time the next school term began, the horse chestnuts would be ripe. We played a game with them. After removing the husks we let them ripen until they were dark brown and very hard. Then a hole was drilled through and a strong string knotted at one end passed through the hole so the chestnut hung loose and free. We then took turns hitting each other's chestnuts. We got to be quite skillful at whirling the chestnut around by its string with great accuracy to strike with real force. The first chestnut that broke was the loser. Sometimes one winning chestnut could last the whole season—for this game, like every other we played, was played in its season. My Aunt Zenia, having seen us in this contest, hearing me wonder why some chestnuts were so much better than others for the game, said, "It's a chance. And it's also that way according to a priest called Mendel." These nuts were bitter to taste and uneatable. They looked just like the sweet chestnuts my father brought home from the Italian grocer downtown, nuts we used to roast and eat after dinner. Zenia loved them. My mother often crushed them and made a filling for small tarts.

I watched the familiar birds who inhabited the trees. Old nests were empty and the birds flew in and out in their sudden way. They too were waiting for something to happen, waiting for autumn and their time to go. When a light breeze came up,

74

the leaves shifted restlessly. Here and there a dead leaf tugged free and tumbled away. In the streets the voices of the very young children playing near Agnes Helder's house always ended in shrieks and running. Far off I heard the fire engines but they didn't come down our street. They had turned away on Crotona Boulevard. There was just nothing to see and nothing to do after so much had happened. It didn't seem to matter then that Laura was going to Minnesota. I knew she would be back for school just as I knew the robins would leave but the English sparrows would stay.

For a long time I lay on the living room rug and watched the reflected lights on the ceiling. Then I drifted in and tried the dining room couch. From the dining room windows I could see the zoo across the lots but all I did was lie there. I wasn't really thinking of anything, just waiting to think of something to do. It was on this couch with the same emptiness that I sometimes lay and listened to rainy afternoons.

The rain isn't always incomprehensible. It doesn't always fall in an unknown language. Sometimes it's as clear as a story and I would lie there listening, waiting for the unexpected but extraordinary moment when it seemed to speak to me. By then, of course, I might very well have been napping. It was hard to tell whether I was dreaming the rain or reading it, the rain in the streets and the rain in the chestnut trees and the rain in the sky and the rain everywhere, falling in windy waves of voices, running in the street gutters with relentless melancholy in the extreme beauty of enormous numbers.

I used to lie on this same leather couch in the dining room after dinner and watch my Aunt Zenia while she half sat, half sprawled, one elbow on the table, cracking nuts and eating them. I had learned to watch her and not seem to be watching. If she caught me, then she would bring me right into whatever she was doing and I lost the unique pleasure of just looking at her. She was taller than most women I saw around, just as she was stronger and handsomer than they were. These were the first things you noticed about her. She was in every way graceful and easy in what she did. She would do things other women wouldn't, like stretch out and put her feet on the couch or a chair or cross her knees. She had long legs with narrow ankles and feet. Her feet had no fat or fullness in them. They were like powerful and delicate instruments and she always had her shoes made to order.

"My feet are evolution's gift to me," was her explanation.

But my father laughed and said, "Vanity."

Her feet were so strong and yet seemed so delicate that they looked as if anything could break them at any moment. It was the same with her hands and her wrists. Her fingers didn't taper. They were long and flattened at the ends. She had great strength in her hands and used to hand-wrestle with my father or with me or with the other young doctors who came to dinner at our house. She was always determined to win and often did, being tricky and quick with plenty of physical strength to back up her cunning.

I got up from the couch and drifted through the apartment again and finally sat on the floor in front of our glass-covered bookcases, trying to decide which of the books I could read. I didn't take any book out. I just looked at them, for I knew them all, read or unread, readable or unreadable. I had a defeated feeling. I just wanted one book to jump out of the case and take me out of this long day of waiting.

In those days, there were lots of books in my father's library that were impossible to read. Now I tried first one and then another. But I soon gave up on them. I kept coming back to one fat book in a reddish cover. It was part of Burt's Home Library. I had tried this one many times but there was too much endless, boring conversation in it about subjects of no interest to me. But now as the afternoon began to get so heavy that I didn't know what to do next, I took out the *Don Quixote* and decided I would read it no matter how bored I felt. I got three or four apples from the kitchen and half lay, half sat on the dining room couch and ate the apples and read. I skipped when I had to, but somewhere in almost every chapter something ridiculous happened, something funny and at the same time something sad, and in this way I read through the afternoon until it grew dark. Then I turned on the electric light in the lamp that stood on a small end table at the head of the leather couch and just kept on reading. I was waiting for my father to come home. I was waiting for Zenia to come, and for dinner, when they would all sit around and talk. By now I had reached the adventure of Mambrino's helmet, how Don Quixote had taken a farmer's brass basin for the magical golden helmet of Mambrino. It seemed to me that the Knight of the Sorrowful Figure always made the same mistake. And I was reading with less and less attention his endless arguments with Sancho Panza when I heard the key in our apartment door. I dropped the book and walked into the hall and there was my father. He had come home a little early and even before he had taken off his hat and jacket he started to tell us all about it.

"Would you believe it?" He was still in a state of excitement. "Two agents from the Department of Justice called on me at the drugstore."

"I knew it." My mother was immediately sad and a silent fear enclosed her face. "I hope you were polite."

He said, "I was polite when they were polite. And I wasn't polite when they weren't." He felt proud of how he had behaved and at the same time I knew as my mother did that he was also a little frightened.

"I knew it," my mother said. "What happened?"

"I sent them on their way."

"I knew it," my mother said. "Then what happened?"

"That's what I'm telling you."

My mother ordered me from the room with an imperial but unseeing nod of her head.

"No, no," my father said. "You want our son to grow up as a backward child?"

She shrugged.

My father went to the great mahogany sideboard where a bottle of Tokay always stood on a silver platter with little wineglasses. He poured himself a small drink and then came back telling his story. "One of them was a lawyer with a very refined voice. Very educated. His name was Stair." My father sat down at his ease and sipped his Tokay. "The other was a detective. He was very big, one of those people who sweat all the time, and when he asked questions his voice had the same accent as Laura's mother does."

"Did he smoke Sweet Caporal?" I was very excited remembering the Sweet Caporals and that accent from Casanova's hut.

My father lighted a Melachrino. "Yes. But how would you know that?"

"He was one of the men in Casanova's hut last night. One of those who ran up the back porch steps and smashed the windows and fired a gun at Antonio. The shots went over our heads."

My father asked, "Have you been trying to smoke Sweet Caporals?"

"Everybody tries them," I said. "I did too but I don't like them."

"Would you like a Melachrino?" he asked politely. He offered me the little cardboard packet, folding back the silver paper with care.

"I've tried them," I said. "They're awful."

"It's better if you don't smoke at all."

"I know," I said, "but I tried. What happened?"

My mother wasn't distracted by this side issue for she had retreated into the gloom of defeat. She knew now that in spite of all her concerns our family was entrapped in the Palmer raids. But I was fascinated.

My father said, "They began with asking just what happened last night and I told them everything as it did happen, including how you ran away with Laura because you thought they were going to come and arrest her. This lawyer, Stair, got very upset when I told him that. He turned to the big detective and asked him in an angry voice, 'What were you people carrying on out there?' 'I never saw the kids,' the detective said. 'I never talked to any of them. But it was pretty rough for a while. We didn't know the kids were still around. They had been playing a game and when the game broke up all the kids went home. That's what we thought. Then we started. We didn't know there were any kids out there in the lots any more. You couldn't see anyway. It was dark.' 'What would have happened,' Stair, the lawyer, asked, 'if you had killed one of the children?' 'It would have been a bad night.' That's what the detective said. 'As a matter of fact we didn't fire the first shots. The first shots came from this man Antonio.' "

"No," I said. "The detective fired out of the window first. He couldn't even see anybody and he just kept shooting into the lot."

"You see," my father said to my mother.

"I don't see anything," she said, "except trouble for our family."

"Why?" he asked. "Why should we have any trouble?"

"Because it's trouble and we're near it, so we're going to have trouble too."

"That could be," he said. "I hope not."

"What happened then?" I asked.

"Stair wanted to know if I knew anything about the anarchist meetings at Laura's father's house. I said I didn't know and Stair asked about Zenia, whether she knew, and I asked him, 'Didn't you ask her?' 'Yes,' he said, 'and she said she wasn't sure what their politics was. They seemed to be very nice people.' 'They are,' I said. 'Nice people don't throw bombs around,' Stair then said to me. His face was very solemn. 'You're right,' I agreed with him, 'but nice people don't run around shooting guns and killing.' 'You're right,' this lawyer said. 'These are very difficult times for the Constitution.' But the detective didn't let that go on and said that he knew I voted socialist and went to socialist meetings and he wanted to know whether I was a member of the Socialist Party. I said I was and he said, 'Why do you come here and join a party that wants to overthrow our government?' That's when I got impolite."

My mother got up then and just went off, saying, "I have to make dinner and this is awful."

"Don't you want to hear the rest?" my father asked.

"I'm worried enough as it is," she said, "or do you have some comfort for me?"

"I have," he said. "The lawyer said he thought that Laura's father was not really one of the men they were looking for. This lawyer, Stair, is quite young and seems to be a man of calm and reason.

"That'll be the day," my mother said and disappeared into the kitchen.

There was a lot of discussion all through dinner and Zenia never turned up. The conversation between my parents simply went on and on.

We were sleeping, at least I was, when our bell rang, and I heard Zenia's voice arriving in a rush and Harry Rivers talking away, flooding the hall with his feelings. The outside door closed and the voices retreated to the dining room, voices repeating over and over again as in a song of shock and sadness. "It's too late. We have to get in touch with Laura's mother. We can wire the train. Too late. Too late." Over and over again I heard the expression. "Too late, too late."

I heard over and over again what I had known all day without knowing, but knowing it as the body knows, waiting, not even dreading but just knowing, in a way, what Laura knew and her mother knew and I knew and everybody knew once this raid on the lots began. Now they said in a dozen different ways, in different voices, over and over again, that Laura's father had fallen or been thrown or pushed accidentally, they weren't sure, but somehow he had fallen from the secret interrogation headquarters maintained by the Attorney General's office in the Woolworth Building. He had fallen, along with another man, from the twenty-third floor out of a window like Salsedo to die in the streets below.

The voices went on and on, as voices will.

By then I was kneeling in my own silence at the open window of my bedroom, which looked out over Agnes Helder's house and garden below with its grape arbor and picket fence, over the lots, past the dark little house of the Greeks with its imaginary smell of roasting peanuts, across the boulevard to the zoo. I knelt there and waited and at last the summer streetcar came rattling along. The voices went on and on. Then as was their habit the lions began and shook the night air from the depths of the zoo, stirring up whatever was ancient and real in them until the insect sounds became irrelevant, and finally the lions exhausted their dreams of Africa and the night of the lots began again. The voices kept sounding on and still I knelt there at that open window listening to the summer disappear as a last wind brushed among the chestnut trees.

I ran out of my bedroom and stood in the hallway and cried out in desperate sorrow and longing, "Zenia, Zenia!"

There was what seemed an enormous space between us. We clung to each other in an embrace and whatever she said to me or whatever I said to her didn't matter, for we both knew, admitting to each other without saying it, while we held each other, that an endless parting had begun. She kissed the salt tears from my eyes.

"Nightmares, poor boy," my father said in his tenderest voice.

But Zenia kept whispering, "It's real. It's real."

I think my mother knew then also. Only my father and Harry Rivers, in their kindness and sadness for Laura's father, didn't know. My mother did as she leaned against the dining room doorway while the others gathered around me to comfort me. She knew and I knew and Zenia knew that something profound, something that included the word forever, had begun. And nothing could stop it. In a way I knew Zenia didn't want to stop it, and if she didn't, I didn't. That was how I loved her.

8

From that night on, I had the uneasy feeling we now call "modern times."

When morning came, I was restless and feverish and then I really got sick. It was an infection, painful and wearing. Zenia said it had to do with my kidneys. I was in bed all the time, with night and day running together in the way I felt and not the way they really are. Zenia stayed with us whenever she didn't have to be at the hospital.

Late at night I would suddenly find myself awake, the room vibrating, my head humming without any help from the insects in the lots, and there my father was, standing in the doorway of my bedroom. He would lean against the frame. I didn't know if he had just come there or been there for hours. The hours of the sickness had no regular time in them anyway. When I opened my eyes there he was, and there was a longing and a comfort in me to find him there, to raise my hand and wave to him. He put his dry, cool hand on my forehead, on my cheeks, caressing my face. His hand was gentle and filled with tenderness.

"Don't be afraid," he told me. "You'll be well soon. The worst is over. You'll feel better." I grabbed his hand and held it. Lying there in the faith of his presence, I know he is always there for me as I wake up to find him standing, leaning against the door frame, watching me as I wave to him.

It turned out also as I got better that Laura's mother had never returned from Minnesota. The body of Laura's father had been shipped there. I heard scraps of information. Many things had gone on. My aunt along with Harry Rivers and some lawyers had been downtown to see the people in charge of this affair. There were meetings with the police and representatives of the federal government. There had been a hearing of some kind and people had testified about the death of Laura's father.

But all this was over by the time I was up and around again, but not yet going out. School had started, not only without Laura, but without me.

Now an early autumn day came, bright and warm like a memory of summer, and I went downstairs. Everybody was at school except the small children. I stood at the side of our apartment house and looked across the lots to Garden Street.

Casanova was working in his garden again. Everything had ripened, including the burdock in the lots, whose flowers were all gone and whose green burs were browning like the leaves and ready to cling at the slightest touch.

I walked down along the path and finally stood at the fence and watched Casanova working in his garden. He was a big man, very tall, powerful and very fat also, with a bright red face and a dirty gray mustache. He worked in his undershirt in the summer. He had a dark brown very wide leather belt, too big for the belt loops of his dirty old pants. He buckled the belt about his waist. His suspenders hung free so he could bend over among the tomatoes, the melons, the last string beans, the cabbage and the carrots he was then pulling up.

He had waved to me when I came to stand by the fence but I didn't say anything. I just watched him. The autumn sun was hot on my back and the lots loud with insects. Monarch butterflies were all over the place, coming through as they did every year on their way south just like birds. Casanova grew asters near the fence line and the bees were lively in them. A last summer warmth rose from the ground.

Upstairs in Laura's apartment the broken windows had been replaced but the shades were down and it all felt very empty.

Finally Casanova worked over close to me and stood up to

stretch his arms and refresh his back. "Where's Laura?" he asked.

"Gone," I said.

"I heard what happened."

"What did you hear?"

"I heard of the tragedy," he said. He stood there looking up at the apartment with its shades down. The sun was on his face. His heavy cheeks bristled with sweat and his eyes narrowed beneath the tufts of eyebrows touched with gray.

"They had your keys," I told him. "They opened your hut and your gate with your keys. Laura and I saw them that night."

He kept looking up at the apartment.

"Does anybody know?" he asked.

"Her mother knows," I said. "My father and mother know. My aunt knows. Harry Rivers knows. The lawyers know. Everybody knows but they don't know how they got the keys. Did you give them to them?"

He didn't answer me. He just looked around at his garden, so ripe with vegetables now in the picking season. He was a marvelous gardener and the garden was like an island in the lots behind its improvised fences that no one dared disturb. He was a powerful man and in general the boys in the block were afraid of him, but Laura had been his friend. She knew where the keys to the locks were buried and often went in to pick some ripe tomatoes for both us. He was fond of her and gave her family presents of vegetables. He also gave her a nickel or a dime now and then which we used to buy ice cream from the Greeks. Suddenly even as I stood there he slipped back into his suspenders and went to the open door of his hut. He was in a hurry. He put on his jacket and an old battered straw hat. He carefully padlocked the door of the hut and then did the same with the fence gate. He didn't say anything else to me but walked into the lot until he hit the transverse path that led to Southern Boulevard. I stood there and watched him. When I lost sight of him because of the burdock I went up along the bocci path beside Laura's house and watched him from the sidewalk on Garden Street. He waited at

84

the corner without ever looking back at me while I watched him. Finally a streetcar came by and he put up his hand and it stopped. He got into it and sat down on one of the benches. The streetcar clattered south while the conductor swung along on the platform and stopped to collect the fare. But now Southern Boulevard took its long curve south and they all dropped out of sight behind the buildings.

He never came back again.

That evening after dinner we had a visitor. Zenia was there but Harry wasn't and my father was still downtown. The doorbell rang and there was a young, attractive man, carrying a straw hat in his hand. He wore a cotton seersucker suit. His face was sunburned, but from the way he spoke I knew he didn't come from New York. His name was Stair. He was about thirty and, in his nice-looking way, embarrassed. But at the same time he was quite determined.

"I called the hospital," he said, "but they said I could find you here."

"I'm surprised they told you," Zenia said.

"I told them it was official business."

"Is it?"

"No. Very unofficial, but I'm going back to Washington and I wanted to see and talk with you before I left."

"Well," Zenia said, "come in now that you're here, but I don't know why you want to see me."

"You're the only one I wanted to see," he said.

My mother offered some coffee which he refused.

My aunt said, "I don't think we should offer him any coffee at all. I think he and those people down there in the Woolworth Building sent Laura's father to his death."

She was sitting in the living room, which faced 182nd Street, with the windows open. Below, the children were playing their last games now that it was after dinner. I could tell they were playing Statues. Their voices rose through the chestnut trees and flitted in and out of the room like invisible night birds.

Stair was on his feet. He was hurt and he was angry, but he was polite.

"You shouldn't say that, Dr. Mont," he said. "It's not fair. It's not true."

My aunt asked him how Laura's father could fall from a window. "You pushed him, or he was crazy. I know that John DiMarco wasn't crazy."

"The problem was," Stair said, "we didn't believe that DiMarco was one of those who had thrown any of the bombs. They do throw bombs," he said. "I suppose you know that. I suppose you believe that."

"Naturally, whoever they are, I've read that people throw bombs. I've also taken care of people injured by bombs. So I know there have been bombings. That doesn't mean I think anybody I know is one of those who throw them."

"Well then," Stair explained carefully, "you also know that DiMarco was an anarchist Italian sailor illegally in this country."

"I don't know that."

"He was."

"I know he left his ship and stayed after it sailed. Is that illegal for a sailor?"

"Yes," Stair said. "That's definitely illegal. But that isn't the point. I don't want you to believe that I agree with everything that Attorney General Palmer does. I'm not here anyway to talk politics with you."

"I hope not," she said.

"I was there when you came down with Mr. Rivers. Do you know that his brother was one of the men arrested in the Green Corn Rebellion and sent to jail?"

"And killed there," my aunt said. "I know that Harry Rivers is that man's brother. I also know that Harry Rivers was a soldier and received two medals for bravery. Do you know that?"

"I know that," Stair said.

"Then we both know all we have to know about each other."

"I was in the navy," he said.

"So was DiMarco, with the Italian navy. Did you know that?"

"Yes," he said. "We know all those things. I just wanted you to know that we were just questioning him about the people he knew."

"How does that explain anything?" Her face was red and white, changing as she spoke. She was hot and furious, but her attitude seemed cool. I was in the doorway listening, and when Stair looked at me and smiled without seeing me, she made no effort to get me to leave. Every now and then my mother would come in and lead me away so I missed some of their conversation. But soon I'd be back and be more or less in the doorway to the living room entrance or leaning against the corridor wall just outside, hearing everything. My mother remained in the kitchen. She had made up her mind to have nothing to do with this. It could only lead to trouble.

"I'd like to tell you exactly how it happened," Stair said.

"I thought you told us when we came down to see you and the other officers. I thought that was what you testified to when they had the hearing."

"I told you what happened and so did my chief, but I want to tell you more than what he said there."

"So there is more!" Zenia cried out. But she composed herself to wait.

I watched them with excitement. The death of Laura's father was a fact whose meaning I accepted but whose weight I didn't feel. It was the night we ran into the zoo. It was the long march to the hospital, the coming together, the excitement, and then suddenly everything that had happened dissolved into fever, so dry, so destructive; it broke into tiny unrelated fragments of memory, of what I'd learned all that week when I lay sick with broken dreams and long heavy hours of sleep and pain. When the fever lessened and I began to get better, I came together in myself, but the fragments never came together. They made a crazy assortment of broken things. Now here was the real thing again, something that had life without fever. Stair was a man to be reckoned with. He was way above middle height, slightly plumpish as if he ate too much, but with a strong face, thin lips, heavy brows; his hair was brushed tight, his eyes were dark, his voice was clear and rich and he used it with natural skill as well as with what experience had taught him. He had come to persuade Zenia. She knew it. He knew she knew it, yet he gave off an air of genuine sincerity and confidence. He was positive he could persuade her. His hands were small, plump, and he wore a great golden ring with some kind of emblem on it.

Zenia asked, "Why did he jump? Why did he kill himself?"

"I'm here to tell you what I saw happen. I can't tell you why he did or didn't do it."

"Did they threaten him?"

"Yes, of course. They wanted him to tell what he knew. It's important for the government to know who's running around with bombs and killing people everywhere."

"But you said they knew he wasn't one of these people."

"They knew he knew men like that, and women like that too. He was in a way part of them even if he never threw a bomb himself. We told him that. I was there with the chief, being an assistant, you understand, but the chief was the one who carried on the interrogation with the help of a translator."

"Who was the chief?"

"Collins."

Zenia's face became quite melancholy, and she said, "Oh, that one."

Stair said, "Collins threatened DiMarco by telling him that he was guilty of murder."

"How was that?"

"Well, legally speaking, when this man Antonio Galli was killed in a fight with the police, that's a felony, and everybody connected with him is equally guilty of murder."

"That's absurd."

"It's the law."

"I don't believe it."

"It is."

She asked, "When Antonio was killed by the police, was that murder?"

"No," he said.

"But if Antonio Galli wasn't murdered, who was? And how could DiMarco be guilty of no murder?"

He said, "You're all wrong about it. It doesn't matter anyway. That's what the chief said."

"Very well," Zenia agreed. "So DiMarco jumped from the window when you accused him of murder."

"No, he laughed at us."

"You see, he wasn't a man to kill himself. That's what I've been telling you."

Stair said, "They threatened to send him back to Italy."

"He would be back by the next boat."

"The Italian government might have imprisoned him."

"Possibly." She thought for a while. "That wouldn't frighten him."

"The fact is," Stair went on to explain, "DiMarco laughed at us, at everything we said. Then Collins told him that not only would he be deported but his wife would be sent to prison as an accomplice and the child would be sent to an orphanage."

She was appalled.

It made Stair nervous when he saw the look on her face. "That's what Collins said. We, of course, had no intention of doing anything about his wife and child. That's nonsense."

"But he believed it."

"I don't know." He thought awhile and she waited as I waited. He then said, "DiMarco looked at us for a long time and then he said to us, 'If what you say is true'—this was being translated all the time—'I might be tempted to talk to you, even to give you names or make up something that wasn't really true, because of my love for my wife and child. I would want to protect them. That could happen.' After the translator translated this for us, Collins went over to DiMarco and said something like this. He put an arm around DiMarco's shoulder in a friendly way, to urge him on, and he spoke in a friendly way too. 'You're a good man, DiMarco. You've been misled by bad people. You're confused. Now you tell us what you know and nothing will be done against you. You help us and we'll help you. We'll see that you stay here in this country with your wife and child, free from all trouble.' DiMarco smiled at Collins then. 'You're right,' he said. 'You don't really give me much choice.' They were standing near the window. 'What would you do,' DiMarco said, 'if I told you I have a bomb in my pocket right now?' Collins said, 'Well, we know you don't have one. You've got nothing.' DiMarco said, 'If I had a bomb, what do you think I would do now?' Collins said, 'You might go crazy, like all the rest of these anarchists, and try to destroy us and yourself with it.' 'But I have no bomb,' DiMarco said. 'No,' Collins replied. It was then that DiMarco grabbed Collins and flung himself out of the window with Collins in his arms, screaming and fighting, and all the while we could hear DiMarco shouting back at us; it was translated for me by the translator. DiMarco said, 'Every man has a bomb all the time, his own life.' I stood at the broken window and watched them fall. I could also see the harbor of New York. And that is God's truth."

"Well," my Aunt Zenia said, "after all, you're just a monster."

"How can you say that?" His voice was desperate with desire that she should believe him. "I've told you the truth."

"You're a monster who tells the truth."

He was angry all over again. "I refuse to take any blame, moral or legal, for this man's death. It was the free act of a man who chose to die."

"No." My aunt was absolutely cold about it. She refused everything in him, his body, his ideas, his spirit, his will, his great desire for her to understand him. "No," she said. "If you give a man of honor a choice like that, you're forcing him to die. He has no freedom. A man without honor, who wanted to live at any price, might well have a choice. He could choose between honor and dishonor. But this man, being a man of honor—why, you just condemned him to death when you lied to him, and you shot him down just the way Antonio was shot down. You're a murderer along with the others."

"You people are all crazy," Stair said. "Why should anyone come to our country and throw bombs around? Who are they to do this? This is our country, not theirs. Let them throw bombs in their own country."

"You're right," she said. "It would be better if they did."

"So you agree that it's right to throw bombs?"

"No," she said. "I'm not sure about any rights in things like that, but there will be revolutions and wars as people fight for what they want or believe or think and believe and want. You must expect things like that, and yet there must be justice for those who have no way to free themselves except through violence and hatred. Somehow that's necessary."

Stair said, "Perhaps that's what they do in Russia, but there's more justice in our country than anywhere else in the world."

She was quite ironic with him. She knew she had him in her hand and that he was unhappy there. "Whom did you ship on the Soviet Ark?" she asked. "Two of each kind, like the Lord did to preserve the race and the kinds from the destruction of the world?"

He laughed. "They wanted to fight a revolution, so we sent them there to do it."

"You sent people there who wanted to stay here."

"They had broken our laws."

"Well," she said at last, "where will this discussion get us tonight?"

"No place," he said. "I came here not to convince you of anything but to express my regard for someone like you who is, I feel, a person of great value, at least to me." He looked embarrassed. "I wished we could have met without this crime between us."

"If you don't commit crimes," she said, "such things become possible. But when you do, you can only wish that you didn't."

He was laughing then. "I see I have nothing to win here."

"No," she said.

"But I have," he said. "I wanted to see your face again, to talk to you, and I have. As for myself, I think the Palmer raids are illegal and I know Charles Evans Hughes is also of this opinion. There are many of this opinion. But there are some things that can be done and some things that can't. It's like a fire raging here."

"Yes," she said. "It's like a revolution."

He looked at me. "What do you think," he asked, "of all this talk?"

Zenia smiled for me. "He knows what he has to know."

"I'll bet he does. Good night, then. I really and truly regret the death of this man, DiMarco."

"They're dying everywhere. What's one more or less?"

"You don't believe that."

"No."

"Neither do I. Well," he said, "on that we agree. So good night." He started to hold out his hand but thought better of it and made instead a small inclination of his head. Then he opened the door for himself and was gone.

She was very sad, for I could see that whatever it was that made her say what she had said to him, she forgave him for something she never could have forgiven herself.

9

Soon everything was the same again but nothing was ever just the same again, although things went on as things must and do. I went back to school. At night we gathered under the streetlamps and ran again. The seasonal games of day and night changed with autumn's being here. We looked forward to the snows of winter. I was able to make my first appearance in the adult library, which was the downstairs part of the public library. This was the calendar of the days.

Actually an exciting drama went on at home, and like the serials I saw on Saturday afternoons at the movie house on 180th Street, each new episode brought its own excitement and left the future in peril. The story was all about whether Zenia and Harry Rivers would be married or whether she was going to Russia. The struggle was between love and revolution, with everybody on the side of love except Zenia.

I never heard from Laura. I looked up Minnesota in the atlas and read about it in the encyclopedia. Zenia had an address there but, when she wrote, the letter was returned so there really was no way to know where Laura and her mother were. The family speculated about it and everybody felt that Laura's mother wanted to break with the past, which was full of tragedy for her. "But," my father said, "we may not know where they are, but you can be sure the Department of Justice does."

"She's not afraid of them," Zenia said. "She wants to forget her friends, not her enemies."

My mother was annoyed. "You can always find new enemies, but new friends are harder."

But Zenia understood in a different way. She looked at Harry across the table from her. She looked at me. She looked into the depths of her own nature and studied the whole of it. She looked at the reflection of herself in the silver coffeepot. "Once you decide that you must have a different life, it's not safe to keep your old friends. It takes courage to live in the future. It takes the courage of forgetting everything you once loved. After all, you can be sure of this: the future will have the same sorrows as the past. And when you look back, old sorrows will show up as a kind of happiness and you'll start living each day wondering what might have been if you had never tried this new future. No, Laura's mother is right. We mustn't feel hurt. After all, a friend who won't let you go is not much different from an enemy."

There was then a terrible silence around the table. I could see my father's sadness, my mother's acceptance, and a new sudden determination on the long face of Harry Rivers.

Autumn finally arrived.

Nights now the dark came soon, and I didn't go downstairs after dinner. I stayed home and read a lot. When we got together, the affairs of the day were talked about: when Zenia and Harry would be married, Prohibition, the Soviet Union, Caruso, the stock market, how to make money. Harry urged my father to go into business with him. They would open up a few drugstores, then have their own chemical manufacturing company, in which, like all the others, they would get permits to manufacture rubbing alcohol in large quantities, which in turn would give them the right to manufacture pure ethyl alcohol. And pure alcohol could be sold into the underground Prohibition market. Times were good. Everybody would get rich. It was, after all, to get rich and free himself from work that my father had become a druggist.

Zenia told his story as a romance of the heart. "My brother, having left Russia by way of the Black Sea, was on a freighter. It stopped off in Sicily and he abandoned the ship. He stayed in

Palermo, but when it was time to go to the university he found that it was impossible in Italy without being rich, so he came to the United States. Being what he is, like my father and brothers —for we have brothers in Russia, Harry, and even a father who may be dead, who knows; we never hear—anyway, he went to night school and quickly learned enough English to pass the Regents examinations. Now he was ready to become a physician, for in our family you are either a teacher or a physician. In general this is what the men became when they could."

"And now the women," my father said.

"And now the women," she said. "But don't forget our mother. She was a teacher for a while too. Don't forget her."

"I'm not," my father said.

Zenia said, "Even if our brothers are writing to us, or even if our father writes to us, we wouldn't get their letters, since Russia is now everybody's enemy and especially here, as we know. Anyway, by then my brother had met the woman who was to be his wife. He lived in Manhattan and she lived in the Bronx and I'm told, for it happened just before I got to this country, that one night it was snowing here and he wanted to see the woman he loved. He didn't have the nickel fare, only the desire, so he walked from Manhattan by night in the snow all the way to the Bronx, and there he appeared, cold, wet, feverish, just the way a lover should."

My mother was smiling to herself then. Her red hair seemed blonder and paler by now, and my father glanced at her with the wonder that people have when they think of the past buried in the spirit that has taken on a new idea of itself along with its new chemistry, physics and biology, complex and real as stars and galaxies. That silence and darkness in my mother's personality which had been a mystery that haunted my father's love for her had now become a mystery that defeated it in so many ways.

"Pay attention!" Zenia cautioned Harry, who was drinking bonded bourbon from my father's drugstore. "Pay attention."

"I'm listening," Harry said. "I can't do more than listen."

"Learn," she said. "Even a dog can listen."

"Dogs can learn too," Harry said. "You want me to have a dog's idea of love?"

There was an answer on her face but she didn't mention it. She just went on. "Now the time had come for my brother to go to Columbia and register in the College of Physicians and Surgeons. The way he went was to take the elevated train that ran up Sixth Avenue after switching from Third. However, like Don Quixote, he met a stranger on the train, a young man who was going to Columbia, and they got to talking. This young man was going to register at the College of Pharmacy. He said he would then open a drugstore and soon get rich, for doctors don't get rich while druggists, being businessmen, can. Since my brother has a secret desire to be an artist—you all know how well he draws, he once went so far as to take lessons—he thought, 'I'll get rich. Then I can have a family and paint also,' since he was in love. Then and there he decided to go to the Columbia School of Pharmacy and become a pharmacist businessman. Isn't that romantic? Think of the walk in the snow, the change in careers, all for love. What do you think of that, Harry?"

Harry smiled in appreciation of love but my father was thinking of something else. He was thinking in terms of 'as if,' 'if only,' but he said in a warm voice, "Harry, as I sit around this table, I think I made the best choice."

"You're right," Zenia told him. "The choice you make is always the best choice once its consequences have begun. On the other hand, it takes courage to throw out a wrong premise and start again, long after one thing has led to another. Sometimes honor is involved, and in reality a premise, whether right or wrong, has become an ultimate."

"The thing is," Harry said, "is not to hang back when the stakes are high enough. We magicians know that, and so I brought a new magic trick along tonight for all of you to enjoy."

I was of course excited at once.

"Let's see," my father said.

We hadn't even begun dinner yet but everything came to a stop and we sat around listening, waiting to see what Harry had.

"It'll surprise you," he repeated.

"We're ready," Zenia said. "What is it?"

He put his hand in his jacket pocket and took out a handful of photographs, opening them like playing cards in a fan shape and then skillfully closing them and then, still using only one hand, he slid a picture in front of each of us, going around and around until he had only one left in his hand.

"Where is it?" my father asked.

"Dutchess County," Harry said. "About fifteen miles from the Hudson River and Rhinebeck." From the inside jacket pocket he took out a deed of sale and laid it on the table. "In fee absolute, forever." And he slapped his hand on it. "I'd like all of you, including Zenia, to come up this weekend or, if not this one, next. We can stay overnight. We'll take the train to Rhinebeck and my neighbor will meet us in his automobile and drive us there."

Zenia was as excited as the rest of us. She too studied each photograph of the dozen or so. They were pictures of the house, the barns, the fields, the hills, the creeks; most of them were summer pictures, but a few were of the winter past with the house buried in snow and the fields and hills white with the black trees and shrubs clumped with snow and lonely in it. There were high abrupt rolling hills and a narrow valley. One giant tree grew over the house, which stood on a small rise overlooking the creek. A narrow dirt road ran in front of the house and joined another, which crossed a wooden bridge over the creek.

Harry said, "No one's been living there for a few years. My new neighbor still takes care of the pastureland and keeps it up but the house is in good shape. It just needs someone who wants to live there to take it over."

Now everybody looked at Zenia.

"Well," she said, "I see this is a temptation. So I give in. I'll go up and look at it. You think this farm will make the final difference, Harry?"

Harry answered her in her own style. "Who knows what makes a difference?"

My mother went out to get dinner and Zenia got up to help. "No, sit down," my father said. "I'll help."

My mother came back in and said, "What's going on? I don't need any help."

My father said, "Let the photographs talk for themselves."

I had them all in my hand now, looking at them with excitement, but I could see that my parents were not going to accept the invitation. They wanted Zenia to go up there with Harry and to be alone and there they could discuss the great question of love and revolution and bring the serial to an end.

"I can't get away," my father said. "Not right now."

Zenia said, "Are you sure?"

"I'm sure," he told her.

My mother said, "And I don't go without him. After all, how can I be in the country with him back here?"

"That happens every summer when you go to the Catskills," Zenia said.

"That's different. This is autumn."

"Well," Harry said. "Looks like my magic is running out."

"No," Zenia said. "I'm coming. We'll take Ram. Do you think it's all right?" She was looking at Harry.

"Absolutely," he said. "I was going to suggest it myself. I want him to see something extraordinary. Up there nowadays, all around, there's a painter who's gone crazy with joy."

I think my parents would have preferred that Harry and Zenia went without me but my father made the best of it and decided to make some jokes about this week-by-week serialized love affair. My mother waited in the doorway to the kitchen, where the smell of dinner had been going on for some time. There was beef stew that night and apple pie and fresh-baked bread. We could all smell it. But we were all more interested in the love affair.

"Well"—my father took a long look at Harry and Zenia, who sat there exchanging an intimate but still unsettled look— "these two are obeying the Darwinian law of sexual selection. However, I'm not Darwin. I would just like them to get married.

Then Zenia will stop thinking about going back to Russia to save the revolution."

"How can you be sure she'll forget?" my mother asked him.

"I'm not sure. I'm hoping."

I asked my father, "What is Darwin's law of sexual selection?"

"Tell him," my father said to Zenia.

"You tell him," Zenia said. "You started this. Besides, getting married would be very much according to that theory, wouldn't it?"

"Listen, Ram," my father said, "when it comes to biology, nature does everything in twos, male and female. God created them. The way Darwin put it, sexual selection works either through combat or display. Males sometimes are much bigger, have big fangs, big horns, big claws, big swellings of blood or feathers that make them seem more powerful to attract the females, or I suppose to discourage their rivals."

"Big egos," Zenia said.

"Or displays," my father went on. "There's the pheasant's tail, the birds of paradise."

"Big I ams," Zenia interrupted him. "Like the mandrill's behind."

My father said, "Read the book. We have it here somewhere."

I said, "It's on the third shelf on the bookcase near the window."

"Did you try to read it?" He smiled at me.

"No," I said, "I dusted it off a few days ago."

Harry Rivers had been listening to this conversation without saying a word.

Zenia said, "Everything in the world has the same secret."

"What's that?" We all wanted to know.

She jumped up, opened up her arms wide and cried out, "Here I am!"

Things like this used to drive Harry Rivers wild. He stamped his feet. He slapped the table. He burst into laughter.

Now he grabbed Zenia in a wild embrace and lifted her high above him, where she looked coolly down upon his uplifted face. She pointed a finger at each of his eyes and slowly moved the fingers closer and closer. He put her down gently, letting her loose, and as she turned away she punched him lightly in the side. "All this," she said to me, "my dear boy, all this you've been watching is Darwin's law of sexual selection. Combat and display combined."

My mother gave up then. "I really don't know," she said, "what kind of a boy you expect this child to be after hearing and seeing such strange events here."

Harry agreed. He turned to Zenia. "Let's have a wedding, then."

"I'm thinking of it," Zenia told him amiably. "But then that's not all I'm thinking of."

"Maddening," Harry said, his long face suddenly beautiful, while he looked at this woman who flirted with his whole life. "Don't you know," he asked, "that if you refuse to marry me I'll become a different man? I haven't the slightest idea who I'll be."

"You know I love you," she said.

"We're long past love." He argued without vigor. Their affair had gone beyond conversation or even those little symbolic acts with which people acknowledge that the obvious is once again repeating itself. His mind drifted about in the unmapped region of what seemed to him an impossible future in which he was here and she had gone off to the Russian Revolution. "We're talking about fate, we're talking about destiny, killing, dying, starvation, disease, hope, illusion, confusion. They'll all swallow you up out there in the madness of change. Here, you're an iceberg, floating in great beauty. But there, you'll be water again, mixed in the heat of Russian H_2O. Gone. I wish somebody would tell me what's supposed to become of me."

Nobody answered him.

While we were having dinner my father after a while turned to me. "I hear," he said, "you've been to the adult library. You went there last night, didn't you? How did you like it down there among all those books no one can read?"

"I took one out," I said. "They told me I could have only one until they sent me my card. All I had was the letter from my teacher, asking them to let me use the adult library." I had the book underneath my dining chair and I laid it on the table. My father picked it up.

"How did you find this one?" he asked me.

"There it was," I said. "So I took it out."

"Are you reading it?"

"I'm through," I said.

The book was *The Romance of Leonardo da Vinci* by Merejkovsky, and like all things I read it without really intending to, just as Zenia said. "In life, one thing leads to another. There's no other way. That's why it's always too late to turn back but never too late to change. Change you will, in any case."

In school two days before, with an autumn rain outside, we had a class in English with Miss Bronstein. She taught grammar and tried to improve our handwriting. She too had red hair, a flaming red, with a busy face and busy eyes. She was small and full of authority and not very old, although old enough for us.

We trooped in and the bell rang. Outside the autumn rain fell without fussing. Every once in a while a wind would take it and fling it against our windows, which ran with water.

"Today," Miss Bronstein began, after a small tap on the desk with a book for silence, "we'll write a composition in which you tell the story in the first person of some object."

The class knew this composition well. You picked some inanimate object, a ball, a desk, a rubber tire, a wheel, a book, a comb, anything, and you wrote, "I am a letterbox and here comes the postman," and so on. Some students wrote funny ones, such as the genius who began, "I am a fire hydrant and here comes a dog." Then he got stuck and skipped the obvious. Miss Bronstein was not amused. You wrote the title, "I am something," on a single sheet of paper. It had lines and a margin. You wrote in good sentences with proper punctuation and paragraphs. After we learned how to use punctuation, then Miss Bronstein said she would teach us how to use as little as possible. "In good writing," she said, "as little as possible is the best for those who don't know how to write as much as they can."

The sheets of paper were handed out, two to a pupil, and soon the room was quiet as the rain fell, murmuring to us. But no one wrote, "I am the rain," for the rain seemed alive to us and we had to be inanimate objects.

I looked at my blank sheet of paper. I dipped my pen in my inkwell. Then, without much thought, I wrote, "I am Mambrino's helmet."

I told how I was really a barber's basin used for shaving or to catch blood, for the barber who owned me was also a doctor of sorts who used to bleed his patients to help them recover when they were sick. I told how it was raining and how the barber had turned me upside down and wore me over his head against the rain while he slowly rode his donkey to the next town. I described how the rain in the story beat down and slowly the rain on the school windows became the rain on the helmet and ran down my sides in little rivers that joined and separated and so on. Then I told how we met Don Quixote and his valet, Sancho Panza, and how the knight had challenged the barber and swore he would seize Mambrino's helmet or die, and charged. The barber jumped from his horse and ran for his life, leaving behind the donkey and me, rolling in the mud. I knew I was a brass barber's basin but Don Quixote took off his own knight's helmet and placed me on his head, calling me the magical gold helmet of Mambrino, although I was only a polished brass barber's basin.

By then I had come close to the end of the second page for I wrote large in those days, filling with size what I couldn't fill with words. I had to have an end, and not knowing what was best, I wrote a paragraph saying that I knew I was a barber's basin and not a helmet at all, but Don Quixote had made me into something extraordinary and I ended with a question and a doubt, wondering could it be, without knowing it, that I was not really a barber's basin at all but Mambrino's helmet? I left it at that.

The bell rang and off we went, after handing in our compositions.

The next day Miss Bronstein read, as usual, from a few of the class compositions. A little from this one or that, always praising what was good, but she read my whole composition.

No one in the class had ever heard of Don Quixote and she told us a little of his story and something about Cervantes.

After the class, she handed me back my composition. It had a few spellings corrected and some punctuation too and one sentence that had begun but somehow never finished. "Did you enjoy reading that book?" she asked. "Was it a version for young people?"

No, I told her, it was my father's book. Very fat and very long but I had read some of it. Did I enjoy what I read? she wanted to know. I said it wasn't easy to answer that. It was hard to read. It had long conversations in it about subjects I didn't understand or care about. But there was always something that happened like Mambrino's helmet or the windmills.

"Well," she said, "I'll write a letter to the librarian and you can use the downstairs adult library if you like. I know the librarian at the public library and you'll be a good addition to her readers." So she sat there writing quickly and skillfully in her neat flowing hand. Without looking up she asked me, "What other books have you read in your father's library?"

I said, "Edgar Allan Poe and Guy de Maupassant." I pronounced it the way my aunt had told me to, and Miss Bronstein looked up. "Do your parents speak French?"

"My father knows a little," I said, "and my aunt knows a lot. I also read *Makers of History,* forty-two volumes."

She blotted her letter and put it in an envelope and addressed it to the librarian, whose name I now forget.

"What's your favorite book for rainy afternoons?" she asked me.

I said in the most casual way, *"Pathogenic Microorganisms,"* and left without looking back.

I heard her burst into laughter. "Thank God," she cried, "for rainy afternoons!"

Since I was going alone and late in the afternoon to the public library, my mother gave me two nickels for carfare, but I decided to save them for something better and walked all the way. The evening was on its way in by the time I arrived and the lights were on in the Carnegie Building, which like so many others in the city had a wide-step stoop and a sort of classical front.

I knew the upstairs children's library well from all the Saturday mornings and Friday afternoons when we went in a pack. There in the great room, flooded with light from the many windows, the low bookcases were arranged around the walls with a few smaller double-faced bookcases placed here and there in the center. They kept the Du Chaillu books in the center. The atmosphere filled with boys and girls waiting in lines at their favorite bookcases until the librarians brought up the returned books, always the favorites and naturally in short supply. In a funny way, the books the boys read and the books the girls read were usually in different bookcases, although occasionally a girl would be on a boy's line. I never saw a boy on a girl's line. Of course, when Laura was around, she used both lines with ease, but she was not the usual girl of the neighborhoods. It was quiet enough in the children's upstairs library; a cloud of imposed stillness hung over the room, filled with lively spirits, and underneath was conversation, some horseplay and an air of excitement and potential breakout. The librarians varied between those who were out-and-out enemies and those who didn't care, with occasionally one, old or young, who tried to palm off some worthwhile reading on the gang of children who waited to grab and run.

In general if someone from the neighborhood got a good book, say an Altshuler, why that would be lent around before being returned to be taken by someone from a different neighborhood. In general we knew each other vaguely, because we mostly went to the same public school. There were boys and girls there who went elsewhere, and of course the usual parochial school children, who seemed to be the best behaved with the librarians and the worst behaved with the other children. In our neighborhood, Siney, the postman's son, with his six brothers and sisters, all of whom seemed around the same age but weren't, were the only ones who went to the Catholic parochial school above Crotona Parkway. But then Siney was part of the Saturday library-goers with the rest, and a friend. His father on weekend summer afternoons would sit his children down on upside-down barrels and cut their hair himself. We all stood around and watched. I once had my hair cut by him much to my mother's horror, for he turned it out on an assembly-line basis, paying no attention to style.

This downstairs library, the moment I walked in, was a different world. It was quiet, because that was its nature. I didn't hear a whisper. Part of the room was furnished with desks, chairs and filing cabinets of wood. The rest of it was corridors of tall bookshelves, rather close together, and wandering here and there within the silence, like tropical fish, were grown-ups, men and women. The place felt dead to me.

The librarian was a young woman about the same age as my Aunt Zenia. She was pleasant and her hair was piled high on her head. She wore a white blouse and a skirt and she had a sweater draped over her shoulders although it wasn't a cold evening and the library was warm. I had my letter from Miss Bronstein. When I didn't move, she finally looked up to see who had come in and, finding a young boy there, immediately lost all interest, expecting me to leave. I think if she had continued to look at me, I would have turned around and walked out, but the detached glance decided me. I went up to the desk and handed her the letter without saying a word. She opened it and read it, smiled at me and handed me a little card. "Just fill it out," she said. There was a pen and inkwell. I filled out my name, my address, my class, my father's name, my mother's name, my date of birth and handed it back.

"Good," she said. She had a very light voice, almost fragile. But she was smiling and helpful. "Tonight you can take out only one book. But when your regular card is ready, then you can take out two books. You can usually keep them two weeks."

So far I hadn't said a single word.

She half turned and pointed to the bookcases. "All the cases on the left-hand side are fiction. I suppose that's what you'll be wanting to look at first." She had a very long, white neck, thin and delicate, and when she turned it, with a heavy pile of hair above, she looked like one of the extraordinary birds in the aviary at the zoo. She spoke in her pleasant way and had a diamond ring on her left hand. It was a very small diamond, but it glittered.

I said, "Thanks," and took my temporary card and walked over to the shelves. I didn't look back, and it seemed to me that the fish wandering among the shelves all were looking at me to see what I would do in this strange place. It wasn't fear I felt but the anxiety of being embarrassed by doing something that wasn't usual in the downstairs adult room of the library.

It was the same as jumping from a place too high or running off at night. Suddenly, now as then, I was no longer deciding what to do but just doing what the moment had decided for me. I walked right to the second group of bookshelves and, without stopping to read what the book was, put my hand out and took a book from a shelf about my height and without reading its title returned to the desk and placed it in front of the librarian.

She was surprised to see me there so soon and even more surprised to see what I had chosen, but I stood there as calmly as I could, keeping an air of knowing what I was doing firmly in mind. She stamped the book and my temporary card and returned the book to me. "I hope you enjoy it," she said. "Good night."

"Good night," I said and, without a backward glance, walked out.

I went down the steps and halfway up the block before stopping under a streetlight to read the title of the book. It was *The Romance of Leonardo da Vinci* by Dimitri Merejkovsky.

I grew hot with shame thinking that the librarian was laughing at me and then and there decided to read that book even if it was as impossible as *Don Quixote* or *Middlemarch*, another book in my father's library, one that he thought was as good as the best of the great Russian novelists, "of whom none are better."

When I got home, my mother was upset, for I was very late.

"Why did it take you so long?" she wanted to know.

I said, "I walked."

"But I gave you carfare."

"I decided to walk to save the fare."

"Good," my mother said. "I'll take it back then."

I was angry. "It's my ten cents," I said. "I saved it by walking."

"No," she said, "it's my ten cents. I gave it to you so that you would get home early and be safe, but you didn't care about that. You went your way, so give me my money. It's not yours."

"But I earned it."

"No," she said, "you cheated me and you made me worry. I owe you a good slap in the face for it, but I'll just take back my ten cents."

I was by then too old to cry or fight with my mother. I just handed it over and said, "You're unfair. It's not right."

"That's what you think," she said. "What did you get out of the library?"

I showed her the book.

She handed back the ten cents. "If you read the book from cover to cover, keep the ten cents. If not, I want the money back."

I returned the money to her. I said, "I don't have to be paid to read a book."

Then she slapped me in the face.

* * *

The next night at the dinner table, when I said I had finished the book, it was with the same lack of belief that my father asked, "Did you enjoy reading it?"

"No," I said, "I didn't. But there's a terrible thing in it which he writes about."

My Aunt Zenia was surprised. "What terrible thing?"

I told them the story of the feast and what happened to the boy they had painted in gold.

"I remember now," my father said.

My aunt explained about the pores and body temperature and how it is all balanced. She said, "They killed him just as if they had choked him to death or burned him in the furnace of his own body."

"I think," my father said, "I'll get you a better book for someone of your age. It's called *Desert and Wilderness*."

My aunt said, "Well, it won't hurt him, but the picture of the young English girl in it is maddening, as is the young Polish patriot. Really, writers are mad, just like people who only read. But then Sienkiewicz won the Nobel Prize." She talked about the way the book dealt with Khartoum and General Gordon. "It's just English imperialism. That was the real enemy and the cause of the revolt in *Desert and Wilderness*. I often wonder," my aunt said, "at the strangeness of it. The Jews, like the Bedouins, are a desert and wilderness people, but look how they've ended up in ghettos, in Middle Europe and Russia, or as Germans in Germany, Americans in America, Cockneys in England or even lords for that matter. They became Frenchmen and along came the Dreyfus case. Yet their story in the Bible is the holy book of the Christians who enslaved them. In a way their story is that of the human race itself, always wandering, killing or being killed like the other animals. In a way their story is the same as all the others, but since we still live in its history, we remember it as something special."

My mother's brother Max, who even then was a well-known oral surgeon who taught at Columbia, was a Zionist. "It would be nice," my mother said, "if we had our own country, even if it was just a desert in a wilderness, but even that is denied us."

My father thought all such notions were old-fashioned. Socialism would bring an end to all these ancient horrors.

"It won't be long before we find out," Zenia said. "Now and then a great idea sweeps across the common mind of humanity. And here we are, about to live in the time of socialism."

Harry Rivers was listening like a new Gulliver in the midst of another surprising voyage. He said, "It's always different and worse than you expect."

"It seems worse because it's different," my father said. "What we want and what we get have to be different."

"Yes, yes," Zenia said, "but no, no, too."

I think Harry's love affair with Zenia was making him dubious about everything, or perhaps it was what had happened to his brother during the Green Corn Rebellion in Oklahoma.

The conversation around the table exploded now and I slipped away to my room and lay there, reading again with a kind of fascinated horror about the painted boy.

10

Along came Friday and off we went to see Harry's new farm.

"You can thank Dr. Sweeney for this," Zenia said. "He's taking my place at the hospital this weekend."

Harry arranged everything. He was there with his automobile and a friend, another salesman named Gil Shelley, whom I had met once before in my father's drugstore. Shelley sold cosmetics and always handed out samples of perfumes, powders, soaps and such. He was fragrant with them. "It's my boudoir aroma," he explained. "Try this." He gave Zenia a half-ounce bottle of Black Narcissus. "It's the real thing," he said. "Let's go, Harry."

While we drove along in the excitement of silence, Shelley, with his pointed long nose, his snappy body and alert air, told us perfumed anecdotes. Magical names floated through each of them, Emeraude, Shalimar, Guerlaine, Worth, Weil. When Zenia thanked him for the Black Narcissus, which was not a sample at all, he immediately began an anecdote of something that had happened in my father's drugstore. My father supplied the makeup for the Jewish theaters around Houston Street and Second Avenue. "I happened to be there," Shelley said, "when the Maurice Chevalier of Second Avenue came in with his Irish setter and his beautiful Russian wife. This actor, as everybody knows, samples every chorus line and leading lady by first giving them a bottle of Black Narcissus. An older actress was in the store that time with her big French poodle who was a bitch in heat." All the rest of it he told while he laughed in and out of the words. "Well, naturally enough, while everybody was bowing and scraping to the Maurice Chevalier of Second Avenue, the Irish setter immediately joined up with the French poodle. Your father was discreet. He pushed the dogs behind the counter into the prescription department, but believe me the actress was in despair. 'I'll have mutts instead of purebreds,' she said. 'I'll have all the trouble without any of the advantages.' You should have seen that Second Avenue gallant bow to her. 'Like every love affair,' he said, 'there's pleasure and there's sorrow.' It was like a line from one of those songs he made famous. And, Dr. Mont, he said to your brother, 'Give the lady a bottle of Black Narcissus.' 'You forget,' she told him, 'that you gave me one years ago.' As his beautiful Russian wife left with him, she looked back to the actress standing there with a bottle of Black Narcissus in her hand. 'He doesn't,' said the wife. 'But the perfume lingers on.' "

We climbed the stairs to the Harlem Station there at 125th Street. Harry's friend took care of the automobile and we took the early Albany train that made many local stops, every one a new world for me. When we went to the Catskills, we always first took the ferry from Manhattan to New Jersey and there boarded the Erie Railroad. This was the great New York Central that ran up the east bank of the river until it crossed over the bridge to Albany.

We passed the red-brick streets of Hudson River towns, the little ports and ferries. We ran into the confusion of Poughkeepsie and now we were nearly there. We passed Hyde Park and finally paused in the Rhinecliff Station of Rhinebeck. Just as we got off our Albany train, an express went flying by on its way to New York, roaring past in fumes of smoke, pounding and savage with raging steel, roaring back from the cement walls that held back the high shore banks on the east side of the station. The whistle stretched and wailed away and off it went to join all the train whistles of distant stations, far hills, lonely valleys, the whistles of trains by day and by night. It was the same train whistle that stayed behind in the sky while evening cooled and deepened on the lonely Big Indian station. There the train lurched off, grinding up into the Catskill highlands. It puffed, it grunted. The grind and gnash of steel became delicate and irrelevant and the acrid smoke from soft coal mixed with night and mountain chill told us we were there.

This Rhinebeck station was big and ornate because many rich people lived on their estates along the river and the station had been built to make them feel at home even when they went away. There was marble and wood and comfortable seats to wait in. But Harry urged us along, and we were so eager we had no time to look at anything. "Some other day," he said. "This is our station now." He held the door with its polished brass handles open for us. He was carrying both suitcases, his own and the one which was Zenia's and mine.

"There's Mr. Waal," Harry said. "His family has lived in the same house since the day his Dutch relatives arrived in Rhinebeck. Our farm is in the township of Milan, not far from a place called Jackson Corners. It used to be part of the Little Nine Partners' Patent. That's what they called it. The house was built in 1790 or a little before then. Later on, they added a big kitchen."

Outside, his new neighbor and new friend was waiting beside a Chevrolet. It was a new car but the roads and the dust had already given it the air of something that had always been in that part of the world. Sumac trees were fiery red above the station hills and every leaf that wasn't a pine had abandoned green. There was an everlasting movement of fragmented sun flashes on the river. I could see a ferry landing and some tugboats drawing a long line of barges. There was a small sailboat where the river stretched wide. Beyond were the mountains, a haze of green and blue, laced with autumn violence. A handful of jays quarreled in the surrounding trees.

Mr. Waal was of middle height, about forty, with thick shoulders, square and strong with health. He was clean shaven, like my father and Harry. He took off a battered soft hat and shook hands. "Call me Peter," he told us.

Zenia sat in front with him while Harry and I sat in the

rear. She wanted him to call her by her first name, but he couldn't. She was Dr. Mont for him, and so he named her as he pointed out things along the way. Zenia wanted to notice everything. Something got free in her, something so free and open to be in the world that Harry began to smile. It was this world of hers that he had seen less and less of ever since the Palmer raid on Garden Street. But up here in the country we bumped along and ran through Rhinebeck, where Mr. Waal pointed out at the Albany Post Road one of the oldest hotels in the East. "It's the oldest hotel in the state," he said. "And we have a sign to prove it." It was a town of elms, of stores around the crossroads. There was also a Victorian house sitting back behind a wide lawn with an elm on either side of it. This three-story private house, Harry said, was one where an architect with a fretsaw had reinvented the pirouette.

We drove through and were at once in farm country. There were pastures on the farms and abrupt hills and herds of dairy cattle. We passed solid rows of apple trees. We ran over a bridge above a creek. Then Mr. Waal took a turn to the left and we were on the Academy Hill Road. The sides of that road were dense with big trees, oak and maple, and clumps of sumac on fire with autumn frenzy. The car was a touring car, of course, open to the wind.

Wherever I looked, leaves were falling. Sometimes one or two, sometimes a flight of them. Colors fell like leaves falling. Colors blew across the windshield. Even in the wide open fields themselves, dosed with bronze and yellow, touched with red and everywhere along their borders banked by trees and brush, with goldenrod bright there, and little pale flashes from the asters, everywhere, in the most open space, wherever I looked, somewhere a leaf would blow by, sailing, and as it fell there would be another and never a moment without a leaf in the air. Yet it wasn't very windy. There were autumn breezes on this brisk but warm day, the sky clear yet hazed among the far hills. Each crest of the road, each dip, had its own secret breath of air to carry the falling leaves of autumn. They came aboard our bumping automobile as flying fish will on small sailboats in tropical oceans. They fell on our laps and we looked at them and set them free to fall again as we went along rising and falling on Academy Hill Road.

The road descended slowly, and suddenly there were other farms with red barns and white houses and fences against which Holsteins wandered, and here and there clusters of Guernseys. "For the richness of their milk," Mr. Waal said. "The Guernseys give less but it has more cream."

There were horses too, work horses in pasture, some of them giants in size like the horses that pulled the city fire engines and slammed down 182nd Street, almost as fast as we did on our skates or sleds in winter.

Everything was more and more.

"I feel very close." Zenia turned. Her face was wild with autumn.

"We are," Harry told her. He leaned forward to put a light hand on her shoulder. "I could say 'Close your eyes' but it'll be just as good if you keep your eyes open."

"This is my farm," said Mr. Waal. His house was a small one made of shaped fieldstone but the biggest part was wooden clapboard and unlike the stone, which was gray, it was painted yellow. It was the only yellow house I had seen since we started. Academy Hill Road ran between his house and his barns. There was a fence on the right side of the road which ran up a very steep pasture with new green showing beneath the dried summer grass. At the top was a line of trees, the edge of a wood.

"From here on," Mr. Waal said, "it's Harry's place. Everything on the right of this road belongs to his farm."

The road went down. There was a creek on the right side and marsh grass and brush. As we bumped by, a pair of wood ducks flew out and beat their way across the fields. "This road goes on to Jackson Corners, but here's where we turn."

This was a dirt road too, narrow and fenced on both sides with barbed wire. "Now everything on both sides," Mr. Waal pointed out, "is Harry's farm."

We crossed a bridge made of heavy planks of wood. The rutted road went up, the automobile bumping crazily, and now a stand of hemlock began on the north side where there was another bridge and a bigger creek which flowed from the south and joined the one we had just passed. Great slabs of stone, all that remained, marked the place of an old mill. We slowed up before crossing the bridge to look north, where the creek fell across massive stone steps with glacier potholes in them. The flow of water was noisy and rushing. It disappeared within the forest of hemlock trees. They were very tall and very thick and they covered the sky so that we were looking through a tunnel of green with patches of sky showing overhead.

"Hudson River peltite," my aunt said.

"Don't show off," Harry said. "I've studied it in order to tell you."

"Tell me," Zenia said, "or I won't believe it."

The automobile crossed the bridge.

"There." Zenia called out to the house as if it were a person. We could see it on the north side of the road up above a quick rise and then unseen level pasture. Hidden among elms and maples, the red of barns and the first glimpse of a white house.

"Stop," Zenia said. "I want to walk. Do you mind?"

We stopped and got out, all except Mr. Waal, who drove ahead.

Harry stood away from Zenia and I stood away from both of them. We just waited there looking around.

"What is there to say?" we all seemed to be saying to each other when we walked toward the small rise on which Harry's farmhouse and its barns, its carriage house and chicken house, stood with the road below and the creek wide and rushing with accumulated autumn rains. No one wanted to talk about what they felt. They just said things out loud, things like, "apple tree," "maple," "but these are ash, aren't they?" They were, with their pale yellow leaves.

"You know," Harry said, "back behind that first creek we passed, where it disappears into the woods, that stand beneath the high hill here, we have a waterfall of a sort. I'll show it to you later. Even in summer, even in dry weather, it always flows. In the spring, they say, it's really a fine waterfall, about thirty feet high, one that can really pour and roar.''

"We'll look at it," Zenia said.

We three then walked toward the house on its little hill, surrounded by its elms and maples. We didn't walk together. We each walked alone, Zenia in front because that's where I thought Harry wanted her to be. I was in the rear. She walked in the center of the road and he walked on one side and I on the other. When we came to where the road divided, the bridge that led over the creek on the right was more modern. I stayed behind and looked around and down into a wide pool of lively water.

I was some twenty feet or more behind the others now, and as I followed them I knew that this was Harry's wedding present for Zenia if she would marry him. I also knew, in spite of the way she walked with him, just ahead, full of animation and pleasure and warmth, enjoying it all as if it were really hers already, that she had that extraordinary bedside manner of doctors. Her enthusiasm, her comfort, her praise, while real, were nevertheless no commitment that these feelings belonged to her alone and were not part of the way she was treating a patient who had just discovered he would live and, filled with joy, included the doctor in his heartbeats. It wasn't that Zenia pretended. It was simply that, unlike the rest of us, her sincerity wasn't simple. It was what she felt as her own self, as a person feeling, and it was also herself as a doctor feeling what doctors should for the patient she intends to cure, both real, often mingled, yet separate.

"Harry tells me you're only here for one night," Peter Waal said before he left us at the house.

I was standing away from them, looking north across a neglected lawn that ended at a picket fence. Beyond that was a vegetable garden grown to seed, the whole surrounded and fenced by barbed wire through which the cattle could go by way of white-painted wooden gates. The great pasture was bounded on the west by woods whose edges were aspen and poplar, behind which, from the hidden ravine where the brook flowed, the tall tops of hemlock emerged. North beyond an open wooden gate, the field rose swiftly to still another meadow, hidden from us by a plantation of red pine. All this dipped west into a narrow valley, and beyond it the hills kept rising, woods alternating with pastures, until they reached a ridge where rock and brush showed, and the skimpy edges of pitch pine. Every blade of grass, like every leaf, had gone dizzy with colors, soft or simple, brilliant and bewildering. Some were purple, some singed with violet.

Some few hundred yards down the narrow dirt road below Harry's house was another farmhouse and a neighboring farm, whose lands ran south from his house and rose far in the distance east and south while Harry's farm lay mainly west and north.

They were still talking as Mr. Waal left. He had parked his car below the dirt driveway, which had been badly rutted by winter snow and spring rains and not repaired. "Might as well wait till next spring," Mr. Waal said. "I know you're just here for one night and my wife thought you'd like to have supper with us so you didn't have to cook anything, although your kitchen stove is burning. I lighted the wood in it for you."

"I don't know," Harry said. He looked at Zenia, wondering what she would want.

"The fact is," Waal said, "I have a daughter, and when she heard about Dr. Mont, she wanted to know if she could come and meet her. She's bright, Ann is, and she thinks perhaps we might send her to Vassar, although I don't know. It could be a waste."

That was all Zenia had to hear. And so we were going to have supper with them. Waal drove off, pleased and excited with these new neighbors of his.

Everybody then stood around and looked at the house from the outside. From below, looking up from the dirt road, it seemed like a big house in the usual style of its time. The second story was really just an attic with small windows facing front and regular windows facing east and west. There were no windows on the north side of the older part of the house. That was the cold side. But the addition which had been built to make room for the new kitchen, bathroom and a small extra room had windows that imitated the beautiful ones in the front of the house. A porch on the kitchen side had been fitted with windows and now had become a room adjoining the kitchen.

When you looked at it on the north side, the house fitted into the small hill and seemed very small, low in the landscape which fell some thirty feet below it to the dirt road and the creek.

We stood there together and separate. The entire landscape had become a presence in our lives. I felt excitement at the way it went, the water talking away, the leaves forever falling, the farmhouse there under the giant maple. Then a flight of crows went overhead like a bunch of rowdies.

So we went into the house.

The house inside breathed wood and wood fire. It also was nearly empty. The floors were made of yellow pine. It was clean but it needed repairs. Most of the floors were painted.

"Under the paint," Harry said, "is the same yellow pine. The day all that paint is gone, the floors smoothed, varnished, waxed, the house will breathe free again. What do you think of that? It needs a lot of things but it has more than it needs. What do you think, Zenia?"

"You're right," she said.

"This place can be anything you want to make of it," Harry said.

Zenia just stood there and sighed with pleasure. "I can't think of anything better," she said. "What shall we do? Do you have a plan for us? You sound like it."

"Yes," Harry said, "I'd like to walk around and show you everything there is here, more or less. Then we can have dinner with the Waals, spend the night and go back."

"How did you find it?" she asked.

"I was hunting here last year with a friend and he introduced me to Waal. This farm was owned by my neighbor you haven't met yet. He was happy to get rid of it and I was happy to buy it."

The afternoon was long and we walked most of the time when we didn't stand still and just look. Harry must have gone over it again and again without telling us because it was a surprise to us that he knew it so well. "But then," Zenia said, "why buy a farm if you're not ready to know it well?"

Now here was Harry, excited by everything new but knowing more about it than anyone who had known the place forever. My aunt watched him and enjoyed being there with him, trying to see everything with his eyes while all the while her own saw things no one else had ever seen there before. I drifted around them, sometimes close, sometimes far away, for this farm now that it was Harry's became full of a special kind of wonder. It was no longer a place I could visit or a place I was now visiting. He made me feel I belonged there along with Zenia and himself. He was giving it to her and therefore to me.

So we walked everywhere, and Harry pointed things out. He said there were plenty of deer and raccoons. There were red and gray squirrels. There were red foxes. And there were woodchucks, too many of them. "You could live off this farm," Harry wanted us to know, "and never buy a thing, but it would kill you with the work it took. You know, no matter how it begins, once you let it alone, whether it's swamp or bog land, whether it's lowland running stream or high land, whether it's ravine or hill, whether the soil is rich or scant, one way or another, by different means the land finally makes its way back to the final forest of this wonderful place. That would be oak and hemlock, white pine, maple and beech, and all the others which manage to get on with them. If we left it alone it would stay the same way for thousands of years and become again the primeval forest that the first settlers found when they arrived here and began the civilization that ended up in the Green Corn Rebellion and the Palmer raid on Garden Street. So here I am. When I saw it, and saw everything was speaking to me of the past and the future—I read a lot of this, you know." He interrupted himself. "It was written by two professors from Vassar. When I saw it, I said I would have a place here. I would find it. I would buy it. I would do it fast."

So we walked and he talked and Zenia listened as I did. It all became one to me, flowing with color and different shapes of grass and weeds and wildflowers and trees. We went up and we went down, sometimes steep and sometimes gentle. Harry pointed out a red-tailed hawk sailing above a distant hill. He said, "The vultures are gone already and soon the hawks will be gone too, but the owls will hang around and you'll hear them. You'll hear the great horned owl, Ram. If you count the hoots, there are usually five and they go like this, 'Hoo hoo hoo, hoo, hoo.' Sometimes there are three and sometimes six, but usually five. If you come up here you'll soon see one. But you'll hear them."

We arrived back at the farmhouse and stood outside pulling all kinds of seeds and burs from our clothes, and for the first time I saw, on the south side of the carriage house, burdock, very tall, almost eight feet tall and almost all dried out.

"Burdock!" I shouted. "That's the forest of my lots."

"Yes," Harry said, "and a terrible weed to get rid of."

"Not where I come from," I said. "We still live in the burdock days in my lots. You may be going back to the maple days here, but that's here and not there."

Zenia and Harry were laughing now.

"A weed," Zenia said, "is what you don't want. But in nature there are no weeds. Weeds are in people's minds. Everything belongs and we do too."

It was colder now and we were happy to get back inside the house, as the afternoon died away quickly. The sky grew luminous and in the west and north, rising higher and higher in vast bulging shapes, were the cumulus clouds, their tops bright with sunlight.

"They're so very still," I said.

"Inside they are wild with wind," Harry said.

Inside the house it was pleasant and warm.

"In a way," Zenia said, "I suppose when early man roamed around in little bands, they had a kind of socialist society. Don't you think so? So I've read. It seems natural."

"Maybe," Harry said. "I don't know. Maybe they weren't so equal as you think."

"Let's pretend," she said. "It might be true. Then it would be like this. There was once a primeval forest here. Then men changed everything and now when they let nature make its way again, just as you said, bit by bit things change, one thing making it possible for something else to live again, and finally in the end you have the primeval forest again. It could be the same way with men. There were the primeval groups living in their socialist societies, and then all the history we knew changed everything, and now at last the dream of socialism is back again and here we are at the beginning of the age of socialism."

Harry said, "Well, it looks pretty still out there, but there's lots of dying and killing going on along the line. It's a kind of natural tragedy."

"How can there be tragedy without hope?" she asked him. She seemed very calm. "Here now, even as we sit in the great stillness here, everything is madly changing, inside and out."

"There's always hope if you're near," he said. "Everybody has hope or hoped, I suppose. How could it be different? But with you, in the end, everything comes alive with hope. That's what you do to all of us."

"I'm not embarrassed," she said, "with your praise. Why should I be? It's only love talking and not common sense. But I'm happy to see you're not feeling as hopeless as you've been lately."

"Not up here," he said, "not with you."

I wasn't near them. I was watching the fire, which like the sea is never still.

Zenia said, "I'm sure we'll never forget this wonderful adventure of first seeing your new farm."

As night fell, we walked over to the Waals' farmhouse.

Inside it was a real place with plenty of furniture and I was very sleepy. I ate a lot and everybody talked and the young girl, Ann, worshiped Zenia and listened while Zenia talked to her and made her talk. Everybody talked. I didn't talk. I was dying to go to sleep. Harry produced a bottle of bonded bourbon from my father's drugstore, so they talked about my father and my mother and New York. They talked about Oklahoma and they talked about Vassar.

It turned out after all that Mr. Waal didn't make a living from his farm. He was part owner of a hardware store in Rhinebeck.

They began to talk of the hard winters and the snow. "Sometimes," Mr. Waal said, "you wake up on a winter morning and the world is gleaming, for every tree and plant is covered with ice before it melts. It glitters like glass. It also breaks off the branches and knocks out the telephone and electric lines. I suppose," he said, "you'll bring electricity in."

"I sure will," Harry said.

But I dozed off, I think, because they woke me and we walked home quickly in the cold night, back to the not-so-warm farmhouse that was Harry's farmhouse. He heaped the fireplaces with logs which he got from the wood house. The logs were dry with dust and age.

They put me into the other big room across the hallway and I was soon asleep, the windows open to the cold outside.

I woke up because an owl had settled nearby in the elm tree and was hooting. I counted the hoots and it was as Harry said, a great horned owl. Sometimes it sounded very near and sometimes very far away but the owl was like a ventriloquist, throwing its voice this way and that.

I listened to the voices of the night. They gave the world in which I lay the stillness in which the leaves kept falling. All that day the leaves had fallen, and wherever I looked and wherever I stood and walked the leaves kept falling. They fell in flocks or one by one, always falling, and somehow that was the stillness.

Once my parents took me to the RKO Theatre on Tremont Avenue to see a vaudeville show. We went at night, which was the beginning of all the excitement. The orchestra played and the curtain rose to reveal the undergrowth of a giant forest. There were toadstools bigger than men and mossy earth and rocks covered with leaves and unknown flowers. There too were enormous tree trunks growing out of the forest floor and disappearing above. Rays of moonlight filtered down through the unseen leaves. Sitting on one of the mushrooms was a frog. The sigh of the audience then was like the sigh of the night outside, where now the leaves were falling as they did all day and where the owl was talking outside as Zenia and Harry were talking inside, to make up the stillness, in the center of which I now lay and listened as then I watched.

The frog was a contortionist. He tied himself into knots that made my blood run cold. Little pains of imagination ran through my flesh, and then he leaped with such height and ease, landing like a frog, this man with a frog's head and frog's skin and frog's feet with great toes like fingers. He leaped and landed softly and then leaped up on another mushroom or toadstool. Maybe he was a toad. It all went on with a kind of ease and voluptuous grace of motion. I was back in the world of children's books where rabbits talked.

The great horned owl threw his voice around the night and Zenia and Harry continued to talk across the hall behind two closed doors, mine and theirs. In this house everything was so much one with its wood from the days when it was built, oak and pine which had been trees outside from which the leaves once fell as now they kept falling while the talk went on.

"There's one more reason why you shouldn't go back to Russia," Harry said. "Or the Soviet Union."

"What's that?" Zenia wanted to know.

"It's a subject I never wanted to discuss with you," he said. "But I have to, now. I'm desperate. I feel desperate. I know what you're doing is bad for me. But even if you forget me, it's bad for you. It's bad for you and for me and everyone who loves you. It's one of those roads people take, and the moment they look back that way is gone forever. You mustn't go back because you're a

Jew. You must never go back to Russia or Europe. That world is poison for the Jews and always will be. It'll take the world as long to change as it took for the apes to come down out of the trees and run around on two feet and pretend they were human."

She said firmly, "There's no anti-Semitism in socialism."

"I'm a socialist like you—or not so much," he said, "to be truthful. But no matter what it is, it's just one more way to run a country. No matter what it is, it's just another government."

"It can be a better one."

"It can be the best we've had up to now, but it will do everything governments do. It will go to war. It'll be like the people who have always been there whatever their government is. And they have been poison for the Jews."

"It could be the answer to anti-Semitism."

"It'll be the answer to everything. The talking will change, but what people have lived and done way back in time they will keep doing no matter what name they call it. I would never speak to you about such a thing but I'm desperate tonight. I know tonight is the last chance to keep you from leaving me forever. Don't go."

"And what about here?"

"It's a novelty here. Nothing changes fast. Nothing. It just seems to."

Her voice was grave but bold. "But what about the millions like me. What about them?"

"A Jew will have to have his own country. He must be a Zionist."

She laughed then. "You're a Zionist? You're telling me that you, a Green Corn Rebel from Oklahoma, are a Zionist?"

"In principle," he said. "That's the only way to make a fight of it."

She was absolutely dumbfounded in silence until her voice appeared again as soft and gentle as if it were a leaf falling somewhere outside with no place to go. I could hardly hear her.

"Harry, I really and truly find you a man to love. That's the whole truth of it."

And his voice began with the monotony and melancholy of the owl at night. "Don't go!" He said it again and again. "Don't go, don't go, don't go, don't go, don't go, don't go."

He went on saying it until she kissed him into silence.

The night poured through the open window and the night wind shook the autumn skirts of the trees. Without end the leaves kept falling. I could hear the brook tumbling and rushing. I pulled the covers over my head with only the tip of my nose out. I didn't want to hear anything. When the great horned owl hooted it seemed this time to come out of the fireplace, where the fire paled and occasional sparks flew up.

I knew that Zenia was leaving us forever.

11

Now all at once yet day by day the time came near which would be the last day in America for Zenia.

She resigned from the hospital. She collected the latest medical books and certain medical supplies and instruments. She bought all kinds of clothing and boots for cold weather. Everything was for over there and nothing was for here.

She appeared everywhere with more and more speed, seeing everyone she knew, going to places she had known. The days were fuller and fuller, the weeks shorter and shorter. She lived with a kind of joyful nervous frenzy and sudden hesitations of sadness, such as a migrating bird must feel as the landscape tugs away at it again and again until the bird begins the journey it can no longer escape.

Almost every day we took walks in the zoo or the Botanical Gardens, by the lake and the river, in the streets and lots of my childhood. The burdock was brown, the burs loose, the stalks stiff and brittle.

Zenia was full of remembering: the Catskills, the Albany night boat, catching snakes at the end of long trolley rides by way of Westchester towns, the swimming, the sights, the taste of apples and the fragrance of roasted peanuts from the Greeks. She told me everything she had already told me and then told it again.

Nothing could prevent that day from coming. There was a cold autumn day when Harry Rivers suddenly arrived and took her off with him. She came home in tears. He had argued and pleaded with her for the last time not to leave. I think for a desperate moment she had changed her mind, felt the enormous relief of remaining with those she loved until, like a fatal disease, her sense of what had to be done set her loose again for the new life she owed to humanity.

She told my father that Harry had shouted at her, "We're humanity!"

"Well," my father asked, "what did you say to that?"

"I said, 'No, we're only human. We're not humanity.' "

That word had haunted so many conversations around our mahogany dining table. It was a guest who never left until she left.

At the pier on the Hudson it was exciting. The passengers were the chosen people and all the rest were celebrating for them. People were mostly on their way to Paris by way of England. It was Prohibition but somehow champagne bottles popped in every corridor behind open and closed doors. People flowed in and out of the ship. It was a time of good-bye laughter and happy tears for almost all. For Zenia, the route was different: England, Norway, then by train to Finland and there, according to some secret arrangements she had made, into the Soviet Union.

I slipped away to the noisy corridor whose open cabin doors were full of good-bye kisses and gifts. Zenia's door was closed and I could hear Harry Rivers shouting inside. I heard Harry say clearly enough, "Good-bye. They'll kill you there, like they killed my brother in Oklahoma."

The scuffling sound of the corridor, the bodies, the voices outside could not absorb the silence within. "Good-bye, good-bye." The voices went on everywhere.

Now I moved away among the celebrating faces as Harry came out. He left the door closed behind him and his face was flushed and beaten with anger and despair. He was taller than most of the people there and I saw his head make its way to another corridor that led to the deck.

I didn't know what I would find in Zenia's cabin. Everybody would soon be there and it was in a way my last chance to see her alone. I knocked on the door.

"Who is that?" Her voice was not hers at the moment. It was broken with feeling. Perhaps she had wept briefly but she wasn't one to cry for long, easily yes, long no, for her spirit would take hold of itself as if it were something crumpled to be straightened out and let fly in the winds of the world.

"Oh, you," she said, opening the door. "Come in. I'm feeling sorry for myself, now that I'm leaving. You think I'm wrong to go?"

I told her, "No."

"How would you know, my dear child?"

"Then why did you ask me?"

"To talk about something. People must talk. Talk to me."

"Stay," I said. "Don't go now. Go later."

"It's now or never. Look at me." And all the while I was trying to swallow her with my eyes. "I'm sweating with excitement. I'm shaking. Would you believe me if I said I want to run up on the deck and cry out to all those people, 'Here I am! I'm going off into a great mystery.' But I'm here with you waiting till they all come to say good-bye. Then after everyone gets off, I'll go up on the deck and I'll lean over the railing and wave to you. 'Good-bye, good-bye,' we'll all say to each other." She went on like this until she turned and took me by the shoulder. She was sitting on the lower cabin bunk and we were about face to face. "You're the only one who up to now didn't say to me, 'Zenia, don't go.' Why?"

I burst into tears and we embraced. I flung myself at her and she embraced me and we clung to each other and she caressed my hair, my neck, my shoulders, comforting me. Just as suddenly I pulled away from her. She wiped my eyes with the delicate little handkerchief with embroidered edges which she always carried, tucked somewhere, in a belt, her bosom, her sleeve, depending.

I said to her, "You want to go. You must. I know all about that."

"Yes." She wiped her own eyes. "Yes, of course. Naturally. You know what's right and proper, don't you? They only know what they want. But we know what we ought to want. Don't think I won't miss America, in spite of all that happened. This country is more amazing than it knows. Who knows, it might even know it."

She was up now and cheerful. "Where's everybody? Why must they wait for the last minute? My father, your father's father, your grandfather, the grandfather you never saw, and who may be dead now, was a district superintendent of schools. He always had everything arranged, if you could arrange anything in the old Russia. That was a difficult place to get anything arranged. You should know that. He said that everybody is born with so many victories and so many defeats. Every time something bad happened, he said, 'That's one less for the future.' And every time something good happened, he was sad and said, 'One less to look forward to.' "

I was laughing. "It's not like that at all."

"Of course not," she said. "But then we don't have characters like his. He was very smart. He could be clever. His life was difficult because he was a Jew, and Jews were not permitted in general to have such jobs. They made it very bad for him. It'll be different now. Who knows? I believe in the future. I hope for it. But I wouldn't say I trust it too much. I think that's what Harry Rivers tried to tell me. He expects bad surprises. I guess"—she turned to me, her arm about my shoulder, and walked me across the little cabin and then back again—"I suppose I was one of those bad surprises for him."

I asked her without intending to. "Did Victor ever ask you to marry him?"

"Victor?" She wondered. It puzzled her and then she laughed. "Oh, him, that darling soldier who took you rowing on the lake? Yes. But before I could answer he said, 'Naturally it would be foolish of you to say yes or no since we hardly know each other. On the other hand,' he said, 'I must go. I can't wait for months and months while everything goes on and we get to know each other. However, if you don't get married very soon, here's my address. I'll be there for just one month. Then I'm going to California.' And before I knew it he was gone. He knew many strange things about life. Did you like him?"

"Most of all," I said.

"He struck me that way also," she reflected. "Who knows? California, Russia . . ."

We were alone for a while in the cabin of the great ship, solid and unmoving as the skyscrapers of the city yet full of movement, voices, winches, the secret throb of engines, and flying through the porthole the smell of the Hudson, which is the smell of the sea, and, high, the gulls flying from river to river with their gull cries. They dropped into the oily water of the docks where scraps from the visitors, passengers in the ship, floated in the water. That water had seemed frightful to me in its dark oily rottenness with the tide beginning to roll out from the mountains upstream, down the long Hudson Basin into the bays, the islands and finally the sea, the very sea I had seen from the beaches of Long Island where the clean waves flung themselves down in protest because they could roll no more. There the sea went on to become the sky on gray days, the two closing together to become the world, or on cloud-strewn windy ones the sea always kept rolling in like leaves falling in autumn, just rolling and falling. I lay on the hot beaches, huddled in a pit of sand, and my eyes like myself seemed to reach out over the water to the dim small outlines of a distant ship, almost sinking beneath the horizon so that I knew the round earth and the sky were real and went round and round to come back behind me to the beach and myself again, while I lay heating in the hot sun like a crocodile and the cool wind touched me and I didn't know if I was a body at all or just myself. Here, too, now, alone with Zenia, it was also the coming together in the illusion of forever. We were together still, although in fact we were parting, she to follow the roll of the ocean around the earth to England, Germany, Norway, Finland, and from there to disappear like the adventurers put on the Soviet Ark, sent back from the new world of the past to the new world, as Zenia said, of the future.

"We'll meet again, believe me, my dear." So she said. She said it in her soft and rich voice. It always seemed as if her voice went on after the words had stopped. Just as she would be there after she was gone. "I'm going home. I'm Russian."

"But," I said, wanting her to stay, as I also deeply wanted her to leave for her adventure; it was then, it seemed, an adventure she was about to sail out upon. "Papa and Mama are Russians. Grandma is Russian. They're all Russian."

"But you aren't. Never. You were born here. And in that way they came to find the new world here and found you. But I haven't."

"You could stay," I said. By that I meant all of us and I meant Harry. I meant the tribe of young doctors who followed and pursued her and had come to our house often for dinner along with her, all wanting her and loving her, rivals for her heart and body. She was, it seemed then to me, someone extraordinary, out of the *Makers of History,* from a book still unwritten, about whom something would be said, as of Alexander it was said that his horse's name was Bucephalus. So of her, I could say, I am her nephew, just myself. But she was going. That brief endless moment went on. She stroked my head and often absentmindedly kissed my cheeks, holding me close or leaving me, to move, to look out of the porthole, which faced not downstream but up into the reaches of the river, the Palisades, the Catskills, into the summers we had spent at Big Indian, into the dried-out mountain streams with their treasures, the giant pebbles and pools of captive trout, to the hot afternoons, swimming in the icy water, to mountaintops and orchards, to pines, to deer and, below, the farms with the thick house smell of cows and milk—all those healthy things she constantly praised to make one strong and happy in nature and progress. I had heard her dream of life so often in those hills, in those mountains, in the mystery of the zoo and the Botanical Gardens, along the Bronx River, beneath the falls or above. We had walked everywhere and taken journeys like explorers on summer trolleys, and here she was going away on this adventure without me.

"We'll meet again one day, you from your country and me from mine. After all, my dearest thing, how can we ever be separated, since we have known each other so long and are of the same blood and mind and so on?" She had many of those late-Victorian words buried in her speech along with the current down-to-earth talk of someone who was a physician and knew death was not a journey but the ending of the one journey that any living thing ever took. She knew everything and yet, like myself, she knew nothing. She had inherited this extraordinary dream of utopia and now she was racing toward it. The ship never stirred, but it would. The smell of river, of sea, the sound of gulls filled the cabin so tiny with its two bunks, one of which was as yet unoccupied but soon would be by another woman passenger.

The trip was beginning well for her. Her beauty and her charm had already worked its way, for the steward, after knocking on the door, looked in. He was a small Englishman dressed in an immaculate white jacket and blue trousers with a little peaked cap, and he said with a strange accent, "Dr. Mont, we won't disturb you with another passenger in here. The ship's doctor wants to know if you'll have dinner with him at the captain's table tonight." So she had already made her mark on the ship. She was in the hands everywhere of friends, surrounded by her admirers, her lovers, her entranced believers.

"You're very kind," she said. "Thank you and thank him."

What was her charm? She was, of course, blessed by the greatest of all blessings. She had beauty, which like every real talent was given, but in her it was in motion along with her character, her spirit and her martyr's belief in humanity. That was her gift to me, that one day because of us, our efforts, our devotion, our courage, something could be done as if we as captains of the future had divided the world and she would go and take care of it from one end while I, as I grew up, would take care of it from another. Now she looked sad for a moment. I knew these moments when she suddenly stopped as if in air, poised, one hand on the porthole window, the other on her weight of hair, and with a kind of secret sadness looked back at me, realizing that this was a new world she was leaving, driven from it by the cry of history.

It was then the boat's whistle blew like the roar of lions on summer nights sounding across our games, sounding across that raid, sounding into my bedroom across the summer trolley, clicking away into the night, sounding and sounding while the whole ship shook. When it stopped, the voices of the passengers and visitors and all the excitement began to flow through the bodies of those going or those who had to get off. For one last moment I think she was impelled to pick up her belongings and run back to the shore, but the gulls cried by through the porthole and the whistles blew and the door flew open and everybody was there, calling, surrounding her, saying good-bye with kisses and embraces, and in the end I was among those she left as we went up on the deck and off the ship and waited there with the others as this giant ship made ready to sail away on the seas.

Fantastic electrical arcs went between the dock watchers and ship-rail faces. Forever went on from moment to moment, until the talking whistles from tugs and ship gave the last command. This great monster began to move, smoke pouring from the tugs and smoke drifting casually from one of the ship's three funnels. Space opened up and water flooded in the dirty, oily surface around the dock. It took so long to move this ship out before it had the freedom to move on its own.

I remembered then as I had noted to remember that at the beginning of the pier they were constructing a new building, still in the stages of scaffolds and skeleton wood. I ran back and soon was climbing up among the wooden struts, using ladders and such, not caring yet that I might be afraid to come down as well as go up if I thought of it. I wanted to be there, to stand there, to be alone, and watch the giant ship take Zenia to the other world.

It was windy and I clung there, watching the ship guided out, saw it turn, watched it straighten to face the hidden Atlantic, the tugs talking to it, heard it answer. The ropes went loose and free and the ship sailed under its own power downriver with the Hudson tide. I watched it sail out, its whistle blowing of the dreams of the past and the dreams of the future opening the distance between us like the distance between sleep and waking, like the distance between thought and motion. It was a separation of the joining that was joining us in the separation.

Now the ship was itself, self-contained as I was myself, alone. I saw people streaming back and leaving. I knew they would be looking for me in the crush, wondering if I were stupid enough to be lost. I felt an extraordinary responsibility, as if I had committed her to this ship and its journey and its end. But if I had committed her to it, I did not intend it. It had happened. At the same time by this action I had also done the same with myself. Our dream, young and loose as it was in me, hardly definite enough to be named, sailed with her on the immense journey each of us takes alone, even when, like Zenia and myself, there is a common yet unshared plunge of sky and gulf and life and memory.

I climbed down and found my parents and their friends and her friends. Everybody was excited and sad at the same time.

My father said, "She'll be back before long."

My mother said nothing.

"No," Harry said. "She's gone forever." He was angry with the world and all of us. He walked off by himself and was gone.

We three went home, but soon left that old neighborhood to move downtown.

Part II

Call from Jerusalem

12

Snow everywhere. When Ram drove up to the farm it had been gray, growing darker, heavier, with the wind beginning to move. By the time he was over the Taconic Mountain ridge which ran through Fahnestock Park before dropping under the Hudson to reappear in New Jersey, it was very cold and snowing. The wind swept flurries against the glass and the road that had appeared to be going somewhere wandered in a spray of space. Everything was filled with the drive and motion of snow. The parkway was slippery and he drove carefully.

It was almost dark when he turned off at the Pine Plains intersection and took the Fishwoods Road to the farm.

The garage was at the foot of the driveway leading up to the house, and when he got out of the car the wind had left. The air lay still while the snow fell steadily. It was bitter outside the car but the sudden silence which wasn't quite a silence was warm and comforting. The brook rushed and tumbled, swollen and high with the coming spring.

He put on the house lights and telephoned his neighbor, Ann, the daughter of Peter Waal, who since her father's death had taken over the Waal farm.

"What are you doing up here?" she asked.

"I don't know, Ann. I think it was the threat of snow."

"I just noticed the lights on and I wondered who was there. I've leftovers for dinner, if you like."

"I'll be there."

"I also have half a pie." And she hung up.

On the radio, which as usual here carried fragmented noise and stations from any place rather than Kingston or Albany, he was able to make out that they expected the snow to fall all night and that it might then turn to rain. As the announcer continued, a Montreal deluge of symphonic music intervened.

A little after seven he walked out into the night. The snow still fell with an unchanging and windless steadiness, sometimes fine and crystalline and sometimes slow, thick and fluttering in gigantic flakes. In the lights of the house every tree and bush had found its way through the touch of snow to its secret shape. It didn't seem so cold any more.

He walked down the road to the small second bridge where the old wood railings still overlooked the black water rushing below. The heavy wooden planks which rattled with each passing car were now covered with unbroken snow. He stood there in the sound of the creek like someone standing in the natural sound of his own body. It had the same mix of the irregular within the regular.

Wherever he turned and wherever he could see anything, the smallest twig was sculptured with snow.

In the peace of windless snow he turned back along this narrow shoulderless road he knew so well. The wire strands of the cattle fences were like the spangled ropes of Christmas, each barb with its decorative tuft. White weightless stones rested softly as snow puffs in the ever-shaping snow, which fell with a steady evenness, clinging to everything, seeking out every twist and turn wherever it could to reveal the shapes inhabiting the stillness of this sudden winter night in April. Usually by this time the big snowfalls of the winter were over, although now and again a fury of arctic wind would sweep down from the north and thrust the last touch of hard winter on the farm. But this snowfall was original, something different for April. This snow was windless, private. It fell upon everything as it fell upon him, with a stillness of imaginary time, the time of big numbers in tiny flakes of snow, so that Ram closed his eyes as he walked over to Ann's farm just to feel the numbers falling by.

When he got up in the morning the snow was still falling in its silent way. He could hear the furnace stir and begin to work. He went into the kitchen to boil the water for coffee. The telephone rang. It was no longer a party line as in the first days when he had come up there to visit Harry Rivers. But it had the long country ring in a personal way. The present kitchen telephone was attached to the wall over the counter next to the electric stove. There was the big window looking north and beside it the kitchen door, the top half of glass, facing in the same direction. The storm windows and doors were still up but through it all he could see the snow still coming down out of a sky that had no shape but that of the ever-falling, unshaken drama of endless numbers of snowflakes.

"Hello," Ram said.

"Hello," Gertrude Killens, the operator, said. "I almost told them you wouldn't be there."

"I'm here," he said.

"Would you believe you've got a call from Jerusalem?"

"Well," Ram said, "it's getting close to Easter."

He turned off the electric burner to wait, wondering who in Jerusalem might call him. Or why. But there were so many people who might be there. He decided it was Leslie, who lived in London but was married to an Israeli woman and therefore might, if it was Leslie, call from Jerusalem just for the pleasure of chatting from there. He waited and started remembering taking a sudden air trip with Leslie from London to Luxembourg to watch the Chelsea team play an international cup match. While they waited for game time, for they had come over in a chartered plane of Chelsea fans, most of whom were loud and drunk before the plane landed, he and Leslie had decided to visit the American cemetery just to stand and remember. They had done so. Then Leslie said, "Why don't we visit the German cemetery?"

The German cemetery was beautiful. Instead of a geometry

of crosses dotted with Stars of David, there had been flat small stones placed on the ground, obscured by bushes and flowers that made the whole place a garden which flowed toward a giant statue of German heroism.

"You know what's buried here?" Leslie asked.

"No," Ram said.

"The Germans who killed the American prisoners of war during the Battle of the Bulge. The Germans would think such men were heroes. You see, if you look at this cemetery, you know that no one ever died. It's heaven and they're playing Wagner in the gas chambers. Why did we come here?"

"Because you were curious," Ram said.

"My curiosity is satisfied."

They hurried back to their car and were driven to the stadium. There they discovered that the English contingent didn't have seats in the grandstands but had to stand throughout the whole game, while Chelsea beat Luxembourg quite easily and the English fans amused themselves by drinking, vomiting and insulting the officials and a member of the royal family of Luxembourg. That had been a long day and one with mixed feelings.

The phone was very lively with noises and Gertrude's voice came back to say she was having trouble.

"If you expected a call from Jerusalem," she said, "you should've let us know."

"I didn't."

"Well, just hang on, if you don't mind. We're having a little trouble, but we're being connected."

It was so like the conversations they used to have in the Bronx apartment in the old days when he was young. After the janitor buzzed the dumbwaiter and they opened the dumbwaiter door, Burrows would call up to say there was a telephone call. Then it would start. Someone would say, "Would you believe you have a telephone call?" And another would say, "Who could it be?" People would discuss it for a while before his father or mother went down the four flights into the open yard, then down the outside steel stairway to the basement hall where the public telephone was placed beside the janitor's apartment door. Burrows, the informer, would wait there with a smile on his face and a joke in his mouth until finally, with the first hello, he left but managed to leave his apartment door open a little so he could overhear the conversation. By now Burrows and his jokes were probably dead. Yet as a matter of fact, Ram thought, he could still be alive and still working as an informer, but now in this different world.

There was some confusion on the telephone and he leaned against the counter and looked out on the landscape of snow.

Nothing outside had escaped its relief of snow, its cap of snow, its highlight of snow. The pine plantation was rich and layered, tufted and heaped. Red-pine snow was bunched; on the yews topped in heaps; on the low pruned hemlocks, thick and drooping; on the mugho pines, club-fingered and club-stalked; on the white pines tufted; on the Chinese elm, traced, etched, escaping from the sudden ending of the limbs in a spray that had been arrested as it fell. The lilac bushes were particularly intricate and woven with snow, a fine black line of branch and bark carrying out the texture against the grayness that pretended to be sky but was only falling snow. Suddenly in the east a very small touch of pale brown and gold—not red, not yellow, but just the smallest fragment and tone of color—showed for a moment and disappeared. The snow continued to fall. The plum tree had launched its snow branches out in incomplete sprigs. The locusts managed to struggle up. The black walnuts held snow cupped and symmetrical, and the last remaining elm in the great pasture was still a great soarer, searching the sky until it suddenly crooked itself on top like fingers, as if the pressure of the immense air were too great to probe. The old sugar maple that held the house remained immense. It had been a giant when he first saw it and in its greatness had hardly seemed to change. The trunk was heavy and plated with white and black armored scales, traced out with snow, and the first giant limbs were as large as great old trees themselves, twisting out of the parent root to form what Ram used to see in his old biology book, a diagram of the tree of life. So the sugar maple was. It held the house from above and below through its roots. In that way the house was almost in the tree, joined to it, and so he felt it, the house alive as a tree because the tree was in fact a tree of life. It held the world this way, not only the birds, the beasts, the insects, the plants that lived there but even the inhabitants of the house and the ghost of Harry Rivers.

There were many voices of men and women on the telephone until finally the male voice of the Israeli operator was clearest and he asked Ram if he was in fact the Mr. Mont they were trying to reach. When Ram said yes, the operator asked him to wait one minute please. So Ram waited again. Finally a new voice came on the telephone. It was a cheerful voice and it was lively with excitement and surprise. "I'm Dr. Moishe Haller," he said. "I'm a professor of medicine here at the Hebrew University, and I don't think we've met."

"I don't think so," Ram said.

"I'm calling for someone who is staying with me as my guest. She is also a physician and her name is Dr. Zenia Mont."

When Ram didn't say anything, a slight alarm came into Dr. Haller's voice.

"Mr. Mont." He said it again. "Mr. Mont. I hope it's a pleasant shock but your aunt is here beside me. She wants to talk to you. Hello? Are you there?"

"I'm here," Ram said. "Thank you."

The great stillness of the image of the maple as the tree of life in the old biology book, and fallen snow, and Zenia's young, excited face were present in the room with him.

"Ram, here I am in Jerusalem."

"If I hurry," he said, "I can be there sometime tomorrow." She laughed.

"Zenia!" He shouted into the telephone.

"Yes. I'm here and I'll be here. Are you healthy?"

"Mostly. And you?"

"The same."

"I'm on my way."

"I'm waiting. Here is Dr. Haller. He'll give you the address and whatever you have to know. Don't you want to know when I got here?"

"You just arrived."

"Naturally." She was laughing now again and again. It seemed as if she was laughing because the telephone sound began to fracture. "I'll put him on," she said. Her English was more Russian than he remembered it but it was Zenia's voice, dismembered by time and the telephone.

Now Dr. Haller came on and he spoke and Ram and he repeated again and again until it was all clear: the proper address, the proper telephone number and the fact that Ram was coming, that he was on his way. There were many good-byes with Dr. Haller and in the end, with a kind of exhaustion, Ram hung up.

He stood there looking around at Harry's house. It was his house now but it had always been Harry's. It was intended to be Zenia's and a wild thought came that now in the end, after nearly fifty-six years, she would return and enter this house for the second time and it would be hers as Harry Rivers had wanted so long ago.

He knew exactly how old she was. She was four days less than eighty-one, and her birthday was on April 21. He knew that. It was all he had to know.

Something ground and rasped in his chest and his heartbeat became irregular. He was used to it. It often did this nowadays. But this time it made sense. At last, his crazy heart had found something to keep time with.

He put a call in to London to talk to Leslie and finally got him at his office. He told Leslie about the call and Leslie, all the while talking to Ram, made arrangements with people around him to have a room at the King David Hotel, high up with a view of the old city. That seemed to be something significant. Leslie was shouting to someone and said, "We're figuring out your time. Don't worry about anything. I'll have a car and a chauffeur there and he'll take you wherever you want to go. What was that doctor's name again? Haller? Was it Moishe Haller? I've met him. I know him. I'll call my wife right away. She knows him. Her family knows him. Haller is somebody you should know anyway. He lives in a house "—he named the street and the number—" and from there you can look down on the old city as you will. You'll see, Ram, everything will be fine." And now he said, his voice brimming with all the feeling that someone could manage at a time like this, "How extraordinary. I'll get to meet your Aunt Zenia one day!"

"Good-bye, Leslie," Ram said. "You're sounding crazy."

"Someone has to. You'll be a great disappointment to her if you talk in that calm and reasonable way that I'm hearing now."

"Good-bye and thank you and your wife and everyone."

"Don't worry," Leslie continued to say, "I'll get reports on everything. Whatever you need, wherever you are, anywhere, someone from our company will be happy to oblige you. You see, it's better than the official service of the government. All these people really want to please us, not because they have to but because they like to."

They said good-bye and Ram hung up again. He replaced the telephone receiver in its cradle, where it hung as evidence that he had spoken to Zenia and that she was alive and in Jerusalem.

"Why not?" he said aloud. He spoke out loud every once in a while in order to lend reality to the feelings he was waiting to feel. "It's a holy city. We know that. Strange things have happened in the imagination of my ancestors there, and later historians have said that such things really happened, if not exactly as told in the Bible, then almost like that. In fact, beneath every story something real happened. The fact that the story really means something means she's there, like all the rest of the stories that have come from Jerusalem. Only she's happening now. I must be very careful not to die before I meet her." Now he knew the meaning of his strange care and calm. He was being cautious with the everlasting threat of death.

Ram put on his boots, which were standing near the kitchen door. He put on a windbreaker and a knitted wool cap and then went out to walk over to the neighboring farm. He crossed the field past the old chicken house and the snow was still falling. He didn't try to open the wooden cow fence because of the snow. He just climbed over it. It wasn't as easy as it once had been but he did it. Then he was on the old dirt road, which hadn't been plowed yet and might not until the next day, and walked the few hundred yards to Ann's farmhouse.

Her golden retriever was romping around in the snow and barked loudly at him while her three geese puttered around the rushing water of the creek where new ice had formed during the night, but only at the edges like a delicate fringe of lacework.

Ann was at the door smiling at him. She looked a lot like her mother when they had met some fifty-six years ago, although Ann now was older than her mother had been then, but not as old as her mother was when she died at eighty. Ann was two years older than Ram. She was sixty-nine, thin, straight, wrinkled. Looking at her it seemed that her smile had never changed, or the straight way she had of looking and talking.

"Come in," she said. "I didn't expect you twice in the middle of the week."

Ram said, "I have to leave right away."

She poured coffee and he pulled off his hat but kept his windbreaker on. He had wiped his boots in the little vestibule but the water melted from the little snow on him and wet the linoleum floor.

"Never mind," she said. "It's winter yet, even though I'd like some spring. You look pretty excited. You look as if you might be getting sick. There's fever in your eyes."

"I'm not sick," he said. "I'm excited." And he told her about the call and Zenia. Ann listened, and as she listened she remembered, and while she remembered she became soft and thoughtful thinking of the days when Harry had bought the farm, of the one meeting she had had with Zenia on the one weekend Zenia had come up there.

"I remember her," Ann said. "Mostly I remember what I heard about her all the years that Harry came up to his farm here and the times you came here and the way you spoke of her."

She talked easily about Harry Rivers and he knew that for years after her husband died they had been lovers, but now she was talking about Zenia.

"When are you leaving?" Ann asked.

"All the arrangements are being made and one way or another I'll be on my way as soon as I can."

"Then just take off," she said. "I'll close up everything for you. Will you let me know how things are, how you find them?"

He got up, put on his wool hat and started to leave, then turned around to look at this woman who had known Harry Rivers so well, whom he had known for so long, ever since she was a young girl. She lived here alone on this farm and with one hired man ran the whole place, the hundred Holsteins, and kept company with her dog and three favorite geese.

"I found fox tracks around this morning," Ann said. "I'm going to have to keep my geese in at night."

They shook hands and then she suddenly embraced him and kissed his cheek. "I hope it's all as lucky as it sounds."

He said, "I don't even know what I feel. I mean every part of me is on the run and it's still snowing."

"They've plowed the parkway."

"I heard them during the night."

"They've been through again this morning. Just drive carefully. It's no use getting killed before you get to Jerusalem."

He waved and left. The retriever ran back part of the way with him, then said good-bye with a last bark.

He drove carefully, and by the time he came down the Taconic ridge the snow had turned to rain. He was in New York in about two and a half hours.

His law partner, Leonard, was waiting for him at the apartment. They stood there looking at each other with a kind of unusual wonder that comes occasionally when the past opens and spills out as if it were just happening for the first time.

"Shall I postpone your appearance in Washington?" Leonard asked. "Do you have any idea when you'll get back?"

"No," Ram said.

"Bring her here."

"That's not up to me."

"Well, then," Leonard said, "I'll take your arguments before the court. Did you read that Columbia piece I left on your desk?"

"It doesn't apply."

Leonard was still gifted with beauty in his old age, a little ruffled like a fine old dress or costume, yet still elegant and lovely. His grace had become an absentminded eccentricity.

"Shall I drive out to the airport with you?" Leonard asked.

"No, it's all right." Ram really didn't want to talk to anyone because he didn't know what to say. He tried not to think. He planned just to keep looking out at the world outside and see nothing within. He couldn't bear the uproar of his senses, his memories, his hopes, his astonishment. He had a hot crazy feeling, as if he were leaping from a high rock down into Garden Street without intending to but there he was flying through the air and the runners were ready to break in all directions, which his feelings were doing without any help from him.

"There's a car and a driver downstairs," Leonard said, "so just go when you feel like. You still have two hours until plane time but they say they want you there an hour early."

"They always do."

They shook hands and then suddenly Leonard embraced him and left.

After all the waiting for Zenia, in the end the waiting had died. When he had thought of her at all he could say to himself, "I suppose she's dead." But it wasn't really like death. It was just that she had gone away and that was the end of it.

The whole trip had no physical continuity. It was a nonexistent interval between two discrete events. He was in the new world and then he was being driven to Jerusalem. No matter how he tried to pay attention to things so that he wouldn't be thinking of Zenia, of wondering why she was in Jerusalem, of how it was that she was alive and, being alive, why it was he had never heard from her or never found her, for he had asked many of his friends to see if they could trace her and they had tried. They had found no trace. Yet there she was in Jerusalem and he was going there. It was impossible to sit out those endless hours of separation and the absolute moment of the meeting which would take place by thinking of what went on between. Oceans, continents, islands in the Mediterranean. Night becoming day. These places refused to exist in him. They disappeared as he tried to observe them. His pulsating excitement burned up objects. Then he tried to live in the memory of her as he had known her. This extraordinary young woman, full of conversation and motion, simply dazzled and disappeared.

All he could think about was the time eight years before on a rainy October when he had nearly died in London. For the first time what happened then frightened him now in a profound way and not as it had then in fits of anxiety about dying, the physical absolute against dying, the need to survive coming up for air between extravagant bouts of pain.

He had been in bed after midnight trying to read the letters of Thomas Mann when death arrived as pain.

Now he was obsessed by the frailty of that time. Had he died he would not be on his way to see Zenia again. And it was still possible she might die, being very old, and he might die since he almost had. In his mind she had been dead for a long time, whatever that meant, since in him she was always alive, sailing on that great ship into the Russian Revolution forever on her way as she always was in his love of her, so open to things as they were and so driven by the idea of "humanity" in a world full of "backward elements."

He must have been smiling because for a moment the young woman from the airline leaping out of the fashion magazine of that day smiled back at him. She handed out smiles with food, with drinks, with the passing hours, while the numbers flashed and the miles became time.

His drift of remembrances found nothing satisfying and he returned again to London and how he had almost died there. It was important now. It was more important now than it had been then.

He was there to meet with an American scientist who had fled the country under the suspicion of having been a spy. This scientist had been named during the McCarthy period by an informer who had confessed to being a Soviet agent and whose testimony was backed up by an arrested English scientist-spy, who had confessed and gone to prison and then many years later had been freed to go to East Germany, where he now lived and worked. The American had fled and now (this was eight years or so ago) had suddenly reappeared in London and wanted to return to the United States. His trouble was that the United States government wasn't particularly interested in getting him back and the English weren't particularly interested in letting him stay. He had, through an English solicitor, appealed to Ram's office for help. There were many constitutional questions involved, as well as personal and moral ones. Was he in fact a man who had once been a spy for the Soviet Union? Had he become in the interim a citizen of one of the Soviet-dominated countries? If he hadn't, he was still a citizen of the United States and entitled to come back, no matter what the consequences might be. In a preliminary conversation with someone in the Justice Department whom Ram knew well, there was mentioned, without being stated, a kind of offer. What would this American scientist know that could be of use to his own country? If he had really in all the years between been occupied in anything of a military or political use to the United States, especially if he knew the names of people in the United States or in the NATO countries who might be spies or potential spies, then the United States government might be interested.

From Ram's point of view, if any of this was true, then naturally he was not prepared to handle the case. His object was not to service the man and get him back home as an informer. Ram's only interest was if in fact the man had never been a spy and was in fact an American citizen who had been a victim of the past and now wanted, for some reason Ram could not understand, to return to his native land.

So that winter in London they had met. Ram knew that this man was already under observation by English, American and possibly Soviet agents to find out what really was at stake in this unusual case.

They met in Ram's suite at the Connaught and went down to have dinner in the Grill Room, where they had a relatively private table.

As soon as Ram saw the man he disliked him.

Ram had seen a picture of this young scientist when he was twenty-six years old, the time when he had fled the country. In that photograph he was laughing, looking at someone who was pleasing him, and the face was open with energy and a kind of anticipated happiness. The headlines after the scandal naturally called him "brilliant," which made his case more interesting. The man who now walked into the sitting room was in his fifties, a shabby creature in every way. He shuffled around the room, cunning and carefulness in his voice, in the random searching glances with which he looked around. He stood for a moment at the window to survey the mews four stories below as if someone might be waiting there to watch him. He was polite. He was artificial. And his suppressed egotism was irrepressible.

"You care if what you tell me is overheard?" Ram asked.

"I have no secrets," the man said.

Ram thought this was strange since he had led a secret life from 1951 to the present moment.

"Good," Ram said. "We can eat comfortably downstairs and talk. If I think you're about to say anything that shouldn't be heard by anyone but me, I'll stop you."

"You may be too late by then."

"Naturally," Ram said. "But you're warned. This is just

our first meeting. If I decide we need a really secret conversation, I'll make some arrangement."

"Is that possible?"

"More or less."

Hume King was tall, somewhat hunched, not so thin, not so fat. He looked like someone who had been sick for a long time and would never recover. But he ate with pleasure and enjoyed the good food they had in the Grill Room. He also drank a lot of wine and smoked most of the time. The story he told Ram sounded completely false, highly improbable, and yet in fact might actually have been true. In the world of conspiracy as explanation all such doubts find new conspiracies to explain them. Ram had discovered that men have a passion for the pleasures of conspiracy, not only in gossip but in science as well as politics. Hume King had spent most of his life since 1951 in a world of possible conspiracies.

Supposing that what King told him was true, and if King was innocent, what he described was an extraordinary adventure and it in turn reminded Ram, as he listened to one story, of another that had happened to someone he knew during the course of the Second World War.

Ram had been with the Office of Strategic Services in Paris when a Washington official, formerly an advertising man and now a colonel in the army assigned to the OSS, had paid a supervising visit. In fact, he told Ram after he arrived, he wanted to see a real battle before the war was over, for it now seemed that the war was coming to an end.

No one in authority in Paris thought this was a good idea. But the man simply wrote out his own orders, commandeered a jeep and a driver and set out for the quiet Ardennes. He was lucky in one way, because he arrived just in time for the Battle of the Bulge. He imagined he was driving through territory safely held by the American troops but suddenly found himself surrounded by German soldiers dressed as Americans, who had infiltrated in advance of the main thrust of the German army.

The Germans were delighted to find a colonel. They

promptly killed the driver because they had no time to take prisoners, but this colonel was carrying all his identification papers, which revealed his position in the OSS. The Germans knew they had someone important, for here was someone from the secret intelligence agency of the United States at the very place where even now a desperate surprise attack of the war was taking place.

The colonel was put into the hands of the Gestapo. They questioned him. He knew nothing. That hadn't been his job in Washington. The Battle of the Bulge went on in its fury while day and night the Germans tried to find out what this important spy knew. They pulled out his fingernails. They beat him. They attacked his genitals. They used electricity. They did everything but kill him, and all this man could do was to protest and say he knew nothing. All he had was office information from Washington. By the time it became clear that Germany's last attack to break out of the encirclement was doomed to failure, what was left of the colonel was going to be sent to Dachau for a final solution. But just as the colonel had been overrun by a sudden attack, so was the Gestapo group. When the Americans found this American colonel and the state he was in, they killed all the Germans who were holding him.

The colonel survived. He was in the end given a formal dinner of appreciation in Paris and awarded the Legion of Merit before being sent home. He told stories of his torture the way another man might tell stories of his pleasures, with great detail and an enormous sense of surprise. He kept saying, "I couldn't believe that such things could happen." And then he'd tell exactly what happened. It was for him a remarkable adventure.

It was this kind of stupid and unbelievable story that Hume King told Ram.

Hume King still had an engaging smile, which had now become a fiction behind which he hid his suspicion of everything in the world. He had had to be suspicious to survive. It seemed that his field back in 1950 had been microbiology and genetics. While he ate his dinner, delighted with every new thing that he had missed during the years between, he denied that he had ever worked on anything but theoretical work. "I was in the mathematics part of it," he said. "I was interested in the nucleic acids and the problem of base pairing."

He told Ram his version of what had happened in bits and pieces. It appeared that just before he was about to leave for a conference in Copenhagen that would take up the microbiological problem in genetics, a fellow scientist in the same field told him that he had been visited by a representative from the Mc-Carthy committee and that the name of Hume King was mentioned. He soon learned that a former fellow worker had confessed to being a Soviet spy and was now an informer and had hinted to many people that King was a fellow conspirator. Nothing of this was true, King insisted. What was true was the fact that he had been close friends with the informer-spy and had been having some financial troubles because of his engagement to a teacher in the same university. As a result, he had borrowed money from the informer-spy on a pretty regular basis.

"What do you mean, 'a pretty regular basis'?" Ram asked.

"Pretty regular" turned out to be five hundred dollars a month over a period of six months.

"That isn't much money," Ram said, "but it's a lot to borrow from a friend in that peculiar way, and it's just about the right amount to be paid to a spy."

"So I understood," said King. "I knew I would end up being ruined. I knew the other man was lying. I didn't know why he had chosen me to lie about. I had no politics. But I was young and I didn't want to go to jail. I wanted to keep on working. I knew that this whole field was the beginning of a new language in biology. Everything pointed to it. And I saw what was going on around me. I suppose you've seen the paper I finally published in East Germany."

"No," Ram said. "What was that?"

"Why, it's pretty well known." King was indignant. "Don't you think as my lawyer you should know my reputation as a scientist?"

"I should," Ram said. "But I'm not your lawyer. I'm waiting to see if I'm going to be."

"Then is this in confidence?"

"Naturally."

The man was silent for a long time. He thought about many things, including the possibility that Ram himself might be an agent for the United States government.

"I believe," King said, "that you were in the OSS during the war."

"Yes."

"How do I know you're not in the CIA?"

"You don't."

Ram made no effort to assure King and in the end King said, "I've decided to trust you."

Ram smiled at him and wondered why this man wanted to return to the United States. He would finally ask that question.

King ate with a relentless desperation and drank in the same way so that they had a second bottle of wine with their saddle of lamb. It turned out that after King arrived in Copenhagen, he simply went on into East Germany and disappeared. His name was mentioned in many of the hearings in Washington and he was called a spy.

When he arrived in East Germany he was immediately arrested but they treated him with respect and shipped him off to the Soviet Union for questioning. When Ram asked him where he was sent, King was vague about the places but said he would give the names and the dates when the appropriate time came.

It appeared that the Russians of course knew that King wasn't a spy. On the other hand, they suspected he might be one sent to be used against them. In the time of the Cold War, all these conspiracies seemed reasonable. However, in the end the Russians were kind to him and put him to work in his own field. King had insisted, as he told them his story, that he worked only on general theory and mathematics. The Russians accepted this.

He found the new life so different from what he was used to that in the beginning he was happy that he had escaped the repression in America in time. Meanwhile the Soviet intelligence services spread information abroad that this young scientist had come up with useful information about biological experimentation in America that could be used in warfare.

In the Russian university where King was now conducting his experiments, he met a young woman who was also interested in this new field of the grammar of inheritance. They soon fell in love and finally married. He told her everything that had happened to him, in the course of which he mentioned the name of a close friend in the Cornell physics department with whom he had gone to M.I.T.

Three weeks later, King was arrested by the Russian intelligence service, and this time they were serious. While they didn't actually physically attack him, they used very severe methods of interrogation, and slowly King realized that this old friend whom he had just mentioned in passing was in fact a genuine Soviet agent and still at work for them.

By now in the terrible world of suspicion, the Russians believed they had received in their midst a genuine agent, and they were trying to find out what he had learned in the Soviet Union that might be of use to the Americans. King spent years in prison under constant interrogation, and it was only after the death of Stalin and finally of Khrushchev that the Russians realized that he was as innocent of being a U.S. spy in their country as he was of being their spy in America. They apologized to him. They released him and told him he could return to America if he wished. His wife, of course, had been the one who had informed on him, since she was in fact working on a part-time basis for the intelligence services, and while she loved him, her duty to her country was paramount.

Naturally by now King hated the Soviet Union and they despised him. They were also ashamed of how they had mistreated and misjudged him but felt that state security justified even their errors. King had decided to return to America, feeling that in the new atmosphere of détente his story would be believed.

"You tell me," he demanded of Ram, "if I ever did anything which could possibly justify the suffering, the suspicion and the treatment I received from everyone."

"What makes you think," Ram asked him, "that the U.S. will want you back?"

King was outraged. "I never gave up my American citizenship. Never."

"Suppose," Ram asked him, "after you get back to America, the Russians say you did?"

"Why would they?"

"For the same reason they thought you were a spy in the first place."

"Are you telling me"—King was furious—"are you sitting there and telling me I'm a man without a country?"

"No. You're a citizen of the United States and entitled to return. You just may have to make a fight of it."

"I'm prepared to do that."

"Can you afford it?"

"The Russians gave me fifty thousand dollars which they deposited in a Swiss bank in my name. They said it was to make up for their mistake."

Ram said, "This looks like more trouble. It looks like they paid you off."

"I want my rights," King said. "I want nothing but my rights. I want to go home and work as a scientist. If I hadn't been forced to leave my country, I might have been the one who discovered the double helix. I was always interested in models and the mathematics of them."

"Do you have any political opinions?" Ram asked. "Are you a socialist or a communist or an anticommunist? Suppose the government of the United States offers you the choice of revealing all you know about your work in the Soviet Union as the price for being permitted to re-enter and be treated as an American citizen again."

"I'll tell them anything. The Russians said to me they didn't care what I told the Americans."

"That's hard to believe," Ram said.

"Here I am," said King.

"That of course is what makes it suspicious."

"Do you suspect me?"

"Of course not. I'm speaking like the American intelligence services. Tell me," Ram went on, "while you were there, in the last years, before you decided to leave, were you in fact working on recombinant DNA?"

"When it comes to science," King said, "Americans shouldn't think the Soviet scientists are behind them. They're first-rate."

"That's what the Americans would like to know in detail, I suppose," Ram said. "I suppose that's what they'll ask you."

"That's ridiculous," King said. "American scientists know everything that Soviet scientists do. It's only the military and the intelligence that don't know. The scientists all over the world know exactly what's going on, more or less. You can take it as a general rule: The moment a fundamental discovery is made anyplace, someone elsewhere is just about to make it or in fact has already made it and not published yet. It's just the question of industrial technology that's different. The countries spending the most money with the fewest restraints on their scientists will advance the fastest and that may make a difference in war. However, it's possible to catch up very quickly. So you see, I have no secrets to tell anybody. It's all a lot of nonsense. I've been a victim of nonsense most of my life."

"I believe you," Ram said. "When it comes to finding out things in nature, anyone who searches will find them. It's only the politics that's different."

"Not so different," King said.

"Then why are you coming back? Why do you want to?"

"Because I miss my own country. I miss being an American. I hate being an American in the Soviet Union. They're like us but different. Even at their worst, it's better to be an American. But you remember how it was in '52. They were after you too, weren't they?"

"Yes, I remember," Ram said.

"Well, then, I escaped being crucified by that lying bastard."

"Let's say," Ram said, "you had an extraordinary adventure and you survived."

"Yes," King said. "Let's say that, and let's also say, 'I have a right to come home.'"

"So it seems."

King thought for a while. The dessert was finished. The Grill Room had emptied and they were finishing the second bottle of wine. It was very pleasant and civilized in that room. It was very pleasant and civilized in the London that was in that room. King was lost in thought and after a while he began to talk again. He said, "I had a long time to think while I was away. There's a thing you can call civilian liberty. It's not just civil liberties, and it's not just liberty. I call it civilian liberty. Nowhere in the world does anyone understand that, except for the Americans and the English and the Jews."

"Are you Jewish?" Ram asked.

"No," King said. "People have their pride and they have the liberties they're used to, but no one understands how marvelous a thing it is to live among people who believe in civilian liberty, even when, as they did with me, they frighten me away from my home. Do you understand that?"

Ram said he thought he did.

King leaned toward Ram and his face was angry. "You know the man who lied about me still lives near Washington. So I've heard. He lives on a farm. He has retired. He has become a born-again Christian and goes to meetings and churches and makes speeches about Jesus. That's what I hear."

"I don't know," Ram said. "It may be."

King brooded about this. "Our President is a born-again Christian too, isn't he?"

"He says so."

"Tell me, Mr. Mont. Here we are in this fine hotel, in this fine restaurant, in a country going crazy with strikes, a country that has a silly semi-socialist society or something. What's going on? Don't you find the world a nightmare that makes no sense?"

"From time to time, I lose hope."

"I hope to go home."

"We'll meet tomorrow. Let me think about your case and we'll meet. Call me about ten in the morning."

They shook hands in the lobby and Ram got a copy of the London *Times* and took the elevator upstairs.

Now in the great darkness of the sky, flying swiftly to Israel, Ram thought how King's story had ended after he returned to the United States. It took about a year before King was able to accomplish what he had in mind. On a cold winter afternoon he had made his way to the farm of the man who had lied and betrayed him for some unknown purpose that no one still could understand. King had taken a Remington automatic shotgun with him and he had killed this man and his wife and his dog. He had left a note. It read: *He cheated me. He prevented me from winning the Nobel Prize.* Then King had shot himself. Ram had not been involved in getting King into America. His own adventure in London had interrupted that.

Even now, with the plane less than an hour from the Lod Airport, Ram kept thinking of how he had almost died in London. It began just after he left King and went upstairs to his hotel room.

Long afterward, when Ram was being finally discharged from the Stanford University Hospital, the young resident cardiologist, making a last examination before Ram went on to say good-bye to the chief, had suddenly, in a more personal way, in that little room surrounded by other little rooms and the active informal life of the hospital all around him, with a kind of springtime of feeling everywhere, had turned to Ram and in a different, less medical voice, asked, "Mr. Mont, do you mind if I ask you a personal question?" It was strange, as if anything could have been more personal than their intimacy with his body. It was there that his body had been pried apart, his life transferred from its own system to the heart-lung machine, his aorta opened and repaired, its arch reinvented so it had a double channel for the flow of blood. They had put him together as if his body were really a machine, obeying the rules of the new language which King had been interested in. Yet it was not just a machine, although it acted like one. It was a kind of sacred machine, for life existed in it. It was then, at his weakest, when he lay wondering after the operation just what he was trying to live for, how absolutely evil it was that men used the same intense care to kill and maim each other and all the other creatures of the earth and how it made no sense unless you believed that in life the very thing that made it a magical existence contained the evil which destroyed it. It was the same in medicine as it was in politics, even in what Zenia had called "the age of socialism." Everything had changed but nothing evil had disappeared. Things were better for more people in many places, and that might be a real good. But then, nothing evil had disappeared and the evil was there in every hiding place of what men thought of as being good. It flowed along as part of life itself. It was, in fact, life itself. It was as much life in its way as anything else, and it was a kind of poetic license to call it evil.

"Tell me," the young resident, Dr. Brandman, had asked in that little room at Stanford, "do you mind? Tell me, when you were in London and you first felt the pain, how would you describe it?"

"I'll tell you," Ram said. "But why do you ask?"

"Because the books describe it as a tearing pain. Was it?"

"No," Ram said. "This was a pressure, a weight, and in the weight was the pain. It was just as if I were having a bad attack of indigestion."

Young Dr. Brandman's face lit up. He was happy to hear this. "That's what I said. How can you call it a tearing pain when there are no nerves in the aorta that can transmit messages of that nature? They don't have tearing pain nerves."

"What kind do they have?" Ram asked.

"The aorta has the kind it needs to carry on its work, and

the information it must transfer does not include the message of tearing pain. What function could it serve?"

It was the pain of weight which Ram had felt that night. There he was, lying in bed, thinking of King and wondering how true his story was. He looked at the bad news in the London *Times* and then began reading the letters of Thomas Mann.

The pain came as he had told Dr. Brandman at Stanford.

He got out of bed at last. He looked around in his suitcase for some tablets to take for indigestion. In those days he usually had some with him because he had once had ulcers and these tablets were a medicine prescribed as liquid or pills to neutralize the stomach acids. That was the theory. Ram only discovered later that they also caused the indigestion he used to take them to prevent. But medicine changes all the time and is full of magic just as it was when it was a brass basin carried by a barber surgeon on his head against the rain and called, by Don Quixote, Mambrino's helmet.

He walked restlessly around the hotel rooms. He stretched. He tried to cough up what he thought was gas trapped in his stomach. He even sat down on the floor and lay back and sat up again. He did all these silly things. He jumped up and down. These were all deadly dangers to what was really going on as the lining of the aorta tore loose. The aorta lining had dissected from the arch and down, and it was his blood finding a new channel that endangered his life. It made the wall of the aorta swell with the pressure, and all the while the tearing went on. The pain was very heavy but it wasn't a tearing pain. It was simply heavy. It hurt in the form of a solid surrounded by an ever-increasing magnetic field of pain.

"By the way," Ram had asked Dr. Brandman at Stanford on that final day, "what do other patients have to say about this kind of pain? What do they report?"

The young resident appeared embarrassed. "We don't know, because in general they die before someone asks them."

Just as the surgeon who was young, careful, amusing, who flew airplanes and made inventions for machines as well as inventions of surgical instruments, had said to his friends after the seven and a half hours of surgery, "If the test we had given him had been accurate instead of being completely misleading, if I had known what I was going to find there, I don't think I would've operated." In other words, the false reports from the test had saved Ram's life.

Now Ram thought of the conversation which he had had with the surgeons before the operation.

"You can, of course," they said, "choose not to be operated on. We have the medicines, and by living with great care and not moving around too much, you might extend your life. In this way you escape the risks of the operation."

"What are the risks?" Ram asked. "How do you figure the chances?"

"A good seventy-five-percent chance of success. Perhaps better. You seem to be in good physical shape. But we think you should know this before the operation."

"I'll think about it," Ram said.

"In addition," the surgeon said, "a nerve controlling the vocal cord is wrapped around the aorta there. We probably will have to cut it and you'll lose your voice. There's therapy for it. But it's almost certain that nerve will be severed and die."

He didn't think about it for long. It seemed to him that his choice had been decided long before by his character. But the decisive factor was in fact the passionate advice of another young resident who had taken care of him during the days of waiting while the Christmas holidays passed and the medicine given in London had a chance to wear off. The London medicine was Inderal, and the surgeon said it had a bad tendency to prevent the heart from starting again when the patient came off the heart-lung machine. "That's the crucial moment," the doctor said.

This young doctor, whose father was a physician in New York and who was going into research and not the practice of medicine, had spoken to Ram with an earnest and positive force. "You must have the operation. It doesn't make any sense not to.

You won't live long the other way because any day the whole thing could blow apart and you'd be dead. This way you have a good chance." That was good advice from a friend, from someone who wanted him to live, as he did, in the way he knew how to live. That was also the time when he knew what every animal knows, that it's important to live. People commit suicide, and suicide was wise in the Nazi torture chambers. But generally, biologically, from the point of view of evolution, so to speak, every animal wants to live and every animal does so and there's nothing to decide about. After all, as Zenia had said long ago, "Just what happens the way it must happen is exactly what evolution is. Evolution is a grand way of describing a universe of chance and change, whether among the living or the not-living."

On that night in London, when Ram had at last called Leslie from the hotel, the doctor had come, a chatty fellow he had met on other trips who thought it was a heart attack. He gave Ram morphine. It didn't get rid of the pain. He gave Ram heroin and sent for an ambulance.

For the rest of that night, the anxiety on the faces of the people who made his life real shocked him. He drifted in and out of the pain.

When they carried him into St. George's Hospital he felt he was in the horrible world that Karl Marx wrote about when he described the conditions of the English working class. Mostly Ram was obsessed by the pain. He drifted in and out of Dickensian brutality. He knew the staff appeared and took X-rays as he lay in the special section which was merely a space set aside in the center of the regular wards where old men coughed and spit through the night without having to pay for the privilege because of socialist health insurance. When Ram went to Stanford and saw a modern hospital, he thought of the London hospital as a literary event in a book in his father's library. It took on the qualities of his reading as a young boy. He seemed to be back on some rainy afternoon reading the titles of his father's library, wondering what book he could take that would remove him from this world of rainy afternoons with no one to see and no one to do anything with. On such an afternoon he had read the narrative of A. Gordon Pym. That was a fever too, a fever that seized him with the first words, a vocabulary of fever, the fever of living, of course.

When he woke up at St. George's Hospital, a dozen doctors of all sorts were standing around his bed. In front of him was a frame that held his X-rays and the chief cardiologist was saying, "It's a dissecting aorta and will probably keep on ripping. He'll be dead by this afternoon."

So it isn't afternoon, Ram thought.

The chief cardiologist had studied with De Bakey. He was wise in his analysis, brutal as a person and wrong in his prophecy. Stanford was a different world. It became the world of humanity again and Ram remembered thinking before he went into his next stage at St. George's, which was hallucinatory, that the English ruling class had treated their working class worse than the Nazis had treated the Jews, for they had killed them without even hating them. What a farce, Ram thought, is written history. What a romance of research and imagination.

Meanwhile his desperate friends who loved him had been in touch with doctors in the United States. They had been warned, "Don't move him. He must lie still. If the dissection stops, get him to us and we can do something."

Then he began to live out the waiting.

He believed his life was threatened and that someone wanted to kill him and that without actually intending it the hospital, given its way, would have accomplished his death. Each night he saw the white tents, lighted everywhere from within, the figures of deformed people, some of whom were nuns or nurses, and they made love or carried on incredible scenes of torture with strange instruments, and all around he heard the screams of the victims. They also wanted to kill him. The ward was lighted in a kind of gloom. There was a London fog there. The wounded lay in rows on their painted beds and swift menacing figures passed, looking with indifferent hatred at those who were being tortured there. By daylight Ram cursed them and struggled to escape. By night he lay with a knife beneath his pillow, ready to defend himself.

The oxygen tents around him soon became what they were and he didn't die. Three weeks passed as the doctors from the United States had advised. At that point, Ram had himself moved to the London Clinic, where at least he could wait to be sent to Stanford and be saved, if possible, or die in luxury and comfort. By this time he had removed himself from his own case. It was everybody's business, but not his own. He read constantly and when the books were too heavy, for he was very weak, he had them ripped apart, much to the horror of the nurses, so he could hold a few pages at a time and read them.

The time came when he left the hospital to wait another few weeks in an apartment. Then he reached the point where he could be moved carefully, and so he was taken to a plane and his own doctor came along with him to see that he didn't die during the course of the journey. He lay on four seats in the tourist section.

In the end he arrived at Stanford but he felt distant from the world.

The operation was successful, but it had a strange wildness about it. He remembered nothing, only the warning which the surgeon had given him. "Just imagine," the surgeon said, "you'll feel like a man who has been run over by a ten-ton truck loaded with elephants."

So it was. He took his first walk in the streets of Palo Alto from a house that he had rented there. It was fine weather and there were flowers in the trees.

When he thought of his case at all, although he knew he had been saved by the skill of the scientist-physicians at Stanford, he understood that it was because of the refusal of those who loved him to admit or accept or go along with anything suggested by the medical ruling class of London. London hospitals had become in his mind the symbol of Marx's hatred of the horrors of the English working class.

He wasn't very interested in anything. He wondered what

difference it made, especially since in the course of the operation, as predicted, the nerve whose end was wrapped around the aorta had died. He found himself unable to speak except in a whisper or falsetto.

The surgeon told him that he had been able to clamp the nerve around the aorta instead of cutting it. But the nerve had died anyway. Specialists told him its death was final but the surgeon said, "No. It's about a foot long. It grows back about two inches a month and six months from now you'll talk again. I know it." More than six months later one night the vocal cord in question had managed a grunting sound and, vibrating again in contact with the healthy vocal cord, had brought speech as sound instead of thought, whispers, falsetto pirouettes. He felt like a lobster with a new claw, a salamander with a new tail, or just a fingernail. No wonder so many ages ago Zenia had cried out across that old circular dinner table, "Never mind the grain of sand. Give me the human body divine and I'll tell you the secret of the universe."

"But what's the secret?" Harry had asked.

Now as the plane began its long approach to where Zenia was, now as he knew that everything that had happened to him had been in preparation for this coming together, now he saw her springing up again, tempestuous, vibrant, her hair flying, her arms outstretched as she called out the ultimate answer to the only mystery, "Here I am!"

13

Security at the airport was tight since terror was always nipping and biting at the people who lived in Israel.

He was soon riding beside the Jewish driver, Fred Segal, on the way to Jerusalem in a Mercedes.

The driver was an older man who had been involved in the Burma Road operation to save Jerusalem during the '48 War, and he had many remarks to make on this subject and others. Fred knew that Dr. Haller was a famous man and he admired him the way people in general always admire physicians. The driver was also amused because he was driving a German-made Mercedes.

"How do you like driving a German car?" Ram asked.

"When it comes to Germans," he said, "I think of it in two ways: Personally, I wish they were all dead and not a single one remained in the world, not even as memory, and to be quite frank with you, I'll throw in Goethe and Beethoven. That and that only would make me feel right after the way they acted in the war toward everyone, and I don't only mean the Jews. I don't care what you read anywhere in history, no one has ever acted as rotten as the Germans. On the other hand," he went on, "if there was no forgetting, there'd be no history, and we'd have no future. Every generation must have its chance. What do you do for a living, Mr. Mont? Or is it 'doctor,' too?"

"I'm sixty-seven," Ram said. "What do I have to do for a living?"

"You don't have to imitate the way I speak," the driver said.

They had a pleasant drive to Jerusalem. When they went through the Arab villages, the driver said, "Trouble. You'll see. This is all going to be trouble."

When Ram saw the lights of the old city, the walls illuminated from below where they rose on their hill out of the ruins, when he saw the new buildings that surrounded them, he felt unexpected affection. He stood at the window of his room at the King David Hotel and looked out upon the old city of Jerusalem and he also felt a great stillness, as if the snow were still falling around him on Fishwoods Road, falling straight and windless, falling into the eternities of the night.

It was very late when he got to the hotel. Fred Segal said he'd pick him up in the morning at nine o'clock.

"Suppose I don't want to wait till nine o'clock?"

"Listen," Fred said, "they expect you at nine. Go at nine."

"That's wise," Ram said.

"I've been around," the driver said.

Ram must have gone to bed, but it seemed he stood all night and simply looked out at the great stillness of the old city in its magical light of white and pink stone where the gods of the believers fought like the men who had discovered them.

He must have gone to sleep because he had to wake up to go and see Zenia. It turned out that Dr. Haller lived only ten minutes away from the King David Hotel.

It was a bright day, a springtime day, a sun-and-glitter day. The air was so bright it hummed and Ram could hear the drone of it, like bees among the flowers of time. Things, no matter how smooth and soft, made hard sounds, grating, rubbing, skittering along as the automobile did, as the driver did, who turned a smiling, springtime smile at him. "Did you sleep well? How did you like looking down on the old city? Tell me the truth, Mr. Mont. Did you feel at home here, or did you feel like someone on a visit, which is what you seem to be doing, visiting here—"

"I was ashamed to feel at home, but I felt at home."

"But why?"

"Because I was content to be in a country where I could say, 'Well, here I am at last in a country of Jews.' I should feel at home wherever there are people, since I'm one myself. But I don't."

"I know that feeling well," Fred said. "But I find it isn't like that. It's always different. Young Israelis run off to live in America where they feel safer, where they can make money fast, and they promise themselves that if their country is attacked they'll run home to defend it, the same way they ran away not to live in it. But the fact is, having at last discovered that they have a country, it doesn't matter to them any more. They just don't feel safe and happy here. And in fact, we're too corrupt here for this to be what it was meant to be, a land of idealists and socialists besides. Then, also, modern people are disgusted with the Hassidim and the Orthodox Jews. They are difficult, backward people. They are backward elements."

Ram laughed at this.

"You think I'm wrong?"

"I don't know," Ram said. "But I spent my life in the company of what my aunt used to call 'backward elements.' I think I'm one myself."

"Listen," Fred said, "good or bad, this is what we have. We'd better make the best of it. And here you are."

In this springtime brightness, Ram felt the promise of a new summer like all the promises that had ever been given him or those he had made to himself. At this moment he believed in immortality, peace, hope. Yes, even in the possibility of accomplishment. Yes, here in a land menaced by constant terror. He had lived his whole life in the presence of promised terror as well as hope unfulfilled.

Sitting that morning in the bright and noisy coffee shop of the hotel (it was something like a New York dairy restaurant, say the old Steinberg's on Broadway and 81st Street), Ram was surrounded by Jews eating Jewish dairy food of one kind or another. It was foreign, of course, for the people spoke Hebrew as well as Yiddish and English. They also spoke German, they spoke Russian, they spoke French, they spoke languages he couldn't identify. He looked out at the sunlight. The waitresses were not like the old Jewish waiters of New York. His taxi driver had been more their style, weary men who knew too much and struck a pose to amuse themselves and their clients. Ram had read at breakfast yesterday's *New York Times,* which someone had left on the seat. It contained news of earthquakes and storms that had killed hundreds and in one case thousands of people. It also reported arson in the schools of New Jersey, an automobile accident or two, a hijack of a South American plane in Colombia, the death of a Spanish liberal official killed by Basque freedom-lovers, the assassination of an Italian social-democratic judge by Italian leftist terror fighters for a communism rejected by the Italian Communist Party. It went on to tabulate the march of history in Iran, where vast populations thronged the streets calling for the return of an ancient religion and freedom from American influence and death of their billionaire shah. It described in detail a combination of strikes which paralyzed the entire British economy. It reported a sharp attack on Israel's policy by a French newspaper with anti-Semitic overtones. There were murders in Africa, apartheid changes which would give the vote to the "colored," meaning Indians from India. A bomb had been found in a Jerusalem market and been defused. Jewish dissenters had been arrested in Russia, Irish dissenters in Northern Ireland, where someone had thrown a bomb into a pub and killed five men, one woman and a young girl. He put the paper down. He was there sitting in the sunlight and the great stillness. The chattering voices in the place somehow made him feel at home, although there was nothing homelike about it. It was an act of imagination and expectation and there he was.

"Are you from New York?" the waitress asked.

"Yes," he said.

"I lived there for years. I miss it," she said. "I hope you like your visit here."

"Why shouldn't I?"

"Because," she said—she had a heavy dark face with thick brows and a flesh-filled figure—"because everybody wants this to be paradise, but it's just another country, this time full of Jews instead of people who aren't."

"I'm enjoying it," he said.

It didn't take them long to drive to Dr. Haller's house. It was a four-story place. It had a stone wall, very low, and over it he could see the house in the sunlight, glowing with extraordinary beauty in the colors of pink and white and beige, a sense of lightness and brightness that flowed out of the old city with its towers, its cupolas, its domes, its religious symbols of belief and death. But here it was quite peaceful. There were trees and there were some flowers visible.

"Shall I wait?" Fred asked.

"Just exactly," Ram asked him, "what are you supposed to do? How were you hired?"

"I belong to you for as long as you want. Wherever you want me to take you, I'll take you. Wherever you want to go, I'll drive you. I'm looking forward to it. I'm getting good pay. This is my own car. I now also know who you are. My daughter would like to meet you. She's a law student. She's a radical. I think she wants to make peace with the Arabs." Fred sighed. "One day." He shrugged. "I should live that long."

"Don't you?"

"I have, long ago. They just haven't made peace with me."

"Well," Ram said. "Here's Dr. Haller's telephone number."

"I have it."

"Call me in a couple of hours."

"You bet." With that Fred laughed and drove off and Ram waited there, took one last glance across the divide that fell away in front of the old city, and when he turned to look at Dr. Haller's house an old woman was leaning over the stone wall, looking at him.

"Have we met before?" she asked. Her smile like a mermaid was caught in a strange net of wrinkles.

He was at the low stone wall and they embraced across it. Everything he remembered disappeared in the frailty and smallness of her. They held hands across the wall and hand in hand that way, looking at each other all the time, walked to the open gate, where they had to let go. She was coming out and he was hurrying in as they met again and he took her in his arms. He was a head taller, younger and stronger than she was. She seemed to float in his arms. He was afraid to hold her too tightly. He bent his head to her and she kissed him Russian-style—that is, everywhere, his nose, his cheeks, his lips. She had never, in all his memory, kissed him on the mouth when he was a child, but now she kissed him that way. Her mouth was as dry as his. They stood there holding each other, their bodies together. They were in Jerusalem. They were meeting in air like two acrobats in time, swinging toward each other, each ready to let go in a fantastic feat of accident. And there they stopped. And it all stood still.

They waited apart from each other, a step between them.

He knew Zenia, recognizing her without remembering her. He saw a small woman in narrow black trousers, wearing a white cotton shirt with an open collar, a jaunty red silk scarf, and loose open dark-red sweater. She had white frizzled hair and sunken cheeks, and there she waited instead of bounding toward him, her wide long skirt flying in a single bronze wing, with her long steps and black wild hair once upon a time down the steep bank of the Bronx Lake.

"Well," Zenia said. "Has anything interesting happened since you walked off the ship and it sailed away?"

"I caught up with you."

"Don't look at me that way. I'm just old."

Her eyes glittered with imprisoned tears. They were the same dry tears that belonged to him. They shared them briefly in the Jerusalem sunlight. They were laughing. They linked arms and stood there looking at the old city looming out of its walls, the ground falling away below them. There was a road, a car, excavations, some houses. There were weeds growing there and he said, "Why, they're just lots, like those we knew when you used to be tall."

"I'm tall enough," she said. "What great things have you done that I haven't heard about?"

"What have you heard?"

"Newspapers old and new."

"That's it, then."

"Who can help it? You accumulate a life. It's a working solution in spite of everything."

"You changed my whole life with your silence," he said.

"How could we be young and live if there was just remembering?" She clung for another long moment, holding him tightly until the goddess of their youth dived into the sea lion pool. Now, almost eighty-one, she stood away from him. "Take a good look," she said. "It's the last one you'll have of what we were." And she punched him lightly in the ribs.

She held his arm tightly against her own and her body against his. A few people walked by in the street; some cars passed, not too many, but there were cars going back and forth there as in all the cities of the world; but beyond this road and beyond what seemed to be an open lot between two buildings, one small and one taller, one recent and one older, there was this empty lot with weeds growing in it. Among the weeds a small wall crumbled in what seemed to be the shape of rooms, just the remains, made of brick and some kind of mortar. Beyond it the ground fell sharply and disappeared into a ravine, out of which once again a steep hill rose filled with weedy growths, some remains of buildings, and then a modern road which ran diagonally up to the walls of the old city to a gate that couldn't be seen from where they stood. Above the pink walls of the city rose the towers and the domes, the crosses and the turrets. The sun glittered on metal and glass, it glowed on the white and pink stone, on beige stone, on stone that was delicate and luminous, and there was gold.

"By and by," she said, "everything will come out, but it all matters very little to me now that we're both here, walking arm in arm as once we did when the world was young."

"At least we were," Ram said. "I was, I know. You were old, I thought. But now I see you were young, and we both are old."

"Don't jump to conclusions," she said in her old voice.

Suddenly he embraced her again and he kissed her cheeks, her hair, now gray and thin, her forehead, the fragile skin with its hieroglyph of wrinkles, and again it was the smallness and the delicacy of her that he felt. She had saved what was left of herself for this moment.

Zenia said, "Let's go for a walk in the empty lots of Jerusalem."

They crossed the street and went into the empty lots among the weeds and the few old ruins.

"It looks," Ram said, "like these are old ruins, after all, and not like the ruins of the Bronx and our wars."

They made their way upon the crumbled, dry soil, where fragments of rock grew in a profusion of frail colors. There was a section of wall a few feet high. Below they could see signs of an archaeological excavation. Around, muted, was the new city and its machines, while close at hand were bees, wasps, butterflies and weeds. He spread his jacket on top of the low, crumbling wall and they sat near each other, holding hands while they looked at the old city.

"Weeds," Ram said. "Weeds grow anywhere."

Yellow flowers and hairy broad leaves grew out of the shady part of the crumbling ruins nearby. "Golden henbane," Zenia said.

Ram looked around him now and saw something like buttercups. He saw the same viper's bugloss of the old lots. This was no place for burdock.

She went on talking about the weeds there and elsewhere, about oxalis, which he knew from the farm and the lots. "Here," she said, "you'll find only one of the three African strains, so there's no cross pollination."

"In California," he said, "they grow oxalis as decorative plants." Was this place like southern California? This was like nowhere. A spiritual drowsiness began to overcome Ram. Her words were like caressing hands, soothing and comforting. She was young and she was telling him about the weeds and wildflowers of Jerusalem. He closed his eyes to the sunlight. He heard her say, "Bermuda buttercups. Jerusalem buttercups. One isn't. One is."

How am I different? And he didn't know.

How is she different?

He said, "Driving here in the night I saw poppies and flowering almonds escaping from our headlights. Where were you all those years? We couldn't find you. When I asked Harry Rivers during the war, because he was there in Moscow for a while, he just shook his head. I'm sure he tried to find you."

"After I got there"—she let him see a little of her old Zenia smile—"I took a revolutionary name. It was the mode. Just as here people find their European names a historical embarrassment, so they take Hebrew names. That's one reason." Zenia went on in her new voice that was becoming her old voice again. "I was in prison twice. Once, before the war. Once, after."

Without knowing this, of course, he had known it. He didn't say anything. He just held her hand and her hand was light, dry. It didn't seek a pressure of reaffirmation. Was there any to give? They were both alive and free in Jerusalem.

Her living voice continued. "I was rehabilitated. All my old medals were returned and two new ones given. I was free to go anywhere, as if all the while I had only been a tourist in history. At last Russia and I had come to terms with our common past, and that included everything I would never accept. So I decided I had to see you."

Now she pressed his hand gently.

"Yes," she said, "I decided to see the land of the Jews, even if it survived only one second more in time."

He saw nothing. He looked at the old city built of human

175

feeling, pain, a lust of spirit for the universe to signify, all in the material form of pink and apricot stone.

"I know," Zenia said, "you had your hard times too."

"Hardly the same."

"It varies," she said, "but it's the same. It's one place in us where very little can be too much. I saw Harry Rivers in Moscow."

"He said he tried to find you and couldn't."

"He said what I asked him to say."

He looked around at the walls and the weeds. He didn't look at Zenia.

"You were in England and then on your way to France," she said gently. "Who knew who would survive that dreadful war? I knew I wouldn't."

"But you have."

"Now, not then. Anyone can argue with history once it's past. I thought I taught you something when you were young."

"You taught me the habit of useless sacrifice."

"Did I? It's not something I believe. Are you sorry I'm alive?"

It was then he burst into tears of joy and she comforted him with old kisses still fragrant with memory.

"Frankly," she said, "I'm in a state of shock. Anyway, with things like this whatever happens is the only way."

"Harry died two years after the war was over."

"It took me fifteen years to find that out."

Ram thought about it for some time, then he told her. "He was in a happy mood when he died. I didn't know why. He was smiling. He said his life in the end had worked out pretty good."

"So has ours. We're together."

He said it bitterly. "If working out in the worst possible way is the best, yes. But it's true. It no longer matters."

She got up suddenly. "Let's walk back now," she said.

He took his jacket, shook it out and put it on. It was warm from the sun and from both of them.

"Let's walk back through these empty lots of Jerusalem."

She pointed to ferns springing from the rocks, the occasional thrust of ruin and tumbled stone. "Rustyback ferns," she said. "Dr. Haller and his family are waiting with a big breakfast and memories. He'll tell you how he was a boy and I came through with the Russian army. It was the first concentration camp to be liberated. That was in Czechoslovakia. And tonight there's a dinner, people who want to see me, but tomorrow . . . "

When she said "tomorrow" her whole body livened. He felt the eager clasp of her hand in his and everything glittered.

"Tomorrow we'll be on our way to Galilee. There's a new settlement there. There are Russian Jews I knew in Leningrad. They expect me and I want to see them. I promised. We'll go. We'll be more alone together there than here. Do you mind?"

"I have the use of a perfect car made by the Germans and a driver made by the Jews."

"How long can you stay?"

Ram said in a lively voice, "I'm in the middle of forever. Don't bother me with large numbers."

She burst into laughter, the first since they had met that day. It ran like a long nerve which, dead for years, had slowly grown back two inches a month and now, suddenly complete again, carried the one message for which it had been created.

He just gathered her to him and held her while a bus rumbled by in the street and in the open door of the Haller house beyond the low wall there were faces, bodies, voices calling to them.

14

Asher was a new settlement in Galilee, about ten miles from the Mediterranean and six miles from Lebanon.

Ram and Zenia arrived there in time for the communal dinner in the kibbutz dining hall.

All these people had been driven from places where their ancestors had lived for at least five hundred and in some cases two thousand years. Those who had money settled in Tel Aviv or Jerusalem. Those who had anxious relatives in America had gone there. The very rich were at home anywhere in the non-communist countries. Here at Asher were Russian intellectuals, teachers, technicians and a few working-class families who wanted to make a different life. A minority of African and Mideast peasants and small traders had the same idea. There were many who had just somehow ended up there, still wondering what it was all about, for to escape is not actually to arrive.

"It works out more or less," Fred said.

"You mean," Ram said, "they don't know what they want and they won't find it here."

"Exactly, more or less."

He and Ram were sitting at a table apart from the celebration around Zenia. There was plenty of food, but nothing exceptionally wonderful. There was a heavy borscht with tough meat in it, white and black bread. There was chicken and pancakes made of dried powdered potatoes. There was tea, coffee, wine, vodka and plain cake. There were radishes and cucumbers.

"It's not bad," Fred said. "Not bad is pretty good in our

country when it comes to food. Arab cooking in Jerusalem is pretty good in a few places, but I'm dying for an Italian meal on Elizabeth Street."

"I shouldn't be eating this anyway," Ram said.

"It's not the Automat. I loved their beans, their coffee, their pies. Their sandwiches were awful but I liked the nickels and the windows of food."

"Gone," Ram said. "I liked the old cafeterias also. I used to go to a Thompson's on Fourteenth Street. Then we'd go to a meeting of the Proletcult."

He and Fred dipped their bread in the borscht. Ram thought back for a moment. "I used to like two terrible dishes in those Fourteenth Street cafeterias. One was peppers stuffed with rice and chopped meat covered with grease. The other was airborne white bread topped with thin slices of cold hard roast beef covered with a thick floury sauce they called gravy."

"What do you like now?" Fred asked.

"I don't eat like this. Not much meat, some broiled fish without salt, fresh vegetables steamed. It's tasty medicine. I also take pills."

"I can still eat everything. I can still drink. I gave up smoking to set a good example once and I never learned again." Fred looked around with pleasure. "I like the Russian Jews we get nowadays. They're really disgusted with the promised land. They keep saying, Keep your promises. Did we promise them anything?"

"Who are we?" Ram asked.

"Not me," Fred said. "Everybody wants out, but nobody wants in."

Ram smiled with pleasure at this delightful man and agreed. "They'll find out they're in. In is where we always are."

"You're right," Fred said. "We're always in for it."

There were bursts of laughter around Zenia and Ram listened to catch her laugh. He heard it now and then. It was freeing itself and gathering strength from the constellation of Russians.

"You remember the Depression?" he asked Fred.

"Of course."

"Nowadays, they remember the beauty of the Depression. How lovely it was. That was life. They also remember the nostalgia of being young in the fifties. It's the beauty of the fifties. Of course, that was the time of the Cold War and death and disgrace in America. So was the Depression. The fact is I remember those times both ways. In the fifties I discovered friendship. In the thirties I discovered myself. That is, I rediscovered myself. I had forgotten myself after my aunt left for Russia."

"What do you think she found there?"

"Old age, at least," Ram said.

"It looks good on her," Fred said.

"She would do it that way," Ram said.

"You know," Fred said, "it's a miracle for you two to meet again this way."

"Or any way."

"Yes, or any way."

"It's the nature of things," Ram said, "that such miracles happen endlessly."

"They happen," Fred said. "They even happened to me, but I never did much with them."

Ram looked around at this low-ceilinged room built of concrete blocks. It had been softened in many ways but mostly with children's paintings which were hung tastefully on the walls. In bright colors they gave a direct impression of the kibbutz, its people, its animals, its buildings. The paintings looked with wondering eye at the hills of Galilee, at parents, dogs and people working in the new orchards of apples, plums, pears. There were also memory pictures of Russian childhood in primary colors. There was no fear in the pictures. The fear had been in the parents.

On one wall an older artist had painted a mural of faces. It was a long wall and it was jammed with hundreds of different faces. On these faces from Russia there was a longing to escape and a longing to return, as if during a bad and desperate dream a good world had been deformed but now at last might come back again. But the faces in their difference asked the same question: Which was real? The artist perhaps was asking why. These were Russian faces but there were also faces from the little ghetto towns of middle Europe, bright faces looking backward at invisible pursuers, the fox faces of a history of persecution. Only faces. Waves of transparent color swept across the painting and these colors made a disjointed word in Hebrew: shalom. There was no peace in the painting at all, but there was no horror either. Wonder. The faces wondered.

Voices sparkled, broke, flamed up, evaporated in pleasure and delight. He didn't understand the words, but they were universally human like any language, if not universally the same.

He let himself float within it all, enjoying its novelty, alien yet homelike. What was it that made it all seem so secure? They were all Jews and they were all free. They wanted in general to be both, and in general they had found out it wasn't enough.

But tonight they were in a dance of spring. Someone sang a Russian song.

As if to spike the already heady mixture of memory and hope, a hungry pack of young girls invaded the dining room. There were thirty of them, dressed for hiking, carrying their packs and sleeping bags and led by a teacher-soldier. They were mainly the sabra children of a Sephardic Orthodox kibbutz about ten miles away, stopping overnight before starting off again to visit a third settlement that was higher up in the Galilean hills. Dark, giggling, laughing, shy also in the company of people who spoke Russian, they were full of vitality. It was just what the party needed to break loose altogether, and so it did when the teacher-soldier, a young woman named Tamar, learned who Zenia was. Now Zenia became a star of their life for that night, although obviously their idea of what she embodied and her idea of who she was were not quite the same. But at celebrations differences matter little while the dancing goes on.

In the end the group of young girls carried Zenia off like a triumphant goddess, tender with her because she was so old and useful to worship. It took pleading, laughing embraces, a flurry of voices, and she walked with them to the settlement schoolhouse where the hikers were to spend the night in their sleeping bags before going on with their little journey among the hills of evergreen shrubs, among the new wildflowers of a new season in Galilee.

He and Fred philosophized over their hot tea while the Russians chattered in Zenia's absence and the dining room emptied with handshakes and kisses.

"Look at me," Fred said. He was easy and pleasant to look at with his powerful merry face, his thick shoulders, his giant wrists, his nearly bald head and his lively body and mind. He had been born on the same East Side where Ram's father had once had his pharmacy, the very neighborhood where Black Narcissus showered rewards on the love of dogs and actors. "Would you believe," Fred asked, "that my father was a tiny tailor? Would you believe he wanted me to be an infant prodigy on the violin and astound the world?"

"No," Ram said.

"You're right. My father wasn't small and frail. He was big and hearty. He flung tons of rags around on Fourth Street like they were bales of hay or sacks of grain. He was Orthodox and belligerent and he wanted me to be gentle and a rabbi."

"Can you play the violin?"

"I can and do. I'm a member of an amateur string orchestra and I never skip a session if I can avoid it. We weren't starving when I was young but life was rough. We lived on First Avenue to the music of the El. Year by year my parents covered more and more of the rotting floor with more and more shining linoleum. Each day my mother covered the linoleum with newspapers. Until I was fourteen I slept in the same bed with two of my four brothers. This, I said, is getting me nowhere. So I ran off to Nowhere. I got to Palestine and joined the settlements at Gush Etzion. If anyone asks me now where I'm from, I say Kfar Etzion. That's home to me. Anyway, here I was and here the war came. I learned to be a soldier in the Haganah and I was one of the five hundred in Jerusalem when the war began. That's why I'm alive. The Arabs massacred my entire village except for four people. But I say let's make peace with the Arabs. The Jews may have come here for the right reasons or the wrong reasons. Here we are. Here they are. History is drek and gives no rights. Think of that old terrorist Begin having tea in Washington. It doesn't matter which way we go. All ways are plenty of trouble. We're surrounded by fronts. The front is also inside our country. Most of all, it's inside ourselves for we see the whole world everywhere as one continuous front. Let's say, it's tough. But we'll manage." In this way he spoke of hope, the most fragile and illusory of all human qualities.

Zenia returned accompanied by the teacher-soldier, Tamar. It seemed that Zenia had promised to sleep that night in the schoolroom with the girl hikers and a cot was being brought up there for her. "We'll have breakfast together and talk before they go on with their hike to the next kibbutz. They want me to tell them the meaning of the whole story of the world. It seems I've lived it without knowing."

"Did you tell them everything?" Ram asked.

"I left out the worst parts," she said.

"It's the worst parts they should hear," Fred said. "They have to know."

"Nobody has to know anything when it comes to that," Zenia said. "In the end you have to live through it and knowing is not living, as I found out."

Tamar laughed. She had a sudden resolute laugh that promised everything. "I'm as bad as they are." She spoke English as a picked-up language. "Your aunt, what's she? An American and a Russian, a woman and a doctor. A revolutionist, a prisoner and one who sets others free." Strong, dark, powerful, she emanated force and will. She was a member of an Orthodox kibbutz of Moroccan, Iraqi, Libyan, Egyptian Jews. In her spirit she was an atheist with strong radical leanings in politics and a fury to convert the heathen of her own tribe. She kissed Zenia and left. "We'll be waiting for you even if we look like we're sleeping," she said. Then off she strode into the Galilean night.

"Israel," Fred said.

"*Makers of History*," Ram said. "My father's books. There I learned the name of Alexander's horse and in the book of Aunt Zenia you'll learn she's a great snake catcher."

Now Zenia and the Russians united in an elegy of remembering, chattering away, and one or two began to cry. Ram and Fred decided to go out and take a walk. They were to sleep in one of the single men's dormitories, but Zenia called to Ram to return in a little while and walk her to the school.

The two men went out into a night chilled with the bittersweet fragrance of the batha, the garigue, the maquis of lower Galilee.

They walked around within the settlement, saw a jeep load of soldiers stop and chat with one of the settlement guards on duty near one of the trenches behind the barbed wire fence. They walked into the orchard where the buds were bursting and the plowed ground with its grassy weeds gave Ram the feeling of Dutchess County. But the hills were different. They were like the hills of southern France, the hills of California.

"It's better than it used to be," Fred said. "We've got friendly Christian villages at the border. We've got our soldiers. We've got the UN and so on. It's safer than Manhattan in a way if what I read is true."

There was no moon but a bright and starry sky, and the gorges, hills, ravines topped each other and made a dark silhouette against a brighter sky.

Fred went off to sleep and Ram went back to get Zenia. He passed the schoolhouse, which stood alone surrounded by lawns, a playing field and a circle of small houses. There were a few lights in the houses and there were the bright lights of security lamps. The two-story concrete block schoolhouse was just a rectangular shape with shallow horizontal windows. It looked like a fortress of learning in the wilderness of Galilee. But this wilderness was itself exhausted with human history.

Ram walked back with Zenia clinging to his arm. She was tired and she sounded so, but happy also.

"I feel refreshed," she said.

"By what?"

"By a vacation from myself."

It felt colder now.

"The air is made of rockrose and terebinth around here," Zenia said. "It's made of fruit blossoms. It's made of thorny burnet."

All the lights of the two-story concrete schoolhouse were out except at the front door. Floodlights at the roof corners lit up the surrounding lawns and paths and the playing fields on one side. There were a few small trees beginning to shape up. This fort of a schoolhouse on its hill dominated all of Asher. Around its edges were the little houses of the five hundred souls and their small flower gardens, their little pine trees and new-tended bushes. Alone a surviving carob swelled out and leaned to one side away from some secret wind.

The air of Asher was made up of more than the new Asher. It was made of rock and ravines, of mountains in the distance and ravaged streambeds. It was made of the forests that had disappeared and the forests that waited to return. It was made of every tribe or nation that had wandered through, killed and set-tled in, only in turn to pass on as others followed. Some like the Jews and Arabs had returned more than once, for like the batha and the maquis, they were the weeds in history, ever alert for another chance to fill in what had been destroyed.

"You remember," Ram said, "the nights when I played in the lots outside the zoo."

Zenia said, "I remember them as if they were always hap-pening all the time."

The janitor waiting for them, a man in his late fifties, was a skinny grouch who spoke bad Hebrew through a fat, outrageous nose. "And worse Russian," Zenia said to Ram while she spoke Russian. The man opened the door for them so they could go in. His voice complained on.

Zenia said to Ram, "I asked him if he liked it here and he said what's to like. Then I said why don't you go back home?"

"Well?" Ram looked back at the janitor, who was standing in the lighted doorway looking out in the night of Asher. His nose absorbed the landscape with disgust.

"He just cursed the bureaucrats at home and the bureaucrats here. I said that he should go to America. 'It can't be different,' he told me. 'How can it be? The world is full of monkeys waiting to be men.' Meanwhile, he's bossing us. Ten minutes, he says, and he's locking up and you'll be stuck here."

"I don't mind," Ram said.

They went up the stairs slowly and softly. When they reached the top, Ram heard laughter below. It was the janitor laughing. There were four soldiers in khaki about him and the tallest soldier was joking in Hebrew, for the janitor laughed again. The inside hall light caught his funny nose in a comic cartoon of the bureaucrat.

"That's funny," Zenia said. They were at the half-closed door leading to the classroom, where one cot stood empty among rows of sleeping girls in their sleeping bags. The two windows were open and a dim brightness streamed in from the floodlit grounds. A small wind, crisp and deliciously bitter, blew in. They both looked down at the janitor and the vague figures of the soldiers. Their Uzi machine guns caught light reflections. Zenia leaned forward to listen. "They want to know if there are any children in the building."

As Ram moved to see better, the tallest soldier swung his Uzi in a small arc. There were fire flashes from the gunshot. There were discrete claps of sound in a roaring applause of gunfire. The janitor like a surprised athlete flipped back, rolled over, came up on his feet, hung there for one moment's forever and flopped forward, totally relaxed. His life had left before his body knew it, so on it went falling face down on the school building steps. The last Ram saw of him, his nose disdained his fate.

The four soldiers, kicking the dead janitor out of the way, jumped into the building and slammed and locked the door.

Zenia grabbed Ram's arm and pulled him inside the classroom. The girls were up, starting to talk, but Tamar was at the window shouting at the girls. A girl jumped out of the window, then a second.

Outside there were shouts. Inside, the girls screamed.

The Arab terrorists were at the doorway, and the one who had been laughing and speaking in Hebrew aimed his gun and fired two quick blasts. The first shattered the window on the left and hit a girl who was trying to get out. She fell screaming with pain. The second blast hit Tamar on the arm but she shoved the girl climbing out through before turning back into the room where the tall Arab was yelling in Hebrew. He kept shouting in brief bursts. Outside there were commands. They heard people shouting. Downstairs from inside the building there were flashes of machine-gun fire and then another voice yelling out a warning in Arabic.

Inside the classroom, those girls still in their sleeping bags lay there, half up, frightened faces turned to the attackers, one of whom was a boy of about sixteen. The khaki uniforms were not Israeli uniforms at all but just khaki imitations. These were Arab infiltrators on a mission and they had a schoolroom of hostages.

Here they were hypnotized by the guns, a wounded schoolteacher, twenty-seven young girls, some standing up in their underclothes as they had leaped out of the sleeping bags, and two old visitors who had strayed in out of a foreign life.

Tamar spoke and the girls moved to their sleeping bags and quickly dressed. The others lay still. The tall Arab kept talking in his little quick bursts to them and there was no more firing from downstairs.

Ram could see only night through the shattered windows. But there were many sounds outside and a voice called back in Hebrew. Then, outside, a voice in Arabic. It was brisk and authoritative. Inside, in the classroom, everybody was still and silent.

Ram said, "What's going on?" He spoke in a quiet, reasonable way.

The Arab looked at him with surprise and grinned. He had a lean long face, very dark, with a small thin mustache. He had black eyes, heavy brows, and wore his khaki with a kind of bravura style, jaunty and soldierlike. His lips were thick, and when he spoke he had bad teeth. "You American?" he asked. His English had a kind of delightful eccentricity to it, a language of playfulness.

"Yes," Ram said. "And this is Dr. Mont, she's a Russian. Who are you?"

"Do you mind if I help her?" Zenia asked. Without waiting, she moved to Tamar and examined her arm. "Do you have any first-aid stuff along with you?" she asked Tamar.

Tamar spoke Hebrew and a young girl who, unlike most of the hikers, was fair and redheaded searched in the bags.

The tall Arab pointed the gun at her. "Don't move," he shouted.

Zenia said, "These are children. They don't have any guns. No one has guns here. Bring it over," she told the redheaded girl, who obeyed without hesitation. The Arab watched her carry the first-aid box.

While Zenia applied first aid, the tall Arab said to Ram, "We're here to exchange these girls for twenty prisoners the Israelis hold. Stand up," he shouted at them.

They all stood up against the walls. It was the position of prisoners everywhere. It was like the photographs of the concentration camps at the killing walls. It was a universal posture of the times.

"Search them," the tall Arab said. The boy started forward. "Leave your gun here, Salah."

Salah put his gun at the feet of his leader.

The boy first went through the sleeping bags and the hikers' packs. He found four transistor radios and a half-dozen pocket knives, cans of sardines. Then, one by one, he searched the girls. They shrank from his hands but didn't resist, except one tallish, thin girl with a now tormented face. She cried out when he touched her and pulled away. The boy struck her across her face

188

and she stood trembling while he ran his hands about her, grinning all the while. His grin, it seemed, was part of his usual expression and didn't perhaps mean anything precise. In the end, he had gathered a half-dozen tins of sardines, the few radios and knives. Now he stood in front of Zenia. She didn't even look at him. She was looking at the tall Arab, who suddenly called out, "Not her. Just the man." This, of course, in Arabic all the time but Ram could understand the dog language of action.

Ram felt the strong young hands upon his body. He looked at Zenia, who never stopped studying the leader.

The Arab boy gathered his findings and went back. He had put them in one of the hiker's packs, dumping other things on the floor as useless. Salah picked up his Uzi and pointed it at the prisoners.

The tall Arab picked up the bag and looked over his hostages. "My name is Ibrahim. His name is Salah. I'm going down to talk to your friends before they try to rescue you. If they try, we'll kill all of you."

From the outside came the same steady authoritative voice, now speaking Arabic, asking questions.

The tall Arab grinned at Ram. "He's a patrol officer with experience. He understands us. We're getting the calm treatment. Reasonable. Let's talk. He wants to know what we want."

Tamar was wearing a heavy pair of pajamas, and now she was waiting to see what would happen. Her quick response had saved three of the girls if the one shot was not dead. She looked at the Arab with steady fury.

Ibrahim said, "You look like an Arab heroine yourself. I tried not to kill you. I need you."

Tamar showed no response, not even to praise. She was as ready to kill as he was.

He said in English, "You're going to take a list of names and detailed instructions to that man outside. He knows everything. He sounds like it. He wants to sound like it. He's what you Americans call a big shot. He has a big-shot voice. I once worked in New York. I took a night course at the City College there."

Ram said, "We're classmates, then."

Tamar said, "Why don't you send one of the girls with your message? I'm their leader and want to stay with them."

"No," the tall Arab said, "you'll make them understand what's going on here. By now we've got explosives set downstairs and we'll blow this building up with all of us in it if our demands aren't met. We mean business. I want you to go and convince them that I'm serious. It's no use believing it after we're all dead."

"Yes, go," Zenia said. "You're bleeding badly. I've stopped it with a tourniquet. But you need surgery. That needs equipment. Ram and I will take care of the girls."

"Come along," the tall Arab said. "My soldier here hates all of you. I've ordered him to kill anyone who goes near the windows. I've ordered him to shoot anyone who does anything without permission." Once again, he gestured with his Uzi at Tamar. "Hurry. Never mind the shoes. They'll have all the shoes and clothes you need. I'll give you an envelope from Damascus. It has all the information. You tell them out there every single order must be obeyed as written. They have till six o'clock tomorrow morning. That's it. Come on."

Tamar spoke to her students in Hebrew and the Arab agreed with her.

Some of the girls began to cry when Tamar started out of the room. She turned fiercely on them and shouted orders and they stopped. Then Tamar looked at Zenia and Ram. "I trust them with you," she said and left.

The tall Arab followed and the young Arab backed out into the corridor and stood against the wall where he could look both downstairs and into the room. His submachine gun always pointed into the room. The wind was cold coming in through the smashed windows.

Fury and hatred rampaged all over Ram, everywhere that he and his body lived together. The hatred went on without any help from him. In all the war no one had pointed a gun at him this way. He had never felt the paroxysms of hand-to-hand fighting. Shots had come from windows and crushed buildings.

They were as fatal and mad as the bombs of London. He had lived in the peculiar presence of death that is the nature of war as it happens here and there. It happens everywhere and somehow doesn't happen to you. He had managed to survive without anything but a wounded hatred of the Germans, a contempt and loathing he still felt for them. This feeling was philosophical. It was final. It existed for those Germans in that time and like radium death filtered through to his life today. Even now he felt no hatred for the Arabs. Their history, both marvelous and pathetic, brutal and brutalized, was simply human.

Yet he was consumed with a killing frenzy against the terrorists.

He was wild now. He leaned against the wall, a man three years from seventy, greedy for youth and strength and guns and killing. He watched the hostages of whom he was one while an Arab boy with a funny green beret pointed that murderous Uzi at them all. Salah wore a nylon khaki vest loaded with clips of ammunition. He had two American army grenades clipped to the vest. He had a grin and good yellowish teeth.

Ram had lived in violence, near it, surrounded by it. They were the large numbers of the time, but here he was beyond the meaning of numbers. The silent monologue of killing went on in his mind. It was his mind. It was everything, burning and beating in the silence of hate.

This boy and his gun had invaded the privacy of Ram's self. The self was a spiritual cell. In every way it opened itself to the world, within and outside its membrane of isolation. Its nature and therefore its desire in life was to be in the world and let all others flow through it. It struggled to achieve this but, invaded against its nature, it struggled in every way to kill the fatal intruder. Without such a self, there was no human creature known as one.

Eyes closed, Ram made himself breathe slowly because any moment his heart, inflamed by secret stimulants and driving his blood with fury through the damaged artery, might explode it and send the blood flying through illegal channels. He would die. He would die before he could destroy those who had invaded his life.

"What are you thinking about, Ram?"

How strange the refashioned yet true voice of Zenia spoke to him at this moment in a classroom in Galilee. The hushed, uncertain voices of the girls trembled fitfully around. They were afraid to be heard. They were even more afraid to be silent. Was that why Zenia spoke?

He smiled. In his life of many smiles this was the most useless of them all. He said, "First, I thought we would never meet again. Then I said, we are about to meet again. Then we met. This is, of course, an accident. But did you have something accidentally in mind that you chose it this way?"

She gave him a worried look and then let go to pay attention to the girls.

"Who speaks Arabic?" Zenia asked.

Most of the girls raised their hands. They came from homes where Arabic had been the real language and Hebrew the language of the Bible and the temple.

Zenia said, "Tell the boy there, I want you to put your warm clothes on. Then start dressing. Sit on your sleeping bags and keep quiet for a while." The girls hesitated and then a plumpish girl with bad acne, a sullen look and very large brown eyes spoke to the Arab boy.

He came closer and looked at them, grinning at them.

Zenia said in English, "Ignore him and get them dressed quickly."

They did while Salah watched. All the terrors of the border war and its history of rape and mutilation by the Arabs against the Jews were known to Ram, and he saw they were real fears in the girls.

Everyone was listening all the time to the shouted conversations below and outside.

Zenia said to Ram, "The building is now surrounded by soldiers. They're waiting to get the terms and they have assured the Arabs in here they will do nothing until they can communicate with the government."

By now a bullhorn was being used outside.

Ram asked the young Arab, "Do you speak English?"

Salah was short, stocky, with a face distorted by a scar and a vigorous hooked nose. He was excited and aggressive as he stood there, every now and then pointing his gun at one or another in the room, but mostly he was listening to the voice of his leader shouting instructions to the people outside and the bullhorn voice answering.

"What are they saying?" Zenia asked the plump young girl.

"Tamar is now going to walk out to our friends with the letter. They also want to send someone to pick up Dinah, who is still lying where she fell out of the window after getting shot. She's alive. Her leg's broken and she's wounded. The tall Arab says they can send one woman to help her. That's what they're doing now."

She started to move toward the window and Salah yelled at her. She shrunk back.

Zenia said, "We're not to go near the windows." Suddenly she sat down on the cot which she had never got to sleep on.

Ram sat down beside her. "What's wrong?"

"My legs," she said. "They need a rest. You?"

"My heart is lively. That's not unusual."

"I suppose," Zenia said in her old young woman's voice, "this isn't either."

"It is for me," Ram said. "This is the first time a killing gun's been pointed at me personally."

Zenia smiled in comfort. "You were in a different war."

They heard steps coming up two at a time and the tall Arab came into the room again.

"Well, we're on our way. We're inside. They're outside. No one's going to do anything till they speak to their government." His words jerked in and out. His finger was on the trigger of the machine gun all the time. He had grenades hooked to his belt.

He had a revolver strapped to his waist. "My name is Ibrahim as I told you."

"So is mine," Ram said.

"It doesn't make us brothers," said Ibrahim.

"We've just met."

Ibrahim laughed with his bad teeth. "What are you two old people doing here with these girls?"

"Accident," Ram said. He watched Zenia. She had evidently had a physical problem but was better now. "My aunt is eighty-one. And I'm here to see her. We're visitors here."

"You're all the same," Ibrahim said. "Zionists and Jews."

Zenia said, "We're all prisoners here and you're the jailers. That's true."

Ram said, "I don't want any accidents to happen. I'd like to be sure of what we can do and not do. It may take a long time to get this settled, all night and part of tomorrow. How can we use the toilet and where is it?"

The Arab said, "There are two in the hall. One has windows, the big one. You can't use that. The other is just a small one with no windows at the end of the hall. You can use that, one at a time, if you ask permission of this commando here. His name is Salah. These girls all speak Arabic so they can ask. Don't go near the windows. You can move a little but not too much. I want you to keep your positions the way they are, near the bedrolls. Talk but not too much. If you need something else, ask for it. I intend to kill everybody if I have to, but otherwise we will run this in a military way. Be calm. Don't do anything foolish. If the Israeli government is wise you'll all be free by tonight. I'm here to free my comrades by tomorrow night and go free myself. But only on my terms, which were set in Damascus. . . . Is everything clear? If you have any doubts, send for me. Once the shooting starts, it's hard to stop." He waited. Then he said some of it in Hebrew, and when there were no questions, he left the room again.

Ram heard him bounding down the stairs two at a time. He heard whispered Arabic below. He heard trucks and jeeps driving. Soon, there would be a few tanks. Soon, there would be helicopters. Soon, paratroopers would arrive, and all the time the waiting would go on. Ram's heartbeat was truly uneven at the moment. The room was dark except for the reflections from outside.

The Arab boy came in, stepped warily, put a quick hand to the wall switch and the room lighted up. He had this grin which he used almost always. It had a special quality of hatefulness in it. It was drawn back from his thick teeth, from the yellow whiteness of them. His lips were heavy also, the hooked nose had spirit. He was dark and covered with dust. Bits of weeds clung to his clothes. He wore a green beret which didn't fit well. He had two grenades and he was loaded with ammunition for the Uzi. The clips were stuck everywhere. He was a young commando and felt himself powerful, desperate and brave. He was probably all those things, but he was also sixteen. Ram studied him without appearing to do so. He was, after all, the only one who could fire at any people in the room. Everything in the room had been emptied out for the girls except for two rows of steel filing cabinets. They were three-drawer affairs, and there were three on one side and two on the other side of the open door. The door was wide and made of plywood, painted over. The plywood was in two three-quarter-inch thicknesses, as best as Ram could judge. Closed it could stop no Uzi bullets. The windows were wider than tall, smashed open, with prongs of glass sticking out here and there. Outside the air was cold, the night had some way to go. By now he heard much movement. The surrounding soldiers were taking positions, the houses were being emptied. There were lots of guns out there but no one to shoot them at.

If Ibrahim was to be believed, the terrorists had assembled some explosive which could be set off quickly. He wondered if it was enough to blow up the whole schoolhouse. The walls of the corridors were also concrete blocks. The floors were cement covered over with some artificial material that looked like wood but wasn't. There was one desk and three chairs in the room, the cot and the sleeping bags and the girls and Zenia and himself. There was a map on the wall and blackboards. There was a bulletin board. It had photographs of children and some instructions thumbtacked to it. There were two wall vents for heating. He doubted they had air conditioning. Everything was just enough. It was strange in this country with its modern army, its technicians, scientists, university, that these settlements all began by scrabbling for life on wild frontiers. Out of it in the old days had come the basic Israeli army but those old communities had no other choice. This was something else. It reminded him in a strange way of the children of America who founded communes out of rags and leftovers of high civilization to regain something human they thought lost. And rags and leftovers, the refuse of life, also become the objects of new artists. They invented sometimes by just presenting something they found and the museums showed these objects, perhaps the very objects thrown out of the museum's back door and now repurchased through the front door by foundations made from the wealth of the industries that made the objects in the first place.

He thought about the explosive being set up below. He wondered what they used and what they could have brought along. He had seen the four men below just before they rushed in. They seemed to have only themselves, their guns, their grenades. He tried to recall but couldn't whether any one of the four had carried a pack. It seemed they hadn't, and he wondered whether the explosive threat was real or false. In any event, they were armed and had enough bullets and grenades to kill everyone in the building. That was true enough.

He and Zenia sat calmly all this while on the cot. Her hand was dry and light. Occasionally she pressed his hand gently enough. She asked the plump girl, "What's your name?"

"Ruth," the girl said.

"You'll be my translator when they speak Arabic, or even Hebrew. I've just a little of Hebrew."

"Yes, Dr. Mont," the girl said.

Ram looked at Ruth with admiration. He let her see he admired her. She was showing great calm. Beside her sat the bright-looking girl with the fiery red hair. Her white skin took the sun badly and she had a snowfall of freckles on her nose, but they too were fair. Her quick blue eyes were in lively discovery of everything going on. Most of the hikers were gloomy, solemn, sad. They woke up with intelligent interest only when voices spoke on the bullhorn outside and the Arabs answered on their megaphone. But this girl was completely alive. If afraid, she possessed the fear and it didn't take her over. Her face was thin but very attractive in its shape, and her body was slender and athletic. She looked as if she could run fast, do gymnastics and pass any examination. She was very interested in the way Zenia and he sat together, occasionally holding hands. "Why are you holding hands?" she asked.

"When I was a young boy and she was a young woman, we always did. We've just met after not seeing each other for fifty-six years. I don't want to let her get away again."

"What happened after you left each other?"

"Just this. Over and over again. Just this. What's your name?"

"Shlamath."

"Did Shlamath have red hair?"

The girl said, "I think she looked more like Ruth. If there's anything you want me to do to help, ask me. I speak Hebrew, Arabic, English and Romanian. My mother was Romanian."

"Thanks," Zenia said. "I'm sure all of you will help. Right now, everyone should stay pretty quiet. It's better not to talk too much until we find out how things are going." Still speaking to the girls, Zenia asked the Arab boy a question in English. "Guard, can you see what your leader is doing down there? How are things going?"

Salah showed no sign that he knew what the words meant. All the while Zenia spoke, Ruth translated for the girls who didn't understand English and so this time they all were looking at the Arab boy, who moved when he saw this happen, suddenly curious. Ram noticed that only Shlamath didn't turn to look and it was Shlamath who said, "I don't think he understands English."

This girl was remarkable in every way, Ram thought, watching her.

Zenia said, "I'm going to find out a few things now." She got up and everyone watched her, including Salah. "I want to go to the toilet," she said to him.

He stood up, pointing his gun not in threat but because that seemed a natural response to her getting up. She was the first who had moved so definitely, but he didn't understand her.

Zenia said, "Toilet."

He just waited.

She said, "Salah. I want to go to the toilet."

Salah addressed the girls and they looked at Zenia.

"He wants to know what you're saying to him," Ruth said.

"Good," Zenia said. "Tell him I'm going to the toilet. Is it all right?"

It was all right and Zenia walked out of the room. She moved a little stiffly and the boy held his gun pointed at her. She seemed the essence of old age, a fragile woman, without much strength, helpless under the gun here, but Ram knew as all the girls did that she was thinking of something to do, to understand, thinking of some action after a life spent in the ravages of history.

They heard her steps going down the hall. They heard a door open.

Everyone listened for the toilet to flush and it did.

One of the girls giggled. Shlamath spoke sharply and there was silence. Ruth spoke to them angrily. The silence was deeper.

Soon Zenia returned.

She sat down again on the cot near Ram. She said to Ruth, "Thank Salah."

Ruth did and he gave them all his same old grin. He didn't feel threatened because these were young girls, an old woman, and an old man. This was why he was their guardian. It was a good choice if he were the weakest of the Arabs. It was also dangerous because he might shoot where another might wait.

Zenia said, "I just closed the door enough so he couldn't look in. I didn't shut it altogether because he might ask you then to open it. When any of you go to the toilet, do exactly what I did. You understand?"

Ruth translated and they understood. A very tall, very thin girl who all the while was most uneasy, hardly able to stay still on her sleeping bag, could no longer restrain her fright. She said, "I don't like the way he looks at us."

"Then don't look at him. In general, don't look at him. People get nervous when they're watched. But you mustn't be afraid now. Ibrahim is in charge. I think he wants everything to work out, and if he does, then let's hope it does."

It was Ruth with her dark sullen face (even when she smiled the sullen feeling was in her face, in her voice) who said, "Israelis don't make deals with terrorists."

"There's always a first time," Zenia said. "It's not for you to decide what the government will do. You mustn't be afraid and you must hope for the best. You girls are worth more than any Arab prisoner the government holds. You're lucky the government has something to exchange for you, or else you'd be dead."

The atmosphere nevertheless became even more gloomy so it was Shlamath who broke it with a cheerful question. "Dr. Mont, will you tell us when to be afraid?"

In spite of everything, the girls laughed a little.

When this little interchange was translated, most of the girls relaxed. They all felt that if the older people had confidence then there was hope. Only Ruth knew better but she said nothing. It was clear she had no hope. It was also clear she would act when told to and act with strength. She was too fat but she was strong. There was no lightness in her. The redhead had enough for everyone.

Suddenly the man with the bullhorn spoke in Arabic. He was answered by Ibrahim on the megaphone.

Ruth said, "This Israeli commander says the government is willing to negotiate with the terrorists and they are studying the demands."

It seemed reasonable but the voice of Ibrahim was angry. He shouted in short bursts like shots from his machine gun.

Ruth said, "The Arabs say there is nothing to negotiate. The Israelis have till six o'clock tomorrow night to satisfy the demands. He also refuses to discuss anything with the commander."

The reasonable voice over the bullhorn explained something. There was a major burst of words from the megaphone.

Ruth translated and Ram saw the girls were frightened because they understood what he had yet to hear. "He is warning them. Nothing can be negotiated. They must follow the orders of the letter exactly or we'll all be killed and the building blown up."

There was silence outside now and the girls had lost all confidence.

"Tell them," Ram said. "These threats and counterproposals are what negotiations are. After all, the Israelis have all the power. All the Arabs can do is kill us and themselves and the mission is a failure. So this is the way they talk."

It was silent inside and in the silence they heard two tanks or more rolling up somewhere in the distance behind the houses. It would have been easier to stay in this classroom if they could look outside. This was forbidden and enforced by the machine gun. Then the little radios down below made their cackling sounds.

"It's all on the radio," Ruth said.

"It's all over the world," Zenia said. "We're famous. The whole world will be listening, so let's survive and enjoy it."

Below the radios were turned lower and the words could no longer be made out.

"Let's all rest quietly," Zenia said in her doctor's voice. "We're going to be here for a long day as well as the rest of the night. Sleep if you can. If you want to speak a little with someone next to you, do so. But don't talk too much."

Without bending down she slipped off her shoes and stretched out on the bed while Ram sat down on the floor, leaning his back against the bed, his head close to hers where she rested it on the pillow. He looked down the length of her and at the room and then noticed through her stockings her swollen bunions and twisted toes again.

On the ride up, Fred had stopped at a hotel on the Mediterranean and before the sun went down Zenia and Ram had gone for a walk along the windless beach and she had taken off her shoes and stockings and walked in the warmish water. On shore were the lights of the small hotel and lights in the villas overlooking the sea. Beyond were orange groves and the air was soft and touched with fragrance. A few miles inland the hills rose and farther still became mountains. Here and there a cluster of lights but mostly tumbled terrain covered with batha and, beyond, the maquis.

"This," Zenia said, "is such a small country. But somehow too big to understand. It attracts remarkable people like any revolution."

He looked at Zenia's feet. The marvelous evolutionary miracle of her feet was twisted now by time and neglect. She had bunions. The middle toes were deformed, overlapping. She ran a few steps ahead, turned back and let him catch up.

"I see," Ram said, "the revolution didn't do much for your feet."

She rested a left hand lightly on his shoulder and lifted her right foot, turning it this way and that as if examining it for the first time. She said, "In general, that's how it all turned out." When she saw his wondering look, she added, "But you must remember that before it began hardly any Russians walked on their own feet at all."

Now Zenia wanted to speak to him privately, but there was no way without whispering. The girls themselves whispered now and then and the hiss of the breaths gathered here and there above a minimal murmur of voices heard but not understood. It was the atmosphere in the room. Zenia began in the same way.

A half-dozen girls knew some school English and three or four knew it more colloquially. He felt Zenia's hesitancy in uttering her thought. She would never hesitate to think of anything real, but she didn't want to be overheard by these hostages. As he did, she considered them completely innocent of the violence of the world. In fact, these children had lived at least through two wars and every day of their lives knew that sudden violence could intrude upon them. Their kibbutzes were armed camps of a sort with places for children to hide and trenches to fight from, and guards on duty in the hills or in the fields. Every man and woman could shoot a gun and every man and woman had one to shoot. Some were army trained and all were ready, even those who weren't ready. Nevertheless, for Ram and Zenia, and this intrigued him, these children were innocent hostages.

In a way peculiar to understand since it wasn't in any obvious sense true, Zenia didn't consider herself a hostage. Nor did she think of him that way. And it was true in that way. He didn't consider himself a hostage. He felt he was in a battle, in a struggle, in an action. All his life had been such an action, sometimes fierce but generally in a state of uneasy truce, like the land of the Jews. This country annoyed him suddenly. It made a demand beyond his habit of not accepting. It insisted it be accepted as it was. It was the way Fred had spoken all along, mentioning the truth but insisting that was the way it was and that was what they had. Fred didn't reject change. He didn't think too much of it, considering, since a change for the better would in the end come out not so different from a change for the worse.

Zenia spoke with a kind of tender softness. It was after all the same voice she used in love. It was a voice he had heard that first night long ago on the Fishwoods farm, it was a voice he knew from the lots and the nights around the table with Harry doing magic and his father delighted. It was the same soft not quite whispering voice in which she had touched his ear tenderly, coming in at last to say good night a long time ago when they were both young and the lions used to roar while in the summer darkness the glittering summer trolley ticked away on the boulevard. She asked, "Is there anything we can do to save the children?"

"When?"

It surprised her. She was silent for some time. "What do you think will happen then?"

"I think this will go on the rest of the night and all through the day till just before six o'clock."

"And then?"

"I think they'll pretend to give in. Would the Soviets give in?"

She didn't answer for a while. "All governments have higher reasons."

"Even if they try, they won't succeed. These exchanges are very hard to work out even when it's one for one. There's always a moment when one side has to trust the other."

Zenia said after another pause, "It's no use just dying. I have too much to tell you and we must save the children."

"I've been thinking about it," Ram said. "Our time will come when the shooting starts. We have lots of time. Mostly we have to see there are no sudden accidents." He got up slowly and the gun of the boy pointed directly at him while he took Tamar's sleeping bag and put it down beside Zenia's cot.

Everyone in the room was alive to his movements. He stretched himself out on top of it. "Let's all pretend to sleep for a while," he said. "After all, men have walked on the moon. Think of it. If we're careful and make no mistakes, we'll get back to earth again."

A voice said, "This is the earth."

"It's the Holy Land," Ram said. "I've been told miracles happen here. Good night."

One girl almost laughed.

They all settled themselves, lying inside or on top of their sleeping bags. The cold wind blew in from the mountains and the hills. Soon it was very still in the room with Zenia lying on her cot and Ram on Tamar's sleeping bag.

He closed his eyes and listened to the voices of the night. He breathed the bittersweet freedom of the maquis.

He heard Ibrahim coming up the steps again, two at a time

but slowly, the way a young child tests the powers two at a time. He asked a few questions of Salah and then Ram saw the two of them standing in the doorway, the young boy behind the tall Arab.

Ibrahim said, "I'm turning out the light here. Sometimes we'll put it on and sometimes put it out." He said it in Hebrew and English. He looked over at Ram, who simply lay there without paying too much attention to him. "I see you know from now on it's just waiting. We don't trust them and they don't trust us."

He stood there as if he wanted to talk some more but the hostages were silent. Then he and the boy whispered to each other in Arabic and withdrew, the boy to his old post seated on the floor, back against the far wall, his gun pointed into the room where no one stirred or spoke.

It was better in the dark. It took a kind of fever out of the room, but it also suited the terrorists' plan which Ram heard them play out. They moved around the schoolhouse, turning on lights and then turning them off. When Ram looked out of the broken window, he saw a glow of light from another upstairs schoolroom. The new plan inside was to make it impossible for the Israelis to know if all the hostages were in one room or in another, upstairs or down. The Arabs could be sure that binoculars were trained on the school from every side along with the guns, the cannon, and the eyes of the soldiers.

For the moment, it was easier to be a prisoner this way than sitting around and talking. There really was nothing to say.

Zenia was motionless in her coat. A brown wool blanket half covered her body. He saw her profile against the light coming through the window, the mix of searchlights and darkness holding still also, but sometimes a great light would slowly pass across the building from some Israeli watching post. Ram saw Zenia's face as a profile of old age in which was embodied like a shattered civilization her youth and every memory he had of her magical presence.

The young Arab was half asleep. The Uzi rested on his knees and pointed into the classroom. He had taken off his silly green beret. His dark, shaggy hair was thick and young. His eyes were open but there was nothing exciting in the classroom. For him, also, the exciting things were in a mystery outside where, against a dike of terrorist guns, the restless motions of arriving Israeli troops assembled, where radios got their messages and strangers around the world speculated in the marketplace with the lives of the hostages, where governments met and in far-off Damascus a last ripple touched those who had plotted this occasion.

Two of the girls closest to the door across the room from where Ram lay were whispering and one finally said, "Dr. Mont, I have go to the toilet."

"Go then," Zenia said, "but do as I did. Ask the boy and do as I did."

"Wait," Ram said as softly as he could and without emphasis. "Can you wait a little while?"

"Yes," the girl said.

Everyone in the room began to stir a little as if to listen to something interesting.

Ram said as before, "Don't move around. Listen." So they did. "We're divided here just the way it happened, some on one side of the room and some on the other." They all observed as cautiously as they could the obvious. "It's not the best way if we have to help ourselves." He glanced into the hallway where Salah was listening. "Tell him you want to go to the toilet, but don't go till I finish talking."

The girl spoke to Salah, who gave her permission. It gave him something to do also as the long night of silence and waiting went on.

Ram said, "There are twenty-seven girls here. Think how you would divide yourselves in groups of three, one of whom should speak English if possible. But more important, I want two groups of three of the six strongest girls. I want three on one side of the door and three on the other. They should be closest to the door. Now, as you take turns going to the toilet, rearrange yourselves when you come back so that happens." He heard the whisper of their voices. "Start going."

She was a smallish girl and her sleeping bag was closest to the door on the far side. Now she got up, looked around. He could see an arrangement had been made. Then she went out and they heard her walking down the corridor to the toilet. Salah was watching her. Inside the classroom one of the biggest girls casually shifted over and took her place.

"In the old days," Zenia said, "we played this game on rainy days and called it Musical Chairs."

"It helps pass the time," Ram said.

He heard tiny whisperings. They ran around the room like mice, stopped, ran back. Ruth and Shlamath made suggestions. By the time the little girl came back, there was a vacant place for her closer to one of the windows.

There was new excitement among those waiting to live or die.

"Think more than you talk," Zenia said.

The mice disappeared.

Zenia didn't ask what Ram had in mind, nor did she look over to him. He realized it wasn't because she trusted his wisdom or ability, although in fact she may have. She had lived as part of an inner circle of men and women who had learned how to act together in crisis and outside of it. It was habit now. But, of course, it could be simple ordinary prudence. There was a different atmosphere in the room. Their thoughts were no longer completely dependent on the world outside. They were no longer waiting for something to happen to them. There was something they were going to do. Anyway, the gloomy silence of waiting was no longer empty of life.

The night went on.

Every once in a while Ram would speak up and say it was time for another girl to go to the toilet. Slowly the girls rearranged themselves. He wondered what standards they used, how they judged. Shlamath and Ruth had managed to be the leaders alongside the door, each with two strong girls lying beside them.

He could feel the desire all around him to know what the next step would be, so he gave them another thing to plan.

"There are two windows in this room," Ram said. "One window is almost in a direct line with the door, which isn't at the exact line dividing this room in two. The window on my side is to the right-hand side of that line from the door."

They all thought about it.

"Let's all rest. If you have to use the toilet, from now on, go back to your present place. We'll make other changes later."

He closed his eyes for a while, not sleeping. He wasn't one to sleep much even when there was nothing to stay awake for. Now he was through with sleep forever. He had a few digitalis pills in the watchpocket of his slacks. They would take him through the next day if there was a next day.

He felt rather than noticed a weakening of the night in spite of the artificial lights surrounding the schoolhouse. The new light was more momentous and subtle. The universe began with light in a big bang. It exploded in photons. Ever since, the universe had grown cooler except in this room. Here it was hot with fury. Did he still feel that way?

A bird chirped.

It sounded like a sparrow.

"Tell me," Ram asked everyone, "what kind of sparrows do they have in Galilee?"

15

"Let's begin over again. Where is the French ambassador?"

"He's waiting for instructions from his government."

"Where is he now?"

"He's on his way here."

"Asher is only two hours from Tel Aviv. They could use a helicopter."

"He is coming from Jerusalem by helicopter."

"Have you been in touch with the Romanian ambassador?"

"Yes. He also needs instructions from his government."

"He must have a code word."

"I don't understand. What code word?"

"Without a code word, it's useless. The ambassadors must have a code word. There must be a code word. Otherwise it's all over. You hear, it's over."

"We'll ask about the code word."

"The code word is essential."

"We'll pass on this information at once."

"They've had that information from the very beginning. They know there has to be a code word."

"Where can they get this code word?"

"Damascus."

"Do they know this?"

"Why are you pretending not to know about the code word?"

"I am only passing on the information I get from you and

from Jerusalem. I assure you the ambassadors are in touch with their governments. Be patient. We'll try to bring about everything you ask. We can supply you with food or anything else you need, for you and the hostages."

"If anyone steps into the grounds that surround this school building, we'll shoot."

"We're trying to work things out."

"Then where is the French ambassador?"

"As soon as he arrives, he'll talk to you."

"He must have the code word."

Such were the intense and aimless conversations that went on between the inside and the outside, between the megaphone shouting from an upstairs school window and the Israeli bullhorn, which each time cleared its mechanical throat with electric rasps and sudden explosions of noise. The words over the bullhorn were always calm and reasonable yet the amplification made them harsh and commanding. The angry megaphone was the human voice itself so that no matter how vivid its threats it seemed more personal, open to persuasion.

Ram could see in every anxious face in the schoolroom the confusion and fear of the loudspeakers. No matter how still the hostages tried to be, there was always some movement in the classroom except when the bullhorn and the megaphone sounded. Then the listeners, forever facing the pointed gun of Salah in the corridor, became arrested in listening. They were enthralled by their own fate. It was they who would live or die, and in the stretch of time, waiting, they became their own witnesses. It was in its way the very replica of mind itself, bewildering and familiar. Seated, or lying down on their sides with one arm bent, a chin resting on an open palm or knotted fist, the different faces struggled to feel hope. Even expecting the worst is a form of hope, that is, if there is time, there is hope.

"Why?" Ram wanted to know. This was a question he asked of himself. "These interchanges are just another form of noise. They carry no real messages, only the appearance of them. The bullhorn uses words that seem sincere and reasonable. The megaphone uses language of anger and plain demand. It breaks off every conversation with an abrupt silence. Silence, it knows, is its greatest threat."

And this was the way they lived in the classroom, in the state of being hostages.

Meanwhile the day advanced like a hallucination.

Suddenly, after a broken arabesque of noises, the bullhorn made a formal announcement as if everything were already solved. "We are making all arrangements for the transfer of your comrades. They'll arrive before six o'clock. We're not sure we'll be able to keep the timetable, exactly. But we'll keep you informed of every development here. We'll let you know the moment we hear from the Romanian ambassador. Perhaps he'll have details or information from your command. Please be patient and don't do anything rash. God willing, everything will end well. We, on our part, will do everything so your comrades reach Beirut as quickly as possible."

There was then a long silence from the terrorists. Ram could hear them talking in the corridor. They were arguing there. Their voices were also in a state of siege.

There were steps and the megaphone broke out. "We can't change our command's orders. You're changing everything. You must release our comrades. You must release twenty, the ones whose names you have."

The bullhorn replied. "We're gathering them. They are in different places. It's the custom here, it's the law, to keep them in different places."

Irritation now from the megaphone. It was Ibrahim talking, the voice of a man who had dedicated himself to a final act and now with horror saw that the final act was coming closer. He shouted, "They must be there before six o'clock. They must be on their way as ordered. The children here with us know we are making our preparations. Act if you want to save them. We told the young girls that we will release them when you release our comrades. They are asking you to do something. Orders are orders. We can't play games with orders. At six o'clock all will be over. Six o'clock will be the end."

His voice had the lunge of heroism, desperate and determined. It also hesitated with doubt.

In the routine vacuum of another silence, a flourish of whispering arose around the tall thin girl with the perpetually frightened face. It was she who often wept quietly, who recited psalms or feverishly opened her Bible and read in a monotone to herself.

Now she let everyone know she had to go to the toilet. She had held out to the last and, finally, spoke up. She was obviously ashamed to let the Arab boy know, but she was just as obviously desperate and had no choice.

Shlamath said, "Dr. Mont, Hannah has to go to the toilet."

"Ask the boy and go, then." Zenia was sitting together with Ruth on a bedroll. They had been talking about life on the kibbutz. It made Ram smile. In this way Zenia hadn't changed. She was improving the occasion.

By then Ram had moved closer to the door which, wide open as it could be, was stopped by the pair of steel filing cabinets standing there against the wall.

The door had ordinary knobs, a keyhole without a key, but it was solid. He had also leaned against the three steel filing cabinets on his side of the doorway. Here, briefly, the boy in the hall couldn't see Ram. It seemed to cause no concern. The cabinets were very heavy and while he could sway and even slightly tip them, he knew they would be a problem to move when it came to blocking the door once it was closed. And for that, the difficult moment would be when Ram had to cross the invisible line that divided the schoolroom in two.

Ram made his way back to Tamar's bedroll and sat there, his back against the wall, and just watched the sunlight gathering force for another day in the long life of the Galilee. Nothing could be seen out of the broken windows but rising, battered hills a few hundred yards away. There were occasional furtive movements of Israeli soldiers, or so it seemed. Mostly the foothills lay in their tormented silence, and in a far gully he saw the upper branches of a carob tree.

Meanwhile, the girls urged the frightened Hannah on. Finally, Shlamath spoke with the Arab boy, who gave his permission. "Go on, Hannah," Shlamath said. "Go now. Do as we all did. We're all here. There's nothing to be afraid of."

"Whoever named you made a mistake," Ruth said. "Go on, go on."

Hannah got up, straightened her wrinkled blue jeans, her dark blue sweater over a white shirt. Her hair was tangled and uncombed, short, just falling to her neck, which was serpentine and strong. She was about fifteen, Ram thought, and her long bewildered face carried a frozen fright. Her nose was thin and her lips were full and never still. He realized that once her body caught up with her age, and once her spirit caught up with life, she might become quite beautiful. Under her frightened face he saw tenderness, hidden in the astonishment of the way things changed.

She walked by the Arab boy and his gun. She stared at the floor, her body hunched together to be smaller. Then she was walking down the corridor out of sight of the classroom while the boy's glance followed her and flipped back to watch the classroom.

At that moment, the Israeli bullhorn began again. It crackled with noise and the commander began, Ruth translating for Zenia and Ram.

The bullhorn said, "I have an important announcement to make."

Then silence. There was no response from the terrorists. There was a restless movement among the hostages, who swayed to look at the Arab boy.

The bullhorn began again. "After a meeting of the Israeli cabinet, which began during the night and has lasted until this moment, they have agreed to accept all the terms of the demands given them. Representatives of our government are in touch with the Romanian and French ambassadors. They are working out the details. An exchange will be made as requested. I think we can all relax now. It's just a question of time." The voice ceased.

From an upstairs window on the other side of the school-house, Ibrahim's voice exploded through his megaphone. "The ultimatum you have is final. Every term has to be obeyed as written. We demand to see the two ambassadors at once. They must come here. They must have the code word. You know that. We warn you. Six P.M. is the final deadline. One second after is too late. You're playing with your children's lives."

At that moment, a frenzy of hysterial shouting burst from the Arab boy. He was on his feet, jabbing his Uzi again and again down the corridor toward the distant toilet, and the gun, swinging on its strap, jerked him forward. He wanted to fire. He cried for help. And all the while he kept snapping his head back to guard the hostages.

The schoolroom came apart in a flurry of bodies, with the girls on their feet. Hannah was shrieking. Her screams laced the air, ripped it to shreds, dug into the senses of everyone in the schoolroom.

"Hannah! Hannah! What is it?"

The fire of her agony pulled them toward the doorway where Salah suddenly turned upon them, shouting at them to go back.

"What is it? What is it?" Zenia asked. She pushed forward, driving the girls away from the doorway, and the boy, tormented by rage, fear and uncertainty, didn't know whether to fire his gun and kill them all or run to the hidden toilet where the screams of Hannah lured him on.

Ruth called out to Zenia, "That stupid girl locked the toilet door. Hannah!" she yelled in Hebrew. "Hannah, open the door. Open!"

The short, hard-faced terrorist was in the corridor now. He aimed his gun into the classroom and the girls shrank back against the walls. The boy ran down the corridor toward the toilet. They heard him shouting at Hannah and kicking and pounding on the locked toilet door. Her shrieks of terror pierced the walls. They flew madly around and escaped through the open windows, through the broken ones. The whole building vibrated with her screams.

Shlamath started to the open door of the schoolroom, but the Arab raised his gun and pointed it directly at her. She stopped dead. She called out, "Hannah! Hannah! Unlock the door. Don't be afraid."

Ruth yelled in Arabic, saying not to shoot.

And all the time the kicking and pounding on the door of the toilet went on and Hannah became a continuous unbelievable redundent scream. It freed a frenzy in everyone who could hear it.

Outside the bullhorn opened up its giant voice again. "What's going on there? What are you doing? We have agreed to your demands."

When Ram began to walk to the door, Zenia hurried past him, pushing him aside. "Not you. Not you," she said.

The short Arab faced her with his gun but she kept walking slowly. "Tell him," she called over her shoulder. "Tell him I'll help them. Tell him that."

Shlamath translated and Zenia kept moving. The Arab pushed the muzzle of his machine gun against her chest.

The fury of the boy's attacks on the door increased and, with it, the screams of Hannah.

Now the bullhorn burst out. "We want an answer or we'll attack. What's going on there?"

Ibrahim's voice now called to Zenia. "Come here and help. This girl inside is crazy."

They all waited in the room listening.

Ram heard Zenia's steps half running down the corridor. He heard her voice speaking steadily and the screams dying down to suddenly stop. He heard the door open, and Hannah's muted sobbing begin again while Zenia's voice soothed her, and all the steps of those returning.

When Zenia reappeared, half supporting this girl, Ram

saw that Zenia was really taller than most of the girls. It was a shock to him, for there she was as big as his real life remembered her, yet hiding in the disguise of time. Hannah collapsed on her bedroll, face down, and continued to weep.

Outside, the bullhorn was more demanding.

Ruth said, "They want to know what happened. They want an explanation."

The Israeli commander was no longer so reasonable. He said, "You ask us to cooperate. We're trying to cooperate. But if you harm the hostages, how can you expect us to cooperate? We won't wait and do nothing."

Ibrahim was furious. He ran off and a moment later his voice sounded over the megaphone. He shouted with the outrage of someone wrongly accused, "We haven't harmed anyone. You want us to kill them one by one, every hour you lie to us and make us wait? We'll throw them out of the windows to prove we mean to carry out our orders."

The Israeli voice didn't speak for some time, then it began in a reasonable way. "The parents of the children are here now. They want to be sure their children are safe."

"They're safe."

"Are they all safe?"

"What do you expect? You keep these girls waiting. You frighten them more than we do, because they know you're lying. Everything you say is a lie. Where are the ambassadors?"

"They'll soon be here. They'll talk to you."

"We won't believe them or you unless they have the code word."

"We are trying to find the code word."

The conversation went back and forth rapidly and as suddenly ceased. Ibrahim reappeared in the classroom.

He stood there, looking them over. He was angry with them. He had lost control because of Hannah.

The hostages were all in their places, and he paid no attention to the fact that changes had been made. They were in a way all the same to him.

"Why did she lock the door?" he asked. "Nobody else did. Why did she?"

"It happened this way," Zenia said. "We just close the door partway for modesty. You understand that. But she closed it all the way. This was different and Salah shouted at her. Then she locked the door. The rest followed."

"What's wrong with her?"

"Nothing."

"Then why doesn't she help like all of you so we can end this mission without further killing? One shot from outside and this would all be over. Is there something wrong with her?"

"She's religious. She's shy. She's ashamed. She's frightened. After all, what could she do in that room?" Zenia sounded sensible enough. "Nothing. It's the boy who got excited."

Ibrahim thought for a moment. "I could keep him down below and send up one of my other men. Is that what you want?"

"No," Ram said. "Salah was right. This girl is stupid. We're used to him and he understands us. It's all right. Don't blame him."

No one said anything but they looked at him with surprise. They were really frightened of the boy and his roving looks at their bodies.

"Everything is as before," Ibrahim said. "Let's keep it that way. They say the French ambassador is here and the Romanian ambassador has talked with our people in Damascus. Maybe the Israelis will show some sense for a change."

"I'm sure they will," Ram said. "Everything is changing. Could you tell us your demands? We'd all like to know. After all, we're waiting too."

Ibrahim was leaving, ignoring the question. He hesitated, then turned and faced the whole room. "I'll tell you. I want you to know we're not being unreasonable. You'll see why it's impossible to trust the Israelis. We've presented them with a simple schedule to follow. First and foremost, they must free twenty of our comrades whom they've captured and imprisoned."

"They've agreed," Ram said.

The schoolroom was tense with expectation and interest, and the girls who didn't understand English were hearing each word translated by those who did. Each phrase Ibrahim uttered released little sighs of whispering. Understanding passed in waves across the faces of the girls. Their longing for life fed on each word they heard, and even Hannah had turned over, not sitting up, just listening. Ram wondered if she had made any use of the toilet except to scream. It was hard to tell.

"They say they've agreed," Ibrahim said. "But what have they in fact done? Can you tell?"

"Only what we've heard," Ram said.

"Exactly. That's why the code word is so important."

Ram asked, "What's next, then?"

"The next step is for the French in Damascus to speak with a representative of the PLO, who will verify to the Israelis the terms in the letter and the names of the twenty comrades to be released. Once this is done and agreed on by the Israelis, the French government will order its ambassador to come to Asher. The Romanian ambassador will be informed by the PLO representative that the twenty must be flown to Nicosia, Cyprus or Damascus accompanied by the French ambassador and a member of the Red Cross. It must be a civilian aircraft. Now, that's not so hard. It's simple, isn't it? It guarantees the safety of all."

"It'll take some planning," Ram said. "Then what, what about you and the hostages here?"

"That's the second part of the affair," Ibrahim said. "It's the important part for us. We're willing to die but we're not maniacs. We want to live also. We want to live to see a Palestinian state here."

"That may take longer," Ram said. "But how do you get out safely and how are the hostages freed?"

"I see you want to live also."

"It's an old habit. You think I should change it?"

"I could be your friend, couldn't I? We're the kind of people who understand each other."

"Not if you hold a gun to my head."

"That's an accident. You can't hold us responsible for the accidents of life. Anyway, on the arrival of the prisoners in one of those three safe places, a code word would be passed back to the ambassador from Romania in Israel. He'll give us the code word by coming here and talking to us. Then we'll release half the hostages. The other half, my men and the Romanian ambassador would then depart in another aircraft. When we arrive in an Arab nation, in the capital of any one of them but preferably Damascus, the remaining hostages with us will be released."

There was a silence now in the schoolroom. Everybody was thinking of all that had to be done.

Zenia said, "That seems like a lot to be arranged by six P.M."

Ibrahim said, "It's very simple. Once the prisoners arrive—and this must be before six P.M., or else we blow up this building with everyone in it—the rest can take a little longer. But we can't believe anyone until we receive the code word which tells us this has really happened. They should all be there already but no code word comes."

Ram pretended to think things over. Then he said, "Governments take time to do anything."

Ibrahim just left. He spoke harshly over his shoulder. "All they need is the code word. Then we know everything is being done."

"I think they're trying," Ram called after him.

Ibrahim left without saying anything more. He spoke in a low and threatening voice to the boy before disappearing in the corridor.

The boy settled down on the floor, his back against the wall, his gun aimed and ready, resting as before on his knees. His young face was more hostile than earlier. He obviously blamed Ram for what his leader had said to him.

All the girls were sadder. It was a kind of general melancholy, and Hannah began to weep again. She crouched up against the wall, a knee raised, her arms folded across it and her face buried in her arms. Her thin back shook. None of the girls spoke to her. They blamed her for all their troubles although in fact her hysteria had finally brought out the truth of the position of the hostages, but no one wanted to know this kind of truth. Zenia went to her. She embraced her and comforted her. Her soothing voice, which the girl in fact could hardly understand since Zenia's Hebrew was minimal, nevertheless caressed the weeping, which finally stopped.

The usual restrained restlessness of twenty-seven lively girls finally returned, but over all a pall had gathered. It was composed of fright diluted with weariness. It seemed normal only because of the explosion of terror that had happened in the toilet.

Some of the girls began to eat and sip water from their canteens. Many had oranges and, one thing leading to the other, very soon they were all nibbling. Then they talked.

In the hallway the Arab boy opened one of the cans of sardines taken from the girls. He had some variety of Arab bread and dipped it into the oil in the can. He also had an Israeli canteen with water, which he drank.

Ram moved closer to Zenia's cot and sat there. He carried the paper bag in which Tamar had packed two sandwiches, an orange, a can of sardines the boy had overlooked, and a piece of packaged milk chocolate. He also had Tamar's flask and unscrewed the cap and took a long drink of water.

When Zenia returned she sat close to him and asked quietly, "Why did you want this terrible boy here? He frightens the girls with his eyes. I think he would like to rape and kill them all. At least, they think so."

"Perhaps." Ram didn't want to whisper, but he spoke as softly as he could, all the while looking at Hannah so that the Arab boy in the corridor would think it was of Hannah they spoke.

"Well?"

"Well," Ram said, "the other two Arabs seem like trained men with lots of experience. What do you think?"

"I suppose so."

"When the crisis comes, and it will, I prefer to have someone who is young, inexperienced and not used to killing."

She thought about it without agreeing. He offered her the food but all she took was a sip of water.

"What do you think?" she asked Ram. Her voice was very low and she didn't look at him.

"Not much."

When he didn't say anything else, she nudged him with her body. "Why do you say that?"

"The instructions are too complicated."

"You think the Israelis don't want to make the exchange?"

"Of course not. They may try. But they'll fail. Or they may pretend to try. Besides, there's the whole question of the code word, the tight time schedule. It would suit Damascus to pretend. Then, when everybody was dead, the Israelis would be at fault. There's no way to know what anybody is doing or wants to do. Ibrahim is uncertain. The only certain thing is the end. He fears that end. He will do it, but he fears it."

The bullhorn broke out. "We wish to make a reasonable request. We want to know that the hostages are all safe."

They heard the Arabs moving around talking. But there was no answer.

A young girl said, "Why don't they tell them we're all right?"

Zenia said, "I don't know."

"Why don't we ask them to tell them? Our parents are there."

"Let's not ask them anything yet."

The girl began to cry. "That stupid Hannah made all this trouble." The girl looked at Hannah with anger.

Hannah faced the bedroll and began to weep. "I was afraid."

"This is silly," Zenia said. "You have books, you have your Bible. You have each other. You have more than a lot of people all over the world. If your life is in danger, so is everybody's. If

220

you can't go anywhere you please, there are millions with this problem. There's nothing special about you unless you are brave and calm, courageous. Think of yourselves as an example for the world to look at. In this way you're stronger than the guns of the terrorists." To Ram, Zenia said, "I'm going to lie down."

He sat down on the floor while she stretched herself out. His head was close to hers as before.

Once when he was young, she was lying on his bed and he had sat on the floor, his head close to hers, and she kissed him and said, "Tell me a story, Ram."

Naturally, he began a story, which one he no longer remembered, but when he looked up, having watched her hand loosely hanging over the bedside as he spoke, he saw she was asleep. Every face has a secret and the magic was that he saw hers, then, and he was in it.

She was awake now, the story was different and somehow the secret he had once seen was gone.

Their faces were close enough and her deep brown eyes as always had little points of gold that appeared and disappeared as she blinked or moved her head a little. Her face was wrecked with age. It had at the same time traces of its youth. Of course, he thought, she is seeing the same in me, what I am and what I was when she left. He said, "A little before six the Israelis will take this place by storm. In that way they'll hope to save some of us."

"And the explosion?"

"It has to be set off by someone. If that someone is dead, there's no one to set it off."

She said, "I think the Israelis will try and make the exchange."

"It doesn't matter," he said. "It's too complicated."

"Is it time to hear your plan?"

"It's not much," he said. He leaned closer to her. "I'll close the door when the first shot rings out. The boy will fire through it as he rushes the door. By then, the girls on the right with Ruth will push over the steel filing cabinet. They'll push it in front of the door. As it falls, the girls on the left with my help will push over the filing cabinet on the other side. We'll do this in turn until all five are in front of the door. We'll lift some to be on top of the others. It won't be neat. But it'll block the door. The steel will help deflect the bullets. Meanwhile the desk will be pushed forward and jammed against the five steel cabinets."

"You may be dead by then. Most of us will be dead."

"This little plan," he said, "is not a solution to our problem. Like all real problems, the solution is to find some way to live through it."

"It's more like just another way to be killed."

He let a negligent glance take in the room. The girls had settled down into a kind of picnic, depressed but not sodden. "Well," he said, "it may work. At the first shot, those not working on the barricade drop to the floor against the walls. There'll be lots of firing. Perhaps grenades. Even if the building is blown up in part, this room may be still able to function. I want you to stand at the window and see that the girls go out one after another. As the barricade grows, the girls on the other side must crawl across to you. They're organized into groups of three, each with a leader. No one must use the center window, which is directly in line with the door. A lot of bullets will be coming through if that boy does his job. I have to assume that the Israelis finish off the other three terrorists in the first few moments. That has to be their plan."

"And the wounded and the dying and the dead?"

"Who knows? The Israelis, once they see the girls jumping out, will come up into this room, using ladders. We have to assume they'll be efficient at this. We'll have help. It's a gamble. But why not?"

"Why not?" she said.

"The raid will succeed or fail. But we must move the moment the first shot is fired."

Zenia said, "Closing the door is the worst. You'll be right in the line of fire. That door won't stop a single bullet."

"Would you like to do it?" he asked.

"I'm too slow and too frail."

"How about one of the girls? Which one would you pick for the job of closing the door?"

"Any one of them would be faster than you. But we can't ask them to do the most dangerous thing."

"How about me?" he asked.

"You're the only one left."

"You see," he explained, "how I was chosen. I want you to take your time, because we have time. This thing'll drag on up to the last moment, excuse and demand without end. You'll sit with the girls and tell them what they should do if a shot is fired. You can also say it's a last resort and so on. But I think it's pretty probable. The Israelis will have sharpshooters and the like. They have plenty of firepower. They can blast out the front door and the man there easily enough. I just hope it doesn't set off the explosion also. But I assume the explosive is wired and scattered around the base of the building, so if the terrorist below is wiped out, someone has to get down the stairs. The Israelis should be in before that happens."

"At least a few girls may escape," Zenia said. She sighed and lay on her back and looked up at the white ceiling.

He was about to move back to his own place on Tamar's bedroll when he heard himself saying, "Listen, Zenia, I want you to visit the farm. You must see it. It's been waiting for you fifty years."

"Of course," she said. "I'm in a mood to travel and visit before the time comes when I must end up somewhere."

A great relief came over Ram. He knew then that she had really come to see him above all. He said, "No matter what happens in this room, I want you not to leave the window. Help the girls get out. If someone is shot, let her lie. In the end the Israelis will come in unless this place is blown up and everybody is dead. You must see to it that they go one by one, quickly but without haste. This room will be full of bullets."

"Have you waited fifty years to give your Aunt Zenia orders?"

"I'm trying to enjoy my last chance."

"Did I always give you orders?"

"Never," he said. "All I remember is a strange land where I got up every morning and went to sleep every night. In between was the world and in that world you were there. You had an umbrella made of magic which you opened every day, and each time it opened I found myself in another place where I longed to be. I suppose for every child there is someone who is a god or goddess that way. But for me, I've always felt I had the only one who never failed to find something original in this world, which is after all utterly original in every way. However, we never know it until too late. Because of you, because it was you and you were the most original thing in it, I was always the first to discover what each day might be."

She caressed his hair briefly. "Yes," she said, "I suppose. Of course, that's how it seemed to you. To me, it was you who did exactly that for me."

This came as a surprise for him.

He looked around this room of hostages, whom now he loved more than any other people he had ever known in the world except his Aunt Zenia. Shlamath had been listening as best she could. Some of it she had heard and under her flaming hair her face opened to him as from across the divide of a mysterious unknown self that only she knew as hers. He felt it as his own too. He wanted to take her in his arms and kiss her, hold her, tell her they would all live to enjoy the miracle of simply being alive. But, of course, he could only smile.

Of all the smiles that flutter through the universe of the living and dead each one is of course unique, and so was this one and it was that way she caught it. Then she leaned back against the wall close to the steel filing cabinet.

He crawled back to his place and lay down and closed his eyes.

He asked himself if he had such choice–and he did not–if there was one person to save in the room, whom would he choose. He didn't answer this question even as he thought it, for his nature refused such a choice. But in the murmur of feeling from which the body is never free, her face rose as the chosen one. In this way love comes without reason or desire. It comes to fulfill the need not to be alone in the mystery of the self.

It was late afternoon and many exchanges took place between the megaphone and the bullhorn. Each one left the girls more upset. So little by little Zenia circulated, and in place of the conflict of those inhuman voices which never tried to understand, there was the plan. It excited them. They were young enough to feel the adventure of doing something.

At one point they asked Zenia to tell them something of her life but she said, "Your own lives are more interesting. Old stories, while sometimes wonderful, are like old stories everywhere. There is more pain and sadness in them than victory. So why listen? Make up your own stories by just living."

The truth of her life, Ram supposed, was beyond such easy telling.

One of the young girls dared to ask Zenia, "Do you have children or grandchildren, and where are they?"

"I once had a daughter," she said.

In this way, Ram knew that coming together is forever different from not ever having parted. Between was the endless dilemma of two separate lives. It was a terrible loss, yet it was a promise also. It told him they must survive and be with each other, for in the emptiness of the years between they would find themselves again in some other way. Of course, there was little hope they would have this chance. The endless changes and chances of existence had little concern for spirit, and it was in spirit, this conventional word that had to include everything that signified, that they had to live again as once they had, close to each other every day, a sort of living proof that a real world existed for creatures like themselves.

"My little daughter died in Leningrad in the war," Zenia said. "She really died of starvation."

That old grief suddenly became deeper than the grief and sadness they felt for themselves. It was a little touch of madness that clarified their fears. Now they knew why she felt her own life was less interesting than theirs.

"And you?" one of them asked Ram. It was little Gula, sitting closest to Zenia, no baby but a girl of thirteen, yet somehow more of a child than the others. "Where are your children?"

"Here in this room," Ram said. "Here we are and you're all my children and we have a plan to live on, don't we? Let's think of it. Let's make it happen, no matter how they plan outside."

Every once in a while, the tough short Arab would give Salah a break and the boy would come into the room while the other waited outside. Salah really was enjoying the sexual presence of these Israeli girls, most of whom, like himself, might have been Arab girls of Arab villages. It seemed to Ram, as the afternoon went on, that Salah had begun to feel something other than hatred for these girls. This time, he stopped in front of Ruth of the sullen plump face and they spoke for a while.

After he left, she turned to Zenia and said, "He said why don't we become Moslems too. We're like him, not like you two. 'You're Zionists,' he said. 'We're people of the desert.' "

"What did you tell him?" Zenia asked.

"I told him we're all refugees and here for the same reason, to live in peace, and that's what I'd like to do. Then he asked me do I live in a refugee camp? He was surprised when I said that we were refugees. My family is from Iraq. We had been chased out, although we had lived there as long as anyone can remember. He said it was the fault of the Jews in New York."

Ram laughed his New York laugh. "What did you say then?"

Ruth said proudly, "I told him that you and Dr. Mont were famous radicals who were friends of the Arabs as well as of the Israelis and that he was a boy who didn't know anything. So he left."

"Are we?" Ram asked Zenia.

"Hardly," she said.

"What are we then?"

"Who knows?"

"Listen, Ruth," Ram said, "when Adam and Eve tried to get back into the Garden of Eden, their way was blocked. Who blocked them?"

"The cherubim."

"What were their names?"

"They had none."

"Because they were habit and history. But Eve looked past them into Eden. She saw empty lots full of weeds."

The sullen-faced Ruth smiled her sullen smile of reluctant warmth. "You two are strange Jews," she said. "You believe in no God."

"How do you know?" Zenia asked.

"I just know. You look at each other. You never look up to see."

Shlamath couldn't wait to speak. Her light eager voice came running in as if winged like angels' feet. "Do you trust them, Ruth?"

"Of course," Ruth said.

"How much?"

"With my life."

"Well," Shlamath said, "so they trust us too. And we don't have to pray to them for help."

Ruth's full face grew morose and bitter. "You're just a Romanian anyway. Romanians don't believe in God. We're all very religious at our kibbutz. You just pretend, not to make trouble. For us, God is real and present all the time. He led us to Israel and he'll preserve us."

They all listened with respect and Shlamath blushed. Her fair face under her red hair bloomed with redness, and her eyes were brighter and more blue with sudden tears.

Ruth cried out, "I'm sorry, I'm very sorry. I'm just afraid. It makes me mean."

"Come here," Zenia said.

Ruth went to her and they sat together, embracing like friends or sisters rather than mother or daughter.

So she has come to love Ruth, Ram thought, as I have come

to love Shlamath. We love all these girls, yet we have chosen without choosing. He felt it would be a good thing for all there to keep their minds on their own salvation.

Ram said, "Who knows Immanuel Kant?"

No one knew. They looked at each other and then at Zenia but she gave no sign.

"Who is he?" Shlamath wanted to know.

"A German who lived in Königsberg in the eighteenth century. He lived all his life there, and all his life he explored the possibilities of what thought can do. One rainy day, wearing rubbers and carrying his umbrella, he walked along the cobbled streets. He was thinking of the nature of things. His mind went on an immense journey to the ends of every possible universe. Suddenly, he ran into a dog who barked at him and ran away. Well, said Kant to himself, it wasn't such a long journey after all."

"But what does it mean?" Hannah asked as the girls laughed a little or just smiled.

"That we're in this classroom in Asher and here we'll be until we ourselves get out of it."

16

The crisis came at ten minutes after five. Something was happening at the radio, and suddenly the terrorists increased the sound. There was a radio upstairs in the classroom toward the end of the corridor, just above the front door of the school, and there was another radio at the foot of the stairs facing the front door. The sound came up but never loud enough to be understood by the hostages.

Someone was flipping dials, somewhere there was a school Blaupunkt that picked up on one of its circuits music from Europe, from Vienna—could it be Vienna and, if Vienna, why *Wozzeck?* It was the wild chaos of all voices at all times in all places speaking, singing, playing music from everywhere and nowhere, mingled with noise not yet become music and music on its way to become noise. It was change with vengeance, accident with aimless intent and the pursuit of an answer, who knew to what. All then grew silent.

Now the voices of the terrorists unloosed in little gusts of whispers and one outburst of anger. It was the man at the gun downstairs. His voice was new to Ram and it shattered the air in a paroxysm of violence, until Ibrahim shouted to silence him.

There were steps all over, positions taken and finally, coming from below where he had been briefly, Ibrahim ascending as always two steps at a time, this time in a hurry.

They all watched as he bent over and whispered to Salah. The boy stood up and pointed his gun into the room. It had always been more or less pointing there. Still, with the day extending, the afternoon wearing on, the sun glaring in and then swinging west and away until at one time the hostages on one side of the room were crossed with bands of red and gold under which they ducked or turned away, a relaxation had taken over both captors and captives.

Suddenly this was gone. The boy was ready to shoot, although in fact nothing had happened in the schoolroom. By now Zenia had spoken to each girl in turn. She was at this moment not on her cot but as close to the far window as she could be, sitting there with charming little Gula. Gula was the youngest. She considered herself the pet of all the others, with special privileges, and her first privilege was that she was closest to the window through which, when the time came, if it ever came, the hostages would flee. Yet they were a good ten feet from it, according to the rule set down by Ibrahim.

Now Ibrahim stood in the doorway. He too had his Uzi pointing in.

Among the hostages suddenly attentive, their curiosity and fears crystallized by the coming on of the unusual, a sickening fear immediately spread around. Against it, Ram, who was wondering, just before all this began, when the right moment would come for him to cross over to the other side of the door which divided the room into its halves, stretched easily out on Tamar's blanket and closed his eyes.

"You," Ibrahim said. His voice commanded. He had, after all, a natural command in him and now it was flung into the room. "You, Mr. Mont. Come out."

Ram made himself get up without haste. There is a whirlpool nature to fear in a group, and it was spinning now among the girls. Zenia also rose.

"Not you," Ibrahim said. "I want him."

A casual look at her, and for the first time Ram saw alarm. It was quickly gone but it had appeared.

"Is anything wrong?" Zenia asked.

"Is anything right?" Ibrahim mocked her. The terrorists had killed when they first seized the schoolroom, yet all that afternoon, in fact ever since the incident with Hannah, they had ignored the hostages, who were as helpless as any people could be. All the attention had been to the outside, where from time to time information came from the bullhorn. It always came as progress, but it was the kind of progress in which, no matter what happened, the Romanian ambassador never appeared with the code word. "Nobody's to go to the toilet. Nobody's to move from their place. You understand? Salah has orders to shoot anyone who makes such a move. Is that clear?" Then he turned his hostility on Ram. "You, I told you to come here. Why aren't you here?"

Now the fear in the room was whirling about, sucking away the confidence that held them all in dangerous safety while the day folded layer after layer of sun and heat upon their room. They all went under at once. They didn't struggle but waited, as if drowning in fear were natural for hostages.

As Ram walked toward Ibrahim and his angry gun he passed Shlamath. She had been standing when the order came and she still stood, leader of the group on the left-hand side of the door, where the three steel filing cabinets were. She showed that something terrible was going to happen to Ram. By now he felt that way himself, but then the worst that could happen was to die and he had already experienced this fear so many times in his life that, without being used to it, being old had finally brought to an end his interest in the subject. It was in a way nothing. It didn't signify. It was dying as process that he didn't like the idea of. But the girl's face longed to hold him back and it took all her courage, all her strength, not to say something to him. So she looked it. But looks are in a way empty things. They can mean almost anything. Everything depends on the conditions in which the look finds itself, in a way expressing through the inadequate the definite that something else suggests. That something else was the secret relation that had all afternoon grown between these two. He had in fact, without being too aware of it, possessed her as his own and she had in a way done the same for him, just as Ruth and Zenia had chosen each other.

Ruth was on the other side of the door, sitting down with the two strong girls who would help her fling the steel filing cases across the door once he closed it. A quick look at her. She expected the worst. A strange creature, he thought, admirable in her definiteness and ability to react quickly and understand, yet always in every way without hope. Her sullenness, like the plumpness, almost the fat, that shrouded her body, hiding its real shape, was a perpetual sadness. It was this sadness she fed on in the form of food. On a day when few had eaten much of what was supposed to be just a lunch to be carried on their broken journey to the next kibbutz, it was Ruth who had eaten everything she had, then some of her friends' food too. Ram had given her his chocolate bar also.

Ram walked past Ibrahim into the corridor.

"To your right," Ibrahim said.

Ram walked down the corridor, which was the way they went to the toilet. All the classroom doors were open and he could see the desks, the chairs in each room. They had been pushed aside so that the windows were clear and easily reached. Most of the windows had been broken by the terrorists to make shooting from them easier.

"The last classroom on your left," Ibrahim said.

Ram walked into it. The short square Arab was standing to one side of the window, and when Ibrahim and Ram were in the room he went out. Ram heard his quick heavy steps run down the corridor to the front of the building.

"You can go to the window and look out," Ibrahim said.

Ram went over to it, standing there in full view for any to see. What he saw was the circle of little houses, their little gardens and beginning trees, touches of red, orange, yellow and blue of flowers, the first green of vegetable patches. What he saw was the village itself, and its fences. He saw nobody. Everyone outside was hidden from view, a difficult thing because the schoolhouse on its little hill, surrounded by its yards and lawns, dominated Asher. But he could see military trucks, jeeps and five tanks. The tanks were set, their guns trained on the schoolhouse. A soldier darted across in the distance from one building to another.

"What does it look like to you?" Ibrahim asked.

It was such a joy to look out and down on the village, a relief after all the time of having been forbidden. Ram answered without turning. "Why, it looks like a village called Asher."

Then he faced Ibrahim, whose gun now hung loosely and who stood there, just inside the room, leaning against the wall. He was smoking a cigarette. And he was smiling. This smile had no pleasure in it. It was the smile of a man who now felt he had nothing to smile about.

"The girls understand Arabic, don't they?"

"They listened, but you never made the radios loud enough."

"It wasn't much," Ibrahim said. "You want a cigarette?"

"I've forgotten how to smoke."

"It was just a general report. The whole world is waiting to see what's going to happen. Reporters are flying in from everywhere, but they can't get to this village. Some are here, of course. Everybody's waiting for six o'clock."

"Well, then?"

"Are you too old to feel afraid?"

"No," Ram said. "Just too old to show it."

It amused Ibrahim. "In another world, I would've enjoyed your company. That general report from Damascus at ten minutes after five was actually a code message to us. I would like you to know what it said."

Ram said nothing.

"I keep forgetting," Ibrahim observed after a long look at Ram. "You're experienced at things like this and perhaps even worse things. We know all about you. The Zionists would not call you a Zionist. Your biography has been broadcast. They consider you in your own country a radical of sorts. They even tried to jail you."

Ram said, "They never actually tried to kill me."

"Neither have I. I want you to do something for me. But

first, listen carefully. The message we actually received in the course of the general report from Damascus was that the Romanian ambassador has asked the PLO to extend the six o'clock deadline. It's been refused. The Israelis don't know it yet. They'll find out at five thirty."

"What's happened?"

"The first group of the twenty to be released is still sitting at Lod. Not a single one of those men is aboard the plane yet. The Romanian ambassador is still in Jerusalem. The French ambassador is here. He's supposed to be on that plane."

Ram said, "He could be in Lod in ten minutes by helicopter."

"He could. But the twenty we wanted released can't be in Damascus by six o'clock. There's no way."

"That's why they want an extension."

"I told you the extension hasn't been granted by Damascus."

"It could be granted by you."

"I'm under orders not to extend the time. No matter what, even if the twenty are on their way. Is that clear? The time has in fact run out."

"Technically," Ram said.

"Actually."

"I'd advise you to wait until six as you promised."

"I want to ask your opinion."

"I'm ready to give it."

Ram leaned against the wall, looking out of the window from time to time as they spoke. It was no surprise to him that the Israelis had failed to make the exchange which all day they had promised to carry out. At the same time, he wasn't sure it was intentional. It might just very well be they wanted assurances that, once the plane was in Damascus and the twenty captives free, orders would not be given for the building to be blown up. The Israelis would have gained nothing by the whole interchange. There was always one last unanswered question, after the last question was answered. There never was a way to get a real balance of forces in an exchange. Even temporary stability was only relative. He knew these arguments. They were as familiar as the senseless deaths that went on constantly in this world of terrorist politics. For hostages and passersby the threat and private death was a personal concentration camp.

Yet he found himself rather liking Ibrahim at the moment, feeling suddenly that this man so committed to what was a brutal mission of death was nevertheless in his own mind deeply committed to life. He wanted a way out. That was the reason for this meeting here in the empty classroom, with its chairs and desks thrown together in a heap against the wall and the way cleared for quick access to the windows.

"Do you really think they don't believe we'll blow this building up with everyone in it, including ourselves?"

"Some believe it. Some don't, I'd say."

"I want to convince them. But they must have our comrades whom they've promised to free en route to Damascus or Beirut or Nicosia or Cyprus before six o'clock. They must have the French ambassador aboard. They must have a representative from the Red Cross aboard. It must be a civilian plane."

Ram was careful now, very. He looked at this handsome man—well, more or less handsome. It was the thin mustache that gave him the dashing look, but it was a thoughtful face. It was thoughtful now, yet it was something else. He felt there was something else being asked, being sought for rather than asked, and he felt that he was in some way the experiment for the answer.

"You said they have a plane. What kind is it?" he asked.

"It's a TWA 747 and the American crew has volunteered. We insisted there be no Israeli pilots or staff aboard. They're just Israeli army, or agents."

"It wouldn't take much, then, to put the first part of the operation in motion. It couldn't be completed before six, but it could be begun."

"That's right. And this is my proposal." He paused, as people do, to emphasize what is already so emphatic it needs no further force. Yes, Ram thought, he wants me to believe something that he's not sure I already believe. Ram encouraged Ibrahim with a smile that waited to hear. "We'll send you out to the Israelis who have us surrounded. You can be the one to convince them they must make this move. If they make it before six, I'll postpone the explosion to give the Romanian ambassador the chance to get the code word and meet with us for part two of the interchange."

"Suppose Damascus refuses to give the Romanian ambassador the code word because six o'clock has passed. Isn't this what the Israelis have feared from the beginning?"

"Our delay of the explosion should convince them of our sincerity."

"That's true."

Ibrahim now walked into the room and stood openly at the window, his gun hanging down, just looking out at the same view that Ram saw. They were side by side. He knew the Israelis hidden from sight were looking at them. He saw all around the marvelous hills, taking on shadows, and the secret rich colors of the fading day. In the shadows there were fine purples. There were blues. There was lavender. There were hills running away and catastrophic gorges where wild rains had beaten their way down into ravines. Everywhere the vegetation of spring was out. Flower bunches like freckles of color dotted the hilly landscape.

Ibrahim said, "Galilee is beautiful. I was born in one of those high hill villages. I have cousins who live there." He stopped, he faced Ram. Up close Ram could see pockmarks on his cheek, and dried sweat. The eyes were friendly enough, but faces had no real meaning out of the context of action, Ram knew. He'd been through this all his life. It was hard to learn not to judge by the way people looked, especially those who were not part of some intimate circle of friends, and even there, the many betrayals of the McCarthy years had revealed completely that no one could be judged by how he or she simply looked or had lived in friendship. Trust, like love, or love as trust, was an act of faith. And even its betrayal was often in the end trust shaken and strengthened. There was no way out of living a thing through. Life didn't invent faces. Painters did that. Life set up complexities, whose meaning came out in actions rather than looks. Beauty, of course, was an easy remedy for disbelief, and as fatal as savage ugliness, if there was such a thing. So he ignored this friendly face in his own feeling but he smiled to show he was sympathetic to the problem, as he was, in fact.

"Tell me the truth," Ibrahim asked. "Do you think you could convince them?"

"I could try."

"If you couldn't, at least you wouldn't die. Believe me. You must believe it. Unless you succeed, this place goes up."

"I believe you."

"I'm sending you out with the message because I believe you want this exchange to go forward. I think they'll respect your judgment. I do. In any event, on the basis that in another world we two might like each other, you as an old man who has been in so many fights and lost so many like us . . . I'd like you to live if these damned Israelis stay stubborn and afraid to trust anyone and force us to act."

Ram looked out at the window. The afternoon was dying, like the time given to save the hostages. He knew they were both already dead, for the earth will turn and governments betray.

"It's now fifteen minutes after," Ibrahim said. "At five thirty, an army general is going to take over the bullhorn. He's going to explain that they intend to live up to their first acceptance but they need more time, one hour, two hours. He's not going to say that Damascus has already rejected his request for more time. He doesn't know we know it's been rejected. What do you say? Do you want to try? At least you'll live to remember I tried."

All the while Ram had been thinking, and he now felt he had seen through to the real question Ibrahim had in mind. He was convinced of it, so he turned to him and said, "It's useless to send me out with that message. I believe, once you refuse to give them any more time at five thirty, that the plane will be off in the next half hour. The Israelis are faced with the parents of these hostages. Governments fall if they sacrifice the children for twenty terrorists no one really cares about any more. Who wants them in prison? Only the government. It doesn't make sense. I'm absolutely convinced of it. Therefore, to prove it to you, I'd rather stay with the others and take my chance. It's really useless. I could never change their minds if they're prepared to sacrifice everyone. Nothing they can do will prevent your man from setting off the explosion. So their delay past six is really an execution of their own children. The parents out there will tear the government people apart if it happens. The Israelis control this situation. It's not the Olympics. It's not the Germans. It's the Israelis themselves with the power to give in or not. They say they are ready to. I simply believe, from my own experience in dealing with governments, that they have to delay until the very end. It's like a peace treaty. It's like anything else they must do. You can act when you're ready. Even when they're ready they find it hard to act. Too many must agree. But they will act when time forces them to. So I'll stay. It makes no difference. I believe they will start the exchange at the last minute."

Ibrahim walked away from the window. He stood by the door again.

"Well," he said. "You surprise me. You trust them more than I do."

"They'll give in. They have no choice."

"I suppose you wouldn't stay if you didn't believe it."

"I'm interested in life."

"I'm surprised you didn't tell us to send your aunt instead, or one of the children, with the message."

"Why should I?"

"People enjoy personal heroics. Look at us."

"Not me. I don't believe in them, although I've been forced to pretend, since others do."

"Well, back to your schoolroom. We'll see if you're right soon enough."

"Will you give them the time if at the last minute they do what in the end they must do and can't avoid doing?"

"Of course. I don't have any intention of dying here for no reason at all. But the time must be before six. We'll wait till six. I hope you're right."

"I'm certain. I believe in the cowardice and brutality of all governments, even those I'm compelled to create."

"Back to the schoolroom, then," Ibrahim said. "We'll learn together."

Ram walked out into the hall. He had a sick feeling which he hoped didn't show. He knew he had not taken a chance but in fact had simply created an impression. He knew that if he had accepted, Ibrahim would then have been convinced there was no hope, and without hope there would be no chance for delay. In Ram's mind, he believed that the Israelis would never get any exchange started. At some moment before six they would attack, and he wanted to be in the classroom then. But the sickness he felt, which he concealed, that sick retching peristalsis of emotion in his guts, told him he was giving up a chance to walk away from it. At the same time his mind rejected his stomach and bowels. His mind told him that Ibrahim needed this tiny fragment of confidence to hold open some solution and wait.

Ram looked at everything. He saw down the stairs the gunman waiting, and he knew one big blast of machine guns through the door would finish him off. He knew that snipers would take out the other two terrorists. Only the boy was safe in the corridor. He was the one to block.

With the savage clarity of fatal choices, Ram gambled and accepted the fact that three of the terrorists were already dead. He knew it all and he knew nothing. It was like all the false choices he had faced during his life. Only those who had decided to yield went through the pretense of doubt. He had seceded from doubt. Ram hoped he had appeared confident. He was confident, but only of the opposite of all he had said to Ibrahim.

When he reappeared in the doorway, a little cry of welcome relief, of smiles, greeted him.

Suddenly Ibrahim touched Ram's shoulder and Ram halted while Ibrahim leaned close. Ram could smell the man's breath. Some spice he didn't recognize discolored it. But the face showed self-satisfaction and a sense of triumph also. Ibrahim whispered, "I just want you to know if you had accepted and said you'd take the message, I wouldn't have let you go. I'm no fool, you know."

Ram said, "I thought it was a genuine offer. You came into my life as an enemy. You then said we might be friends."

Still close to Ram, still whispering, Ibrahim surveyed his classroom of, for the moment, happy hostages. "They're happy to see you. They thought I might kill you. They don't know of our friendship. I'd like to save your life. I think we could be friends. We could talk. We could see each other. You're so old you could almost be my grandfather. I would trust you. But you see now that I don't have much hope. Suppose you went with the message, could I, who so doubt myself, trust someone who thought so little of himself as to abandon these children and this old woman to their fate? Never."

"You mean, you wanted to find out if you could trust me to die with the others?"

"And with myself."

Ram spoke loudly. "The exchange will go through."

"I'll wait," Ibrahim said, and turned away, pausing only to say, "From now on, no one is to go to the toilet. Stay where you are."

He disappeared down the corridor and Ram was alone in the doorway. It was his last chance and he made the move. He joined Ruth and her group on the side where the door swung on its hinges. He flopped down on a bedroll and sat with his back against the wall. Everyone was looking at him. They needed an answer. They needed a way and he said as casually as he could, "He wanted to be sure that I thought as we all do that the government would make the exchange. He too believes it'll be at the last moment. I believe that also. We're all ready now to wait for that moment we've been preparing for all afternoon."

Alone himself, with himself, he wondered briefly if Ibrahim's last words had been the truth or just another fiction in the many of that day and his life. He would never know, of course. Now, the next big moment would be five thirty, the demand, the refusal, and the waiting until six.

Across the invisible dividing line, he saw Shlamath. Suddenly she turned her face away and crouched down on the bedroll there. She had tears in her eyes. Her face spoke to him with truth as his did to hers. They trusted each other in the sudden exchange which, meaningless in general as an event, is somehow more total than any profound abstract truth. It was a release. It was the end of the tyranny of the self, the spirit, the soul, that accident of evolution which like any other changing constellation of matter had finally come up through so many billions of years with this fantasy of an I.

Just before five thirty, Ibrahim returned to the schoolroom.

Up to then there had been scurrying movements on the floor below. Ram listened to the whisperings, silences, and a few muffled commands.

In the winter months up at Fishwoods Road farm, the pretty little field mice came into the house, and in the winter silence of deep night, when Ram lay in the downstairs bedroom, after the furnace rumbled to a halt and the inner silence matched the weight of winter and snow outside, he used to wait for sleep and listen to the field mice scurrying around. Like bats they could always find a way in but, unlike bats, they were hard to get out again. When Ram first went up to live on the old farm, sometimes for a month or two and once the whole year round, he used to catch these little white-footed mice with their golden brown fur in traps that killed them. He spread food poisoned with warfarin that sent them dying of thirst to find water outside. They devoured this poison food by the pound. But in recent years he caught them in cagelike traps and then carried them out in the morning, across the snowy fields to the pine plantation. Here he set them free and watched them run for cover. It wasn't the safest place for them, but they were out there running.

In a way, he no longer tried to defend the house in any particular way against the invasion of natural things, and each year the wildflowers came closer, as did the woodchucks, the rabbits, the deer, but Ann kept some lawn free, and the fields in condition for her cattle. He had worked out a kind of compromise. He lived there as best he could and let time go by.

The terrorists moving quickly about, stopping, considering, had other plans in mind for him and the rest of the hostages.

Everybody thought the same thing but no one said it. The explosives which had been laid out around the inner base of the schoolhouse were being checked.

Now, Ibrahim was in the room with his hostages. Having made certain preparations, he was ready to try something different.

He has that different look about him, thought Ram. He has dropped the hardness of the brutal terrorist, and there he is with a soft face, with a look so common in that room of young people, helpless but ready to be helped.

"The whole world is listening," Ibrahim said. "They're all hearing about our problem."

But he was their problem. I could tell him, Ram thought, that to begin with it's the same old world. Does he think he's changed it by descending on Asher with three other terrorists, his guns, his grenades and a few explosives? There are wars enough, some going on, some about to. There are disasters in full motion from earthquakes through floods, fires, murders, passions rummaging through every life. Meanwhile, the mesons fall. Meanwhile, the atom bombs lie in wait while the plants that spawn them leak waste throughout the earth. It's all going on as it always does.

Ibrahim went on, "I must tell you the whole world wants our problem to come to an end. The Pope himself has sent a message. Presidents have offered their aid. The world is condemning the Israelis for saying they are making the exchange when they haven't even begun to take the first step."

Shlamath spoke up, surprising everyone else if not Ram. In

general, the girls had been afraid to confront the terrorists, but even without realizing it, they had noticed the change in Ibrahim's attitude. "If the whole world's listening, they know what you want them to know. What good is it to kill us and yourself?"

Instead of being angry, he challenged her. "What choice do we have?"

"You can only find out if you live."

All at once then the girls began to speak up. They were all in one way or another saying the same thing. They had been so obedient and silent in their fears, except in the case of Hannah, and she like a secret sin had been hiding among them all that day. Now these girls began as if this schoolroom were really a class and Ibrahim their teacher.

"If we die, what good happens?"

"We too want peace."

"We're not born to die like this."

"How can we be friends, if you don't offer us your friendship and only threaten to annihilate us?"

Their questions flew about Ibrahim, darting at him to sting like paper wasps from a broken nest. Ram saw clearly that Ibrahim was encouraging them with his silence.

The questions hummed from everywhere in the warm room, luminous with reflected light from the sky, which still caught the sun from behind its shield of distant mountains.

"All of us are refugees who once lived in countries under your power."

"You oppressed us."

"Did you have your own country under the Turks or the Jordanians or the English?"

Ibrahim seemed bewildered. A sly man, thought Ram. He had given up his early brutality toward them, his harshness and easy command. He had asked a human question, and now every girl was alive, all except Ruth, who had no question she would trust this man with.

"Why don't you try to work it out with us?"

243

"If you're desperate, so are we."

"Yes, yes . . ."

Their yeses ran on around him, stinging him from every side. Ram watched it all as a game in which the loser lost life and not just a chance to play again. Life rippled in every face, in every gesture. Without leaving their places they were all in motion, and the questions darted in and out.

"All we want to do is live here and be human."

"This land is here for all of us."

"Let's forget the past and begin again."

"Wait, wait," Ibrahim cried out as if defeated. "One at a time."

They couldn't wait. Each moment of freedom expanded, doubled, and now there was a kind of revolution. They felt the touch of freedom again. They glowed with it. They hoped.

This was Ibrahim's awaited moment and he shouted at them. He actually waved his gun at them, swinging it around on its strap. It surprised them. They were hostages once again.

"I didn't come here to argue with you. I came here to tell you we're close to the end. Your government is unreasonable. I've sworn to carry out my orders and I will. I'm not a tyrant. I'm not a Nazi. I want to work this out."

"Then do." All the voices began again. "We'll help."

"No more talk," he said. "No more. Just listen."

He looked desperate to Ram. In fact he was in a desperate situation, since the Israelis controlled whether he lived or died unless he chose to surrender. Even if he considered surrender, his fellow terrorists might have other notions. Yet in a strange way, beneath his difficult choice, he seemed amused. It could be amusement. It could even be self-amusement. Ibrahim might be exceptional in more ways than one, and Ram felt a sudden sympathy with him who was now launched, as Ram himself had been launched so often in his life, on causes that somehow once begun became unexpected worlds so changed as to be revelations undesired and yet to be endured and lived through.

Salah, the boy with the gun, didn't know what to make of

this sudden outburst of democracy in the room of terror and discipline where he had reigned as king. He couldn't shoot. He had nothing to do. The argument was in all languages, Hebrew, Arabic, English. He didn't know what to make of it. He watched his leader for some sign and received none.

The room was still and attentive again.

Ibrahim now faced Ram. "I told you what's going to happen. I want to help, the way we spoke. As soon as we hear from them and I reply, I want someone to speak for the hostages. That bullhorn wants to know if we've done you any harm. They haven't asked to hear what you think. I want them to hear. Let the whole world hear what you think. Is there anyone here in this room who thinks it's wrong for the exchange to go on, lives for lives?"

No one answered.

"I want someone to speak for all of you and tell them what you feel. One of you girls," he said, looking them over. "Who's the smartest one here?"

"I am," said Zenia. "I'm also the oldest. It's always hard for people to understand each other. I've lived through this a hundred times in peace and war." Meanwhile she moved forward toward him. "You think you're the only one who ever found himself in an awkward position? Awkward is the position. I'll make them understand they must act at once. Let me speak to them."

Ibrahim looked at his wristwatch. "I thought one of their own girls would be better." He surveyed the hostages.

Whoever Ibrahim chose would die. Ibrahim didn't know this. He thought he was choosing someone to live, to help them all live.

"I think," Zenia said, "they'll pay more attention to my arguments than they would to a frightened young girl. Let's go."

She took it for granted to convince him that he had already agreed. She had lived a long time in an uncertain society and knew the rules of certainty. She exchanged one look with Ram and it went back to their earliest days, her left brow arched high, a hand to her hair. It called up the secret meanings he had shared with her. It told him not to interfere. She didn't want Ibrahim to hesitate, to think, for then he would choose one of the girls.

The terrorist said, "You." He pointed to the redheaded girl. "You're smart. You know how to talk. What you said was true."

"Let me try first," Zenia said.

She knew that whoever was with Ibrahim was going to die. She had made her choice and her look had warned Ram to keep silent. She had given him an order, a command, she had spoken with love for him and the girls in this room, and she wanted no interference. After all these years, after so much history and the waywardness of time, they were together and it was coming to an end. At any moment in Ram's whole life since Zenia had left on the great ship, if he had been granted any wish, it would be the wish to see Zenia once more. So it had happened and it was now over. He kept quiet. She had in effect said it's no use living to see each other if these girls die.

There was Shlamath standing up. She wanted to be the one to speak, this girl with her red hair, her slim athletic body and lively face, made like some marvelous work of art of flesh and bones and mind, or of biological wire by some casual artist of the times who sketched in glittering red-gold wire shapes which once could only be made from stone.

To go out with Ibrahim was to die. Ram was now certain that while the talk of postponement went on, the Israelis would attack.

Zenia started to walk past Ibrahim as if all had been settled. "I'll do it right," she said. "I want there to be an exchange. I know what has to be said. I'll say it."

Ram was sitting close to Ruth and the two girls who would help with the steel cabinets on their side. Across from him, close to their cabinets and the door, was Shlamath and her two aides, one a small stocky girl with very black hair and a strangely remote face, as if in constant dreaming. The other girl was tall, perhaps sixteen, womanlike in figure and strength, a sturdy girl who spoke no English but had explained that she worked in the fields of their settlement driving tractors and could also shoot a gun. Shlamath was proud to be chosen and showed it.

Everybody was quiet watching this little drama. They understood everything but the ultimate meaning, that the end would happen soon, that whoever left with Ibrahim would die. There was Zenia. Her age in spite of her lively walk, her talk, had become ancient. She was flying away from him at an enormous rate. She would leave the room. The guns would go off. He would slam the door and their room like a spaceship would roar off in a rage of bullets and action while everything else would be outside on the earth they left behind. So Zenia was already growing older and older. Her youth was more alive in his memory than in her living body, in her face, in her stride.

Ram kept his silence. He listened to it as he had once before in London listened to the pain which flowered with lifelessness in his body. He kept silent. He felt he was helping end the meaning of his life, which had begun with a kind of transcendent flourish when the call had come through from Jerusalem to the farm on Fishwoods Road.

He even had contempt for his desire to go with Zenia. In fact, he had no choice and it was only a weakness of his spirit to think he had some kind of choice. He had no choice.

He kept quiet. She knew that he knew. He knew what she knew. The vacuum of the years, his other life, like hers, which they had lived apart, would remain separate.

A sudden turn of Zenia's head. The frizzled short whiteness of her hair bloomed out in the long black shower it had once been, a flicker, and gone. He couldn't see her face. It was that other face in her cabin, before the ship sailed into the other life he could never know, which now reappeared to offer life and parting.

Just as she was about to walk through the doorway into the corridor where Salah waited with his Uzi ready, Ibrahim said, "Wait. It's no use your way, Dr. Mont. They don't care about old people out there. They'll only care if one of their own talks.

You and your nephew don't count. You're nothing to them. You're like us. You're not even their own kind of people. You," he went on bitterly, "you're not even a Zionist."

"I am now," Zenia said.

He laughed at her. "You're just angry. I know all about you. While we waited here and listened to those Israeli lies, they filled time by telling us about you and about him. I don't want you." He faced Shlamath. "You, what's your name?"

"Shlamath."

"You're smart. They'll listen to you. They don't seem to hear me. But when they hear you, then all the parents and friends, all the relatives of these girls will tear those officials apart if they don't go on with the exchange before the time runs out. Come along."

"I can reason with them," Zenia said.

"They don't want to hear reasons. She may make them feel something." He looked around with a kind of sudden fright at what would certainly happen. "I want them to know you're all alive and want to be saved." He turned to Zenia. "Go back."

She hesitated, wanting to make one more effort to save the girl, and Ibrahim hesitated again.

The bullhorn erupted with electric madness. "We have," the unreasonable reasonable voice began, "an important request to make."

"It's five thirty," Ibrahim said to Ram. "You see, it's begun. Now, I'll see if you're right." He took Zenia by the arm and swung her back and out of the way. But she was too old for that kind of movement and started to fall. A young girl jumped up and caught her, steadied her.

Shlamath shouted at him, "Watch out. She's an old lady. Are you crazy?"

"I'm sorry," he said. "Let's go."

He commanded the young boy, and he and the young girl both went out, Shlamath in front of him, and neither looked back as they disappeared out of sight into the corridor, this time on their way to the front room from which the megaphone answered the bullhorn, which now began again to ask for a conference.

The bullhorn began without any haste in its flow of words. "The exchange is in process as agreed upon. However, we have run into certain technical details and would like a short extension of time."

There was no answer to this.

Once again then the bullhorn tried. "We have been unable to get the code word through the Romanian ambassador. Nevertheless, we're prepared to let the plane with the twenty prisoners leave for Damascus. In return, we want your agreement to extend the time past six o'clock."

Now the megaphone answered. "Only when the plane arrives in Damascus with the French ambassador will the Romanian ambassador get the code word from Damascus."

Ruth was close by Ram and she asked with a breathless quiet, "We have to wait till Shlamath comes back? I mean, if the shooting starts?"

"Well," he said.

Her dark eyes sought the glance that would freeze her heart. "I couldn't," she said. She hardly sounded these dreadful words. She meant to say it but she formed the words without letting them breathe through. She knew the answer, and now she knew what had happened. She looked for some help, something, anything, across the diagonal of the schoolroom but saw at once, as Zenia watched them, that Zenia knew also. One wild look then around the room of girls, all listening to the dialogue between the megaphone and bullhorn. Then Ruth looked no more. She took Ram's hand in hers. She pressed his hand. She told him she would do what had to be done. Then like any true heroine she looked with hatred at the boy listening in the corridor. She was ready to kill him.

But then he was quite ready, perhaps even looking forward to the heroism of killing her.

The bullhorn began again. "We'd like to explain the reason

for the delay. It's only a slight delay. Otherwise all is proceeding exactly as we agreed."

Ibrahim surprised the bullhorn now, the way he had planned it. "One of the young women here with me would like to speak with you."

Stupidly, the bullhorn asked, "What did you say?"

Clear, girlishly clear, in spite of the effort to speak loudly and be heard, this new voice flowered among the memory of those dead dialogues like the coming on of spring itself. Shlamath spoke without fear, without trembling, the clarity of her own self. "Listen," she said. "I'm speaking for all the hostages. I'm Shlamath. Do you know how we've been waiting for you? Do you understand? We're waiting and we're ready."

She said it in Hebrew, she said it in Arabic, she said it in English.

It was strange how each time she repeated her message, the girls listening heard in a different tongue but in that same lively voice that the time when they would have to defend themselves was there.

"Are you all ready?" Ram asked. Little Hebrew ripples repeated his question, and he looked around and saw them ready, three girls at the steel desk, Shlamath's two helpers close by their cabinets, Ruth and her two close to theirs, the girls on the wrong side of the room, already sliding down to be low against the wall, the girls behind Zenia close to their wall, crouched ready to take their turn at the window of escape, the middle window empty, a shard of broken glass protruding from its lower frame.

The terrorists felt safe at their windows with the hostages inside guarded by one who couldn't be touched by an outside bullet. That boy was their guarantee. Nevertheless, the Israelis had to hope they could get in and take him before he killed all the hostages. At some high meeting they had sat around and figured the time and hoped for the best statistic in their favor. In the end they had decided to rush the building.

It had to be any moment now.

"We want you to make the exchange," Shlamath said. "We

want to live and we know we shall. This man Ibrahim is telling the truth. He'll wait if you really do what he asks. We want you to work with him. We want you to do your best."

It's impossible, Ram thought, she sounds like Zenia.

"Otherwise, we all die." Shlamath said this without fear, without her voice shaking. Then in a sudden resolution, an overflow of confidence and courage, she cried out louder than before, shouting through the megaphone, "We don't intend to die. We're ready. All of us!"

When she stopped the bullhorn answered. "You must believe and trust us. We have nothing but your safety and lives in our minds. We're prepared to save you. Don't lose hope. Be ready."

"Ready," Ram said again.

The room stiffened as runners do before they leap into action.

"I believe you," Shlamath said, "but we—"

Her voice was wrenched out of the megaphone.

Now Ibrahim's voice raged out of the megaphone. He could hardly shout clearly. He was yelling through it with all his strength. "Liars. You're lying to her and all of us. I know you're lying. I know that Damascus has refused to give you any more time. Tell me the truth. Then we all can live. Keep lying and I swear to you, we die. I—"

Ram knew it at the same time Ibrahim did.

Machine guns chattered suddenly in a fury of small explosions.

Ram flung himself against the door, slammed it shut, letting himself fall as he went across.

The corridor Uzi went off, shattering its way through the door in a spread of bullets and splintered wood. Something on the ceiling broke and fell in a puff of dust.

Even as Ram was falling, still falling as the door closed and the bullets ripped through, the first steel cabinet from Ruth's side slammed down behind the door in a loud crash. Its file doors opened and paper scattered on Ram.

Twisting away, still lying on the floor, he had one wild look around. All the girls on the floor against the walls, Zenia standing at the window, little Gula just disappearing out. One. Another girl was scrambling, a third crouched waiting.

Below, the building shook and shook up its dice of bullets around its concrete walls. Everything was smashing below. A whole battery of machine guns was pouring its bullets in without pause. That overwhelming assembly of explosion there absorbed all sounds. If someone else fired a gun in any room, it couldn't be heard. Only Salah's gun sent little fast bursts through the door, where now the second and third steel cabinets had been rammed over, piled one on the other in disarray.

Still lying there, Ram pushed one up, then leaned against it, trying to keep his head below the barricade as the fourth and fifth steel cabinets were shoved or tossed in a jumble before the door. He slid out of the way and helped the three girls from Zenia's side push the steel desk up against the cabinets.

Below, the machine guns still poured fire in.

Salah lunged against the door, fired through it, and the schoolroom caught bullets on its walls, high above the girls. Bullets careened off the ceiling.

The waist-high barricade against the door was in place and now the girls on Ruth's side came crawling across the room to join Zenia, all but two. Then one of them crawled, crying with pain, but crawling nevertheless.

Cries and shouts of men's voices all around the building.

All the guns were silent except Salah's.

In the crush of the barricade, one steel cabinet dislodged and slid under the table.

Ram crouched near it, started to pull it free so he could fling it against the door. It was beyond his strength. He saw Hannah break free from the line of girls, one after another going out of the far window. He saw Hannah screaming with death in her voice and wild with flight in her long legs and flying arms, scramble to the middle window and then go limp and loose as one of Salah's bullets hit her. Or two. Or three.

The muzzle of Salah's gun was shoved high through the door. It fired.

Struggling to lift the steel cabinet, whose weight was heavier than the whole earth at the moment, Ram found it moving easily as Ruth was beside him, and they both flung it against the door, where it rammed against the now silent gun.

Ram collapsed on the floor. There was roaring in his ears louder than all the guns. It was like Niagara Falls, which he had once heard as a child. It buffeted and roared in the nerves. Through the roar he knew that the guns had ceased firing. Through the roar he heard the shouts of the girls, he heard their joy, he heard the Israeli soldier voices. "Get out," he heard his own voice saying to Ruth. He tried to look at her. It was hard to see her. There were dark rings in his eyes, dark blots took over in sudden eclipses but in between he saw Ruth stagger over to the wall. Saw her sit down against it. Her neck was red. Her shoulders were red. Her blouse was red. He crawled toward her. He thought he said, "Ruth."

He crawled. It was taking forever to reach Ruth and he looked through the blots of black around and saw Hannah's body tumbled from its straddle into the room and the face of an Israeli soldier.

Outside Israeli voices.

Inside Israeli voices.

Zenia was sitting on the cot. There were still girls there, jumping around, leaping, crying out their names. There were men coming through the windows.

He was close to Ruth, who was slouched against the wall wearing a short red veil that dripped color from her throat, and when he touched her, her head lolled to her side and he saw that a bullet had severed her throat. She was dead in her thickening cape of blood. He tried to hold her.

He was standing up then. His ears were so loud if people talked to him—were they talking?—he didn't hear their voices. The whole flood of noise was in his head, pouring and pouring.

His mind was cool but his heart was mad.

Was it over?

Covered with Ruth's blood and death on his face, Ram collapsed. His knees gave way. He simply lost his balance and vertigo corrupted his brain, breathless for oxygen, and he went down as all the while he tried to keep his balance and stand. He wanted to stand but he was going down, and there he lay beside the dead girl. That's Ruth, his last thoughts recited as they faded. That's Shlamath. Where's Zenia?

Then he came into a world of joy and shouting, of girls shouting everywhere and the voices of soldiers. Zenia was beside him, looking at him. There was horror everywhere and mostly in her voice as she spoke to him. She was speaking to him. "I didn't come back from the dead to see you die."

There were young girls everywhere in the room. They ran after their voices, penetrated the commands, calling from the windows, waving. Those who had escaped were fighting their way back in as armed young soldiers pulled the barricade apart and the room filled from outside pouring in through the corridor now. Here were the living all escaped from history to play again and forever their natures, their hopes, their grief, their joy, their fate.

Ram lay there without strength, listening to those outside him and living within with the death of Ruth, of Shlamath, of himself having returned once too often from the dead to find his Aunt Zenia, who had come from the grave of memory.

He asked himself, he was like that in that old mood of those days around the table in the dining room where Harry flicked the coins from one stiff wigwam of napkin to another. In those days they asked these questions. It was so common an occurrence, and so they spoke of anything, asking each other questions. Am I dying again? At last, perhaps. Is it too soon? Have Zenia and I met yet as I longed for forever?

He was already saying it aloud for her. Hands sought out his wounds, touching him lightly while Ruth's blood dried on his hands, his chest, his face where he had bent to kiss her. "Where are you wounded?" Zenia asked.

"I'm not," he said. "It's everybody's blood, but not my own."

And he got up.

They both stood up.

They held hands in the empty lots of memory.

17

It was a long day of sunshine and despair, for they were burying their dead.

"Come with me," Shlamath said. "We'll walk under the pear trees."

She just wanted to be alone with me when we said good-bye.

"One day," she told me, "I'll see you in America."

"One day," I said, "I'll meet you again. Not here. In Asher."

Here was closer to the sea, here anemones grew violet or scarlet bright, here a gust of rain had blown in while they wept over their dead. Later, the mourners stormed the automobile of the prime minister. They beat on the closed windows of the car and tried to jump on the hood. His security men and soldiers kept the shouting, biblical voices away. The voices wanted vengeance. Two quick air strikes had already bombed Palestinian guerrilla bases, or armed refugee camps across the borders. These pious Jews wanted an eye for an eye, but Shlamath was not like that in any way. She seemed to be a hostage herself in this village of Orthodox belief.

"She's a free soul," my Aunt Zenia had said. More and more Zenia sounded like someone walking in the Bronx Zoo half a century ago, or around the lake, or in the Botanical Gardens. She breathed the sea-hill airs, she saw a black snake wriggle away, she cried out, "Asphodels."

Shlamath and I walked under the pear trees. I wanted her

to tell me what had happened when Ibrahim seized the megaphone from her and began to yell at the maddening bullhorn whose lies he had endured all that day of negotiation.

"Just tell me how it happened there," I asked her. "You were speaking through the megaphone. We heard you. You stopped as if your voice had been torn away."

"Outrage," she said. "He was outraged. He grabbed the megaphone from me. He was very angry, not with me, not with any of us, but with those outside. You know, by then it had changed. There were those inside and that included him. And there were those outside. And outside was Jerusalem. And Damascus. He said, 'They don't care who dies. Not you. Not me. They just can't agree with each other.'"

She stopped then and looked up into the blossom-heavy pear trees. The ground was thick with a weedy growth which soon would be plowed under as fertilizer. The air was heavy with bees and with the fragmented sunlight into which each flowering tree had dipped its branches. There were flowers everywhere. The morning rain still dripped, collecting new springs from the higher hills, and even bare rocks were covered with wild geranium. A quick heavy gust of many rains all that morning had helped bury the dead in their simple coffins.

"You see," Shlamath said, "it was lucky I went. Zenia would've died."

Her face was always so lively, so ready with every motion of her mind. Her red hair like the leaves of autumn was never still, always finding some little current of air to move with. She took my arm. She let go again.

"I was the sacrifice," she said. "Yet I lived and Ruth died."

I followed her out of the orchard up a small hill. It was spring and the same old gods were at work remaking the earth as was their custom and habit. Dots of flowers found life from under the damp ledges of breaking stone. There we stood to watch the sea. We knew the borders were heavy with soldiers. We could see far out the gunboats of the navy sweeping up toward the Lebanese coastline. The human race drifted through this world like a

257

cloud of radioactive dust, bringing death and the surprise of everlasting change. "Tell me," I asked her again.

"So much went on," she said. "Ibrahim yelled at them, 'Tell me the truth.' You're always yelling in a megaphone. Even if you're not angry, it makes you angry because you find yourself yelling as if you're angry. But he was also angry and he yelled, 'Tell me the truth. Then we all can live. Keep lying and I swear to you, we die.' Then all the guns went off at the same time on some signal. The snipers hit him."

"There were two aiming at the window," I told her. "That's how they explained it to me. They both shot as the machine guns smashed everything behind the front door. They killed the other Arab, that little short square man with the hard and angry face."

"Ibrahim fell," she said. "He went down, falling backwards. The whole building shook with the shooting. I heard that boy who got away shooting through the door. I heard it slam as the first shot went off. I knew what was happening there. I was just about a foot away from the window. When Ibrahim grabbed the megaphone, he pushed me aside and there he was alone, just in front, yelling out at them when the bullets went off. He fell past me. His face went right by me as he fell, and the Uzi swung on its strap. The megaphone went up and hit the ceiling."

"Did you see his face before you jumped?"

"His face was alive yet. He tried to say something to me, but there was blood and bone on his cheek and blood in his hair. I just then thought *jump* and out I went, head first through the window. It was the only way."

I had spoken with the officer who led the attack on the front door. Their barrage of machine guns had torn the door apart and destroyed the Arab waiting to set off the charges.

This young Israeli officer's name was David, and on the night of liberation Fred brought him in to see me.

I was half asleep, having been examined and explored and rejected for dying. "You'll live," the doctor said. Zenia stood there with him. "Your pressure is up but going down. This will help."

He was a middle-aged man, very physical and athletic, and he was a soldier or had been or, like most Israelis, was still a soldier and civilian at the same time. He excused himself. "I didn't have a chance to shave. I'm one of those men who has to shave twice a day."

"Why don't you grow a beard?" I thought that would be a pleasant thing to say.

I was feeling fine by then, just sleepy, and I had sent Fred to find the officer who had led the attack and was there when Shlamath came flying out of the window.

It was then Fred came in with David, who shook hands and hurried to say, "Call me Dov."

"Tell me, Dov, what did you see?"

"We thought they had thrown a dead girl out of the window. That's the way she came out: as if flung out head first, her hands loose. It was extraordinary. And all the while that shooting went on inside." The very idea of what-might-have-been excited him again. He was tall, somewhat thin, somewhat handsome and he liked the look of himself. He had very thick brows, very dark eyes, and he looked out at the world with astonishment and disbelief. "Do you mind if I smoke? I can't understand how that boy got away. We've got patrols out everywhere."

"He must be back in Lebanon by now."

"I doubt it," Dov said. "It's a hard five miles. We're all over it."

He lighted a cigarette and smoked, first one long inhale and then another. Then he put the cigarette out. "Actually I've stopped smoking. Anyway, we knew or thought we knew that all the hostages were in that side room. They were. But here this girl came flying out. I thought there would be another and another as the bullets went off inside. Our first men were already storming through the door and here she came and then she did the incredible thing. She seemed to rearrange herself as she fell and we saw that this girl was alive and a gymnast of some kind for she took a turn, her knees close up to her chest, and then she was ready when she hit the ground, taking it at a run. Meanwhile, we held fire, watching the window, not knowing what would happen next. She ran this way and that like someone dodging fire although no one fired at her." He couldn't believe it still. "She landed like a paratrooper, took the roll, and was off running."

I smiled at him although I knew if the young girls hadn't saved themselves, the attack would have guaranteed the death of all the hostages. But none of this mattered any more. Ruth was dead. Shlamath was alive. Hannah was dead. The janitor was dead. Three Arabs were dead and Salah had somehow escaped.

The soldiers were everywhere by then, covering the hills all the way to the border, fanning out through the night, helicopters with searchlights, squads of fighting men ready to kill anything that moved. But Salah was gone. He too had saved himself. But there was more and I wanted to know about it. All these factual events then seemed to me to be of extreme significance. "But you saw Ibrahim, that was the leader who was in the classroom with the girl, you saw him alive, didn't you?"

He hesitated, thinking of what came first. "We knew by then, of course, we heard it on our walkie-talkies, that the girls were really where we first thought they were. They were coming out of the window there and that's where the blasts of machinegun fire inside were coming from also. Our men went up with ladders, but you know that."

"Yes," I said. "Tell me about Ibrahim."

"We saw his fingers on the window ledge, you know, just his fingers and then slowly the head came up. He was alive, all right."

"And you shot him down."

"We had no choice."

"Why?"

"Because of the grenades, because our men were already

through the front door. And the girls were still jumping out while our men broke their falls below. It wasn't over yet."

When I didn't say anything, neither did he. Fred sat on a wooden chair not far from the bed. He was looking at me and Zenia and the doctor listened too.

Dov said, "The reason he didn't shoot the girl was she jumped as he fell."

I said, "Perhaps he wanted her to live."

Zenia said, "He was the one who shot the janitor."

"That's true," I said. "But I knew him best. If he was still alive, he could've killed her."

"Anything's possible," Dov said.

We all shook hands because I was very tired and some drug was working on me, taking me out of this wild world of passionate conviction.

"You had to see," Dov said as he left. "She just came flying out of the window and then, like some fabulous athlete, turned it into an act of . . . well, call it a miracle of self-control, and intelligence. You know, she's a gymnast and has competed in Tel Aviv. She was like a great dancer." He stopped and looked back again into the room. I watched him with half-closed eyes, fighting off the emptiness of falling away out of sight of myself, but still I clung to hear what his last words might be.

"It was extraordinary," he said. "She had red hair."

She still had red hair and it blew in the wind which as the afternoon went on now flowed from the land to the sea. It wasn't much of a breeze. Below us the heavy blossoms stirred and trembled with fragrance and grace. We were, of course, saying goodbye.

Now the time for leaving no longer could be postponed again.

The whole kibbutz was present, parents, relatives, friends. In one way or another we had met and shaken hands, embraced and been embraced, kissed and been kissed by all, but now, with a kind of secret understanding, Fred at the car, a jeep with four Israeli soldiers and a small truck with a half-dozen others were all waiting at the open gate. The settlement had its schoolhouse. It too had those permanent temporary buildings as well as a few built to last made from stone brought down from the mountains. Everything was there to say peace and farewell, including the Mediterranean, shining far off in a wrinkled deep blue, browning along the coastline, with some clouds, like half a flock of distant sheep in the sky. The whole scene, touched and sprinkled with fragrance from the hills, was there in wait for us to depart, and to top it all, as it were, this bouquet of girls, our fellow hostages with their teacher, Tamar.

We walked over to them. We had already had more good-byes than any parting could absorb. We had also more promises to return and meet again than a life could exhaust.

Actually they were there because we were one, intimately one in life and death, and just being there as we left, as we separated, I suppose, for a kind of forever, considering their youth and our old age, well, there they were and here we were.

They brought up their presents.

It was Tamar who carried one to Zenia. Everybody knew that Ruth and Zenia had become very close in those last hours.

They had brought, for my aunt, Ruth's Bible, her precious possession, one her family had given her, one her family's father had owned, one that would have gone to the oldest of her three brothers, all three now standing back from the girls. Tamar, after embracing Zenia, gave the Bible to her, explaining what it was and how Ruth's family felt.

Then Shlamath, red hair carefully ribboned in spring green, gave me a cardboard box, wrapped in a pale yellow paper, with a green bow like the one that held her hair.

"This," she said in her lively voice, "is a fragment of a little figure from the ruins of Byblos. My cousin is an archaeologist, and he's also a soldier. When he went into Lebanon once, he traded something for it from someone among the United Nations soldiers who somehow had bought it. It's not much, just part of an arm, resting on the hip. The whole figure never was bigger than three or four inches. So it's just a bit."

The people from the settlement listened to this invasion of their deepest beliefs, but everybody was happy and sad that afternoon. There was no other way to be.

"It's my most precious possession," Shlamath said. She kissed my cheek and I kissed hers, which was hot and flushed as she whispered, "And so are you."

Then with everybody waving and crying out their peace, our little convoy drove off for Asher, where we again would say goodbye and leave before nightfall in another small convoy for Tel Aviv.

"As a child," Zenia said above the engines around us, as the landscape slid past and through the open window blew the aromatic air of the coastal spring, "I could read Hebrew. I suppose I could learn it once more and read these histories and dreams all over again." She gave me a cheerful look, one of the first I had seen in some time. "They all thought we needed help from the gods. So did Shlamath."

I said, "It's springtime in Galilee. That's the usual season. It's growing time."

I opened the box carefully, cherishing the ribbon and paper. The box was created out of cardboard and tape. Inside in dried grasses like a bird's nest was the fragment, the worn naked arm and gowned hip of some Astarte. There was a note. I read it and showed it to Zenia. It was printed gracefully, with a small flourish. It called out: COME BACK, COME BACK. SHLAMATH.

There was nothing to say, so I rewrapped it carefully and put it down on the seat and sat back and watched the landscape disappear and thought of nothing.

After a while, Zenia said, "Fred, are you sick?"

"No," Fred said. "I'm healthy."

"Is your voice sick?"

"No, it's healthy."

"Then why haven't you said anything at all?"

"Don't worry," he said, "if I had something to say, I'd say it."

"It didn't stop you before."

"There's before, and there's after," he said.

"That's a good beginning," she told him.

He now began talking like the obliging man he was until we reached Asher.

We had tea and good-byes, cakes and good-byes, and finally, as we waited for a section of the convoy to join us, Zenia and I decided to get away for a few minutes and we walked out of the settlement and up a dirt path that led right into the scrambled foothills that climbed and climbed on their long journey to Lebanon and farther north through the mountains until finally they would fall to ancient Byblos, in whose ruins someone had found that bit of stone which now waited in Fred's car to go home with me.

Patrols were still searching the terrain, and two helicopters buzzed far off while the bees buzzed close around us, since every step we took was among the spring wildflowers. There were all kinds of insects, and darting birds.

More than a mile ahead I saw about a dozen Israeli soldiers fanning out, and now and then as we climbed in a slow walk, just looking and not speaking, we would see two or three appear to our right or left and wave to us.

The path straightened out and we stopped. It seemed far enough. We were after all only a couple of hundred yards from the settlement below and would be able to see the convoy when it pulled in.

That morning's rain had found its usual places and water still trickled between the rocks, among grasses and shrubs. Zenia took a few steps forward where a thrust of rock had hidden a turn in the path.

"Come look," she called.

I joined her and saw that on the right of the path a sudden very steep incline ran down into a bed of asphodel. They were there as thousands of white flowers touched with the faintest yellow and from their wet depth, where a crevice of rock closed in, their sweet musty fragrance eddied up to us.

The searching patrols had been through there also, scrambling halfway down, trampling down the flowers, but in the very depth of it the flower faces all turned the same way toward the light that came from above the rocks.

The helicopter buzzed by and was gone. We looked up at it and around and just for a brief moment no one was to be seen and in that brief moment I saw the boy. He was hiding partly under a rock. His legs were bare. He wore shorts and a grayish sweater. He lay very still. He might have been dead, wounded from the fight. How he made it into the very throat of the crevice without crushing the asphodel was difficult to understand. Perhaps, desperate and dying, he had climbed down from the rocks above him.

Zenia looked around to be sure there were no soldiers to be seen. There were none for the moment, even though we knew they were everywhere.

"Salah," she called to him.

He waited there absolutely still, and it was then I realized he might be armed. But it was too late.

He looked like any Sephardic boy from the settlement, and he climbed up, not toward us but away from us, so that he came out on the path about fifteen feet from us.

Zenia called out to him in Arabic one of the few words she knew, the word peace and that meant escape.

He had no gun. He had nothing, no socks, just some heavy shoes, his shorts, his sweater, and his dark mat of hair. He smiled.

He turned and ran away, up toward the hills; then, when he was about fifty feet away, he cut off from the path into the steep hills, among the shrubs and stone that made up the batha.

He stopped, and after a quick look around at the empty landscape he faced us and smiled again.

Zenia waved to him.

He gave a vigorous wave back and took off again, disappearing around a small overhang of rock where a stand of broom angled up.

I put one arm around Zenia's waist and pulled her violently toward me as we both fell down the steep incline, rolling over and over among the asphodel. Their musty fragrance over-whelmed and their tight leaves scratched as we slid and tumbled down the steepest part where a water gash in the abrupt ledges formed a covert of pure rock. Here, cranesbill dropped tendrils decorated with flowers red as blood.

And all the while as I counted off each second I hoped the grenade that Salah had thrown would land on the path and stay there, for if it rolled down with us before it exploded, I knew that at last, in spite of every miracle of these last few days, in spite of the years that had failed to block our lives from coming together again, it was all over.

The grenade exploded above the path before it struck it. I pressed up against Zenia in the broken flowers. I held her close.

The sound went round and round, it leaped from rock to rock, it boomed and crashed as one, and splinters of metal hit the high rock above us and let loose a hail of crushed stone and chips. Then a shower of mixed earth and tiny bits of stone fell in a bristling rain upon the flowers that stretched up the steep in-cline to the path.

Zenia and I were looking at each other.

She said, "I thought he wanted to thank me and wave good-bye."

I left her there, sitting up, and scrambled up the path, sometimes on all fours, up that hill of asphodel.

Before I could see anything I heard the shouts of the Israeli soldiers everywhere, out of the nooks and crannies of tormented earth and rock that endlessly climbed toward Lebanon.

I reached the path and looked away in the direction in which the boy had run. He was not too far away yet, but he was leaping from rock to rock, climbing, jumping, going deeper into the twisted shrubs and earth which formed the runs for the win-ter rains. But ahead of him were three Israeli soldiers, and out of a cleft where they had been searching, as they had searched the cleft in which we had found Salah, appeared two other soldiers.

They yelled in Arabic and Hebrew for the boy to stop.

He never stopped. He went madly on, risking every fall,

straining to escape where he had just been free less than a minute ago simply to disappear.

All the guns went off together and separately. They caught him as he leaped for some hidden cover I couldn't see. The bullets netted him in the very air through which he flew, tangled his body in a flail of arms and legs, and he fell, destroyed before he hit the ground, where his body disappeared from sight.

I waved to the soldiers and they called back to me. Some ran toward me as I let myself slide down among the asphodel, crushing the flowers, feeling their leaves and plant stems holding me back.

Zenia was standing up, leaning against the rock.

"I have all my bones in place," she said. "Have you?"

I took her arm. Above us two soldiers were scrambling down to help. They wanted to know if we were all right.

Zenia clung to me as we waited for them.

"I wanted him to live," she said, "but he had other plans." Here among the trampled asphodel she called out to history, "It's always that way."

The young men were excited and happy that we were both unharmed, and triumphant too, for as one of them said, "He was the fourth one, the one that killed the girls."

He was.

Back on the path, with the light continuing to fail but with evening still in wait, hiding in the west behind the mountains where the sun, obscured, still lashed the sky with color and the blue was tinged with pink as if the wildflowers had lost their petals overhead, we walked hand in hand. One soldier led the way, some twenty feet ahead, and one soldier brought up the rear, some twenty feet behind.

We were, in a way, alone, just the two of us.

My Aunt Zenia didn't use my hand to help herself walk down that dappled stone path. She simply held it as she often had when I was very young.

"I was going to tell you many things about my life," she said, "all of it as it happened the way it did. I planned a lot of it

267

all that long afternoon in the schoolhouse, asking myself, What should I tell him, what should I not? But . . ."

She surveyed the foothills as she walked beside me, her hand lightly touching mine. Below was the settlement of Asher. There were soldiers still working the hills with care, but now and then their voices carried to us as they spread the news that the hunt for the missing terrorist was over.

"But truly," Zenia said, "what we've just survived today and yesterday and the day before, what we've lived, was and is exactly the way it has been again and again. Yes, exactly. Well," she added in her ever reasonable and questioning way, "a little different each time, after all."

I kept quiet, just walking with her, not even looking at her although I wanted to look at her always.

Below I could see the small convoy arriving and Fred standing beside his car. There were people beginning to climb up to join us as we came down. There were voices carrying the news all over.

"Anyway," she said, "the defeated are not always the most defeated." She sighed. Her mood changed. She pressed my hand, she smiled. "Dear child, have I anything else to tell you? Is there after all anything else ever to tell?"

I was really thinking about it all, since my life, like any life, had many meanings. I had felt many things, moving from hope to pain to despair by way of joy and passion. I had always managed in one way or another to find something to hope for, if not really to expect. Yet this was different. My world now signified again. It no longer needed still another explanation after every explanation of its mystery.

Everything mattered except all of it, and all of it signified because my Aunt Zenia and I were together again.